WINTER'S FATE

THE POISONED KINGDOMS
BOOK ONE

AMELIA MACLEOD

Cover by Maria Spada

Editing by Erika Steeves

AUTHOR'S NOTE

Dearest Readers:

For your convenience, you can find a glossary of terms in the back of this book, as well as some other fun extras.

Note: Skip the remainder of this note if you prefer not to read content warnings.

CONTENT NOTES

Winter's Fate contains some consensual on-page spice, though it's rather a slow burn by many estimations. Later books will absolutely have more, so be advised

While not an overly dark book, it does also contain violence in the form of fantastical fights/battles, near drowning, kidnapping (*not* perpetrated by the main characters), attempted murder, and death. Substance abuse (alcohol) is also depicted.

Take care of yourselves while reading, my friends.

Sincerely,
Amelia

A sacrifice of pain, but not thine own
Nor from an enemy's veins may it flow.
Only blood claimed from one that you love
The highest price yields the greatest trove.

CHAPTER 1

*T*he garden smelled wrong.

Laena Felicia Montrose-Aboret, once heir to the Etran throne, left her cottage shortly after sunrise to tend to her vegetables, as she did every morning. Birds hopped from branch to branch, as *they* did every morning; and Brin, Laena's newt-like companion—commonly known as a shimmerling—dropped from the eaves and landed on Laena's shoulder with a pink beetle clamped between her jaws. As *she* did every morning.

Laena paused on the threshold, drawing in a deep breath through her nose. Beneath the expected scents of damp earth and ripening tomatoes, there ran an unmistakable undercurrent of rot.

"Did we lose a chipmunk to the walls again?" she asked.

Still on her shoulder, Brin spiraled in a tight circle and plopped down to begin devouring her beetle. Not a particularly helpful response. Brin had simply appeared one day shortly after Laena's arrival, back when she'd been foolish enough to dub the place Sunflower Cottage. Now the name only reminded her, with bitter irony, that she'd once felt hopeful, even cheerful,

1

about the prospect of living here. Some days she wished she could take it back.

But even as the shine of idyllic cottage living wore away, Brin's companionship remained constant. Laena found she was glad for it. Shimmerlings were rare enough in Etra, and rather untrusting of humans. Laena considered it a distinct honor to be singled out—not that she'd ever say as much to Brin.

"I wish you'd do that elsewhere," Laena said, nodding to the beetle.

Brin ignored her.

Laena sighed and retrieved her gardening bucket from its place on the porch, noting a new patch of chipped paint beside the window. Which reminded her of the splitting rail to the right, and the shutter that the last storm had left ajar. Keeping the house together by herself was quickly becoming more work than she could handle. But any worker she brought in to help would charge triple the usual fee without hesitation, and that was assuming there was someone who would agree to show up at all.

No matter. After the harvest, she'd have time to care for the house. In between all the canning, smoking, and jamming she'd need to do in preparation for winter.

As Laena hauled the bucket toward the vegetable garden, the smell of rot grew stronger, and the concern over the prospect of an unlucky chipmunk twisted into a real thread of fear. If the garden had contracted a blight, she might very well go hungry come winter.

Everything had been fine yesterday. More than fine.

And to all appearances, it was fine today. The tomatoes were plump and green, the barest blushes of orange beginning to suggest oncoming ripeness. The carrot fronds were undisturbed —she'd had to install a fence to oust the hungry groundhogs— and the zucchinis, as usual, bore more fruit than she could hope to consume on her own. Even the strawberries looked perfectly healthy.

Laena followed the rotten smell to the end of the garden, where—in yet another fit of optimism—she'd planted a trio of butterfly bushes. The blossom-stuffed stalks made her think of fireworks after a ball, and her heart lifted every time she spotted a pair of orange, blue, or black wings alighting on the flowers. Even now, with all those early hopes dashed, the bushes felt like a promise. Like everything would turn out just fine, as long as she could attract throngs of pollinators to her garden.

A thin stone path separated the bushes from the vegetables, and even on her worst days, she still thought they lent the garden an air of luxury. Usually, they filled the garden with the delicious aroma of honey, a wonderful accompaniment to her weeding. Only yesterday, they'd been flowering in luminescent shades of fuchsia and purple.

Now, Laena had to blink hard to make sure she was indeed awake, and that her eyes were showing her the truth.

Overnight, her prized butterfly bushes had turned brown, their blooms drooping low to the ground as if bowed with weariness, petals scattered on the garden stones like discarded scabs. Laena placed a hesitant finger to one of the stalks, and the once-silky flowers crumbled beneath her touch.

She wrinkled her nose, venturing closer to sniff the air. The rot was most certainly coming from this corner of the garden, if not the bushes themselves. Laena could barely choke in a breath, the smell was so strong.

"They were fine yesterday," she said. "Weren't they?"

On her shoulder, Brin swallowed the last morsel of beetle and rested her head on her front leg. Time for a nap.

Laena set her bucket down on the path and tugged on her gloves, then knelt before the destroyed bushes and dug her spade gently into the dirt. It sank in almost too easily, as if a pocket of air had been blown beneath the soil. When Laena pushed farther, the spade struck something hard. A rock, surely. Though how it had come to be here, she couldn't say.

With her gloves as armor, Laena plunged her hand into the dirt, wrapping her fingers around the offending stone. When she pulled, it came right out of the soil.

And it kept coming, until she was on her knees holding what looked for all the worlds like a midnight-purple icicle. It was twice the length of the dagger she kept secreted away in her trunk, and when she held it up to the light, she could make out sparks within it. Like stars shining through the black of night.

It was, without a doubt, the source of the rotten smell. Her stomach roiled against it, and though she'd experienced many an unsavory moment since taking up residence at Sunflower Cottage—there was a reason she associated rotting smells with dead rodents in the walls—this otherwise innocuous-looking object might well be the first to make her empty her stomach.

Warmth seeped through the fabric of her gloves, quickly heating to the point of discomfort, and she laid the icicle on the path before it could burn her hand. Actual heat? Or cold so deep that it burned? Impossible to tell, and she'd be a fool to test the question with bare hands.

"A prank," she said, though her voice sounded uncertain even to her own ears. She wasn't immune to pranks, certainly. People knew who she was, and many of them disapproved of her choices. But to murder her butterfly bushes so cruelly? That was beyond the red paint someone had splashed on her front gate, beyond the usual snubs in the market, the stalls that closed just as she arrived, and the potatoes swapped in place of steaks. Perhaps the villagers, who she'd once thought of as her people, had decided she should not even be able to grow her own food.

Surely there were easier ways to poison a neighbor's garden than burying this untouchable icicle. What *was* it, really? Holding her nose, Laena leaned in closer, squinting to inspect the thing, its depths tugging at the pit of her stomach like it meant to draw her in. To hold her attention until there was nothing else, only the star-like glitter and the burning cold.

She shook her head, sitting back on her heels to put more distance between herself and the artifact. It almost looked mage-made.

There were not many things left in Etra—probably in any of the three kingdoms of the Vales—that were mage-made. Few enough, in fact, that a typical citizen would not recognize the material well enough to suspect it. Most such artifacts had been destroyed long ago, though as one-time heir to the throne, she knew that some of the more powerful or indestructible items were hidden away in the castle vaults.

The rumble of wheels on dirt made her straighten. She shielded her eyes as she looked toward the road. A delivery for the neighbors on the next farm, perhaps. But even as the thought crossed her mind, she knew that wasn't true. No one delivered this far down the road. It was part of the reason she chose this cottage in the first place.

Sure enough, the vehicle that emerged from behind the trees was not a delivery cart, but an unnecessarily large coach. She'd ridden in its twins more times than she could count, but it looked swollen to her eyes now, devouring the road as greedily as Brin had devoured her beetle. Laena wished she could have seen the looks on the villagers' faces when that monstrosity rumbled its way past the shops.

And there was no doubt as to its destination; from wheel to roof, the coach bore the rose-gold paint of the royal family. The spouting-whale of the Montrose-Aboret seal glinted in the early-morning light, making it look like the whale were truly drawing in a breath.

"Damn it," Laena muttered as Brin skittered into her hair. "My sister is here."

—✳—

KATRINA SAT DELICATELY on the edge of the settee in the parlor. The polite smile on her lips might as well have been a twist; in fact, Laena thought she'd have preferred that. She hadn't been in the garden for more than ten minutes, yet she felt filthy compared to her sister, whose pristine white gown practically glowed. She smelled of lilies, a scent no doubt concocted by the palace perfumers.

Laena never grew lilies in her own garden.

Kat still wore her golden hair in ringlet curls, though she was a year short of twenty and would be officially taking up the crown next year. She looked like a child.

And Laena could see through her sister's eyes, well enough. To Kat, the cottage would seem cluttered: the butter churn in the corner, the extra gardening bucket by the door, the collection of mismatched tin plates and jugs she'd obtained from the market at great pains, the spinning wheel edged up against the settee. The wooden floors were swept but not polished, the glass windows thick and wavy.

To Kat, every point of pride for Laena—from the hand-woven woolen cloak hanging by the door to the wobbly candlesticks she'd boiled herself—was nothing but an eyesore, evidence of the life Laena had abandoned. It was obvious in her frozen smile, the too-frequent blinks. And the way she kept checking to make sure her gloves were wrapped tight around her fingers, as if one touch of her skin to anything in Laena's home might cause her to burst into flames.

Laena wasn't sure whether to hug her sister, thereby dirtying her gown, or to sit on the opposite chair and begin with a passive-aggressive 'how lovely to see you.'

She wasn't even sure whether she ought to sit or wait to be invited to sit. At which point she would have to decide whether she would obey such an invitation or continue to stand.

Laena was still considering her first move when Kat opened her mouth to speak first. "Where is Ben?"

Air rushed out of Laena's lungs before she could stop it, a painful squeeze tightening her chest. She was too long outside of court, and getting unpracticed at controlling her reactions.

Where *was* Ben? A question for the ages. A question that had, for several months, plagued Laena's every thought. Where was the lover who'd swept her away from the life she knew, with promises of everlasting love and only a spark of disappointment in his eye at the fact that the laws of the land had not in fact bent for them and he would not, as she had told him from the beginning, go from stablehand to king? Where was the man who'd played house with her for months? Who'd been there one night, arms wrapped around her body, legs tangled with hers in the darkness one last time? And the next morning gone without so much as a note...

But the note would have been unnecessary. Laena had awoken to the silence of the cottage—as silent as a country cottage could be, with mice in the walls and wind in the cracks —and she'd known.

He'd left her in the depths of winter, when she had never experienced it outside the palace walls, when their garden had been new and the canning scarce. But she'd taken his bow and taught herself to aim, firing again and again with numb fingers until the arrow struck true—true enough to hunt, anyway—and then she'd traipsed through the woods chasing after deer and rabbits and barely scraping up enough food to survive.

But she *had* survived. And she'd emerged with the skills to live out the rest of this life as she chose. Which, she reminded herself firmly, was all she'd ever truly wanted.

Where was Ben? Laena didn't give a damn where he was, as long as he stayed away.

Yet Kat asked after him as one might ask about the weather, or the type of tea Laena had hastily brewed for them. Kat had not yet taken a sip; she cradled the chipped mug and saucer as if they were merely props.

7

Kat had no reason to know that Ben had left, and she did not need to know. Laena simply needed to breathe, to get through this conversation and push Kat to ask for whatever it was she wanted so Laena could say no and get back to her garden.

As Kat had taken her favorite seat in the room, Laena settled into a wooden chair she kept by the window, reaching for the well-toned muscle memory of court life. "Oh, you know," she said, trying to match her sister's offhand tone. "He's off doing stablehand things."

Kat lifted the teacup to her mouth and took a sip, then suppressed a grimace that no one else would have noticed. But no one else had the benefit of knowing Kat as well as Laena did. "He left, didn't he?" she asked.

Of course, Kat would have given herself a reason to know. Was she here to gloat over Laena's spectacular failure? If so, she might have come months ago. Though her sister wouldn't realize it, Laena was faring quite well in her cottage.

She might be rusty with the games of court life, but she hadn't forgotten how to play. She made a point of leaning back in her chair and crossing her legs. Most improper, even with her skirts still covering most of her. "Yes. One will be inclined to do that when his woman throws all his earthly goods into the river."

That had been a satisfying day. The river was nearly a mile out, but it had been worth trundling the wheelbarrow to a spot where the mud was particularly thick. Though, to be truthful, Laena had done that a month *after* Ben's disappearance.

Kat merely raised an eyebrow.

Laena waved away the unasked question, settling her gaze directly on her sister's. "How many spies do you have watching me?"

"Enough."

At least she didn't bother to deny it. Anger burned in Laena's throat, hot and bitter. Had the palace spies come near enough to watch her starve? Had they seen the villagers turn away, watched as she taught herself to survive? Had they seen her tears?

But no. Kat would not have bothered. Not until there was something she wanted. So Laena waited, keeping the smile on her face, as if Ben's disappearance was something she had orchestrated herself. All part of the grand plan.

Kat set her cup and saucer on the table. "I need your assistance. As an emissary."

And there it was. "No." Laena didn't have to think about that one. She was done with palace life, with all the bullshit manipulations, the stifling rules and the lies. Always the lies. "And you're not even queen yet. So *you* don't need my assistance. The council needs it. The regent needs it."

It was as close as a 'you can't make me' as Laena could get without saying it outright. As tempting as that would be.

"But next year I'll turn twenty," Kat replied, "and then I will be. Declan wants me to begin taking more responsibility. In preparation."

Declan. The regent, elected by the council to rule until Laena came of age after the deaths of her parents. That power was transferred when Kat was named heir.

"Still listening to everything that dried-out old goat has to say, are you?" Laena said.

Irritation flashed across Kat's face, there and gone in an instant. She straightened her spine, defensive on behalf of Declan. For reasons unknown. "He is no such thing. He is a mentor and a true friend to Etra."

Katrina wouldn't recognize a dried-out old goat if it walked up and introduced itself as such. Not even twenty years old and she was one herself. Just sitting there, watching Laena, ignoring the tea she'd set aside. Like she could wait there all day for Laena to ask why she needed an emissary, and to where.

Because as well as Laena knew Kat, Kat also knew Laena.

She knew that Laena would be itching to know the details. And though she hated herself for it, she *did* want to know. With a palace teeming with advisors and courtiers and dignitaries, why did Kat want *her* to do this?

Another sister might want to bring Laena back into the fold, to welcome her home after the trials of the last few years. But not Katrina. Laena should punish her for it, banish her and her scowling guards from her home and demand that she never return.

Curiosity won out, though Laena took care to maintain her casual posture. "All right. I'll bite. Why do you need an emissary?"

Kat rewarded her with a thin smile. It would have been triumphant but for the shadow of worry in her eyes. Whatever this was about, Kat was concerned. "Silerith is stirring," she said. "I believe they mean to break our peace."

Laena snorted, and Kat raised her eyebrow once again. She'd really been practicing with that thing. But though they'd attended all the same tutoring sessions and studied all the same histories, Kat's attention hadn't turned to diplomacy until well after Laena had mastered the subject. As the second daughter, she'd had the freedom to daydream and doodle instead of paying attention.

Silerith was a behemoth of a country, one of the two that made up the mainland. They were secretive to the point of hermitry, but aside from overeager border patrols with a tendency to scoop up inattentive hunters who accidentally crossed into its lands from Aglye, the country had not caused trouble in decades. True, its current king was an unknown entity even after near a decade of ruling. But the same could have been said of his father.

Mainland politics. Mainland problems. Etra was a small island nation, barely holding its own, but neither Silerith nor Aglye had shown any interest in attacking or conquering. They weren't precisely friends, but Aglye at least was a reliable trading partner. What signs could Silerith possibly have given to make Katrina believe they meant to break the peace?

"I doubt the Ruthless King will listen to anything I have to say," Laena said.

"I do not need an emissary to Silerith," Kat replied. "I need one to Aglye. To cement our alliance in case Silerith does grow ambitious."

Cement the alliance. Those words had a tendency to be paired with a commitment far beyond that of an emissary. Laena narrowed her eyes. "Are you hoping to marry me off?"

Kat's expression didn't change. "Would you accept such a plan if I proposed it?"

A clear deflection. Laena watched her sister for signs of the truth, wondering if the ink was still wet on some ill-conceived marriage contract. Certainly Aglye's king should have no interest in 'cementing an alliance' through marriage, especially to the disgraced princess of what he would view as a forgettable island nation. King Hawk was young and handsome, and Aglye was powerful enough to negotiate whatever marriage contracts it might desire. It was generally expected, or had been during Laena's time studying in the palace, that he would marry a rich courtier from his own lands and add to his already bursting treasury.

But it was impossible to tell whether marriage was indeed Katrina's plan, or if she truly wanted to send someone to negotiate a firmer treaty. Laena had been gone a good five years now, and Declan had trained her sister well; Kat's expression was inscrutable. Wide-eyed and guileless, the picture of innocence. Why *shouldn't* she ask her sister for a favor? What in the worlds would prevent Laena from helping the country that had shut her out and shunned her?

Laena didn't trust it. "How long have you known Ben was gone?"

Kat flushed, and Laena felt a surge of satisfaction. One could never school all her expressions, no matter how much she might wish to. Her sister brushed a hand over her skirts, smoothing unnecessarily. "Well…"

But Laena had no intention of allowing her sister to finish. She rose, brushing off her skirts and sending a scatter of garden dirt out over the floor. She'd regret that come cleaning time, but Kat's horrified look made it worthwhile.

"Get out," she said. "You're no longer welcome in my home. I will not serve as your emissary, or your marriage bargaining chip, or whatever else you have in mind."

Kat waited a beat, then rose with a grace Laena had once aspired to. She made her way to the door, lifting her gown as if to protect it from the filthy accommodations. Not that Laena had done anything to dispel that notion, but she knew Kat would act this way no matter where she lived.

Laena had chosen to give up the throne to live, unwed, with a commoner. Their abode, no matter how clean or cozy, no matter how happy—and he was gone, so it was not that—would never have met her sister's standards. Katrina didn't know, couldn't know, that Laena's reasons for leaving went much deeper than Ben. The heartbreak was real enough, but leaving had never really been a choice. It had been a necessity. Far more of a necessity than love alone could ever warrant.

When she reached the door, Kat paused. "I hope it was worth it," she said. "Your little scandal with the stablehand."

With a final glance around the room, which suggested she very much doubted it had been, the queen-to-be opened the door and flounced out into the sunlight.

CHAPTER 2

*C*allum didn't know what hour it was. He was aware, dimly, that his first-favorite pub—which he preferred for the central placement of the hearth as much as the quality of the ale—had kicked him out several hours ago. The scrapes on his knuckles suggested he might've indulged in a fight, but his memory was already scattering the incident to the winds.

His second-favorite pub was his second favorite because the proprietor gave little care to anyone's behavior. The old man kept the bottles beneath the bar in case of fights, which were common enough. Short of lighting the place on fire, the patrons could do little to attract the old man's notice. Callum had seen them scratch their marks into the antlers that graced the walls and spit tabac in the corner, hoping no one would notice. He'd seen punches thrown for bets, dice thrown on bad faith, and men thrown into the street by lovers who deemed it well past time for bed. The owner never so much as batted an eye. Just kept serving.

Paradise, as far as Callum was concerned. Though the hearth was sadly inferior.

He leaned his elbows on the bar and buried his nose in his

ale, trying to mask the smell of sweat that otherwise permeated the place. Rarely did music play here, and the conversation was muted where it happened at all. Though that might just as well have been the roar of ale in his ears. As long as that roar remained loud enough to drown out the whispers of the past, the drink was doing its job. His skin stuck to the wood as he adjusted his arms, but he didn't much care. He'd bathe come morning. Or perhaps the next. What did it matter?

The door crashed open, but Callum didn't bother to glance over. He merely signaled for another ale, since newcomers meant the barman might be busy for a while. Callum had been coming here for years, and he didn't even know the skinny fellow's name. Which suited him just fine.

One of the newcomers swaggered over, bringing the cloying scent of over-spiced soap as he set his elbow on the bar, intentionally invading Callum's space. Out of the corner of his eye, Callum could see the man grinning, satisfaction oozing even more potently than that eye-watering cologne.

Of course, Landon Moore would not have chosen this pub randomly. The king's favored general would no doubt prefer to frequent a more high-class establishment. Or perhaps one that served whores alongside its refreshments. But such a choice would leave Landon Moore with no one to torment. Though Callum supposed the whores might not agree with that assertion.

The bartender delivered his ale, and Callum swallowed half the glass, ignoring the way Moore sidled up close enough for his sleeve to brush against Callum's.

Callum had to resist the urge to take the man by the throat. The pub's proprietor might not lift an eyebrow, but the king certainly would. And Callum was in enough trouble as it was.

"Captain Farrow," Moore said. "What a delight."

Yes. Callum supposed it was. Moore would just love to goad him into a punch, to sport a black eye that Callum would have

14

to explain away. And the king did not accept 'he was being an ass.' Callum had tried it.

"Your cologne doesn't disguise the stink of your breath, Moore," Callum said.

The general didn't budge, and the grin on his face didn't slip. He was too pretty for his own good, Moore. All blond and rugged, with that square jaw of his. He looked like a prince out of a fairy story, and he made good use of that likeness; the man had a reputation for tricking innocent debutantes into thinking he planned to marry them. He'd bed them and then jilt them, leaving them heartbroken.

And now he was the Aglyean general. A post that ought to have gone to Callum. He couldn't begin to guess what King Hawk had been thinking; he only knew it wasn't his problem. Not anymore.

Moore tapped a fingertip to his bottom lip as Callum lifted his glass again. He could no longer taste the stuff, and might be paying top prices for the lowest on the shelf, but he didn't much care as long as it did the job.

"Can I still call you Captain Farrow?" Moore asked. "Perhaps not."

Callum grimaced. Not only had he failed to secure a promotion, but he'd been removed from his post altogether. From Defender of the Realm to nobody special in the time it took to say a few irretrievable words. Hawk hadn't waited long to start spreading the news.

"It's a pity," Moore continued. "We could have used you on the journey. Someone else will have to get his hands dirty this time around, eh, Farrow?"

Callum couldn't even fault Moore for the taunt. Not when it was true. Not when Callum had forged that reputation for himself. When borders needed crossing, when laws needed bending, when blood needed spilling... it was Callum who saw it done.

I need a captain who won't flinch from the difficult work, the old king had said, time and time again. He never called it the 'dirty work,' but he didn't need to. Callum knew what he meant. Just as Moore and everyone else knew.

King Magnus had relied on him. And Callum had failed him, in the worst possible way.

Moore knew it, too. And he wasn't finished. "As it stands," he went on, "I suppose we'll have to manage the trip to Etra without you."

Callum snorted into his glass. If a single jibe from Moore was enough to push the memories to the surface with such force, then Callum needed a great deal more drink. "Just now promoted and already going on a fishing trip in the farthest backwater? I wish you well."

Moore clapped him on the shoulder, and Callum tensed. It was all he could do to keep his fists wrapped around his glass instead of swinging them in Moore's face. A solid elbow to the cheekbone would mar that pretty face for a good week.

"Not a fishing trip, Farrow," Moore said. "An official delegation."

"What the hell for?" The words left Callum's mouth before he could snatch them back, the drink loosening his tongue along with his thoughts. Whatever it was, it didn't matter anymore. It had nothing to do with him.

Moore actually threw his head back and laughed, showing off his too-white teeth. Callum wasn't sure he'd ever heard the man express such glee before. Had he even had a single drink tonight? It would be like him to stay sober just to goad Callum further. Just to lord his worthiness all over town like a shining trophy.

"You don't know? Of course, I suppose you wouldn't." Moore affected a slight frown as if in pity, but the laugh shone too brightly in his eyes. "We're going to get the Etran emissary. Escort them here to speak with the king."

Why in the mages' tits would Hawk summon an emissary from Etra, of all places? They traded together, certainly, and relations were better than with next-door Silerith. But unless Callum had spent a lot more hours in this pub than he thought he had, Etra's newly appointed heir to the throne would not have come of age yet. And would not for another year still.

Callum scowled into his drink. Be it Etra or Silerith or the Miragelands themselves, a mission like that needed an experienced commander. Admittedly, he'd been out of touch with palace workings for a few months now, but it was the kind of mission he'd have expected Hawk to put him on. Maybe even as a leader. His new pretty-boy ass of a general would offend the emissary, particularly if she was a woman—which was all too likely, in a country that took pride in its long line of queens.

Hawk clearly felt that Moore was better than the alternative. And the alternative was Callum. It was too much to bear.

Worse, Moore knew it. "But I've said too much, Cap— Callum, I mean. Too high-level a mission for you to know about, if the king didn't tell you already."

Callum inhaled a long breath, the thrum of his boozy blood urging him to overcome his few remaining logical instincts and throttle Landon Moore until he cried. He was already reaching for Moore's wrist, imagining the crunch of sinew and bone between his fingers, when the scent of burning incense stopped him. No mere marketplace trinket this incense, no sandalwood or cinnamon. This was the distinctive burn of heart-tithed magic. Acrid and smoky, it followed the user throughout their pathetic days, creating a trail that he'd learned to track through any terrain, be it forest or city. Or ale-drenched pub.

In Aglye, heart-tithing was a crime, which meant that *magic* was a crime. Second only to murder, and often accused along with it.

Regular citizens might not recognize the smell, but Callum had spent much of his career breaking down doors to rooms choked with the stuff. He'd spent endless hours trying to scrub that scent from his own skin. From his own memory.

A fool's errand. Should he go a century without crossing paths with a heart-tither, he'd still never forget it. And Landon Moore should damn well recognize it, too.

Shoving Moore out of the way, Callum slid off his stool, barely managing to stay on his feet as the extent of the night's indulgences pulsed into his head. He shoved the dizzy sensation aside, scanning the room and ignoring whatever driveling protests were coming out Moore's mouth.

In the back corner of the room, partially obscured by one of the pub's wooden columns, a group of men sat hunched over a game of dice.

Callum crossed the pub quickly, pushing chairs out of his way without caring whether or not they were occupied. When he reached the table, three of the men squinted up at him, confused. If they recognized him, they didn't show it.

The fourth man took one look at Callum, then scrambled out of his chair and skirted toward the wall, tripping over the table leg. That didn't stop him, though; he flailed, scrambling along the floor like the rat that he was, intent only on escape. Callum almost admired his perseverance.

Not that it would do him any good. Callum stalked toward him, easily grabbing hold of his shirt and hauling him up in the air, legs kicking. "I wasn't cheating," he said. "I swear."

Callum gave the man a shake.

"Farrow." Moore's tone was a warning, but Callum could hardly hear. Nor would he have cared, in any case.

He slammed the man back into the wall, the acrid smell of the heart-tithe churning the ale in his stomach. It was like burning hair and sulfur, always mixed with that hint of sweetness. As if the next time, the magic would be kinder. A promise. A lie.

"He was only cheating at dice," Moore said from behind Callum's shoulder. "It's hardly a capital offense."

"We prosecute heart-tithers because of how they got the magic, not because of what they do with it." Callum could barely force the words out. He slammed the tither against the wall again, forcing himself to breathe through his nose, to experience the full effect of the heart-tither. "Who bled for your power?"

The man whimpered as Callum raised a hand, ready to strike.

Moore caught his fist before it could fly and dragged Callum back a step, forcing him to release the tither, who crumpled to the floor with a sob. Callum dragged Moore forward, but though the general did not share his muscle mass, he had one thing tonight that Callum did not: sobriety.

Moore twisted his arm, whipping him around and landing a solid blow to his face. Callum felt like he was watching from outside his body as his head slammed against the bar and his body dropped to the floor. Hard.

Moore bent over him, flicking a lock of hair out of Callum's face. "*You* don't prosecute anyone. Not anymore. You got yourself demoted, Farrow. You're lucky the king didn't exile your disgraceful ass." Moore straightened, gesturing to his friends. "Arrest the tither. No need for force."

Callum was aware, dimly, that he ought to be experiencing pain. Physical. Emotional. Spiritual. Hell, probably all three. But the only thing he could feel, as the soldiers formerly under his command ushered the magic user into the streets, was the absolute certainty that every word Landon Moore had spoken was the truth.

—*—

THE FIRST SLICES of dawn were beginning to lighten the sky by the time Callum picked himself up off the floor and made his way through the streets of Vunmore and back to the palace. Shopkeepers swept dust from their front steps while apprentices scurried around with buckets of water and window-washing rags. The smells of baking bread and freshly stoked fires set his stomach turning uneasily, foretelling the coming unpleasantness of an after-drink morning.

For now, though, he was still just soshed enough to face the king.

He'd much rather face his own bed and nurse the tender bruise that Moore's punch had left splashed across his cheekbone. But the new general had no doubt gone straight to Hawk after last night's altercation, and the king would be wanting to see him.

If Hawk didn't understand Callum's reaction, then there wasn't much Callum could say to explain. But he'd damn well have to try. Landon Moore was Aglye's general now. He couldn't allow magic to fester and seethe in their midst, inviting the mages of old to taunt them, pushing the door to their lands ever wider with every cursed trade.

Except that Moore *had* arrested the heart-tither. He hadn't let the man go. He'd acted, Callum thought bitterly, with the sort of professionalism the old king would have praised. There were times for knives in the dark, Hawk's father would have said, and times for restraint. The thought made Callum want to take it all back.

The palace courtyard was already bustling with activity when Callum arrived. Stablehands urged horses into the walled-off plaza while servants and enlisted men ran about with supplies, following orders barked at them by the officers who were clustered in groups and clutching mugs of steaming coffee as they oversaw the preparations.

Callum nearly asked what the excitement was about, but then he remembered what Moore had said about the Etran mission. The delegation was readying to set out. And its general had spent the previous evening pissing away the hours, chasing after Callum just for the sake of gloating. How many pubs *had* he peered into before landing on Callum's? Vunmore was a large city. If Moore knew his favorite haunts, he might well have been watching for some time. A fact that Callum should have noticed.

Callum might have proved he couldn't be trusted with a command, but Moore was no better. The eve of such a trip required focus and planning, discussions with officers. And a good night's sleep.

Not that Callum had always been decent at fulfilling those tasks himself. But he was better than Moore. And he would never have let his officers stand idle while their soldiers did all the loading. In fact, the mere sight of him made a few jump into action, abandoning their coffee mugs to join the rest of the soldiers in preparing the horses.

At least he still inspired *some* discipline. Though he might have expected more whispers. Even a question or two. Could it be that they didn't know?

As he crossed the courtyard toward the warmth of the palace, a young soldier came running from the direction of the barracks, nearly crashing straight into Callum. The soldier swerved at the last minute, slamming into the wall instead.

"Watch yourself," Callum said.

"I'm sorry." The kid's eyes widened as they landed on Callum, and he appeared in danger of fainting on the spot. "Captain Farrow."

He said Callum's name with a hint of wonder, the kind that always made Callum want to box people on the ear. But then again, the kid was young. Scraggly blond whiskers poking out of his chin suggested an attempt to grow facial hair—or lack of a razor—but by his gawky posture, the kid couldn't be more than eighteen.

Judging by his reaction, the soldiers truly didn't know that their captain hadn't earned the role of general and that, worse, he'd been relieved of his position.

And Callum wasn't going to be the one to spread the news before it was absolutely necessary.

"My apologies," the soldier said, his eyes darting around the hall until he looked completely frantic. "I didn't mean... that is, I've lost the key to the... but I needn't bother you with... if I may?"

Callum waved him away. "Never mind. Be on your way."

The soldier took off at a run. Callum shook his head, remembering his own early days in the King's Guard. It felt like a lifetime had passed since then. He hadn't been raised in any palace, and he'd always felt more comfortable in the spare accommodations of the barracks. To him, they'd represented the epitome of luxury.

Despite the early hour, King Hawk was already ensconced in his study, a fire burning on the hearth as if it had never died overnight. Perhaps it hadn't; Hawk was as likely to work through the night as he was to rise early. The king sat hunched over his desk, a quill in his hand. The pinched look on his face made Callum consider suggesting a trip to the privy. But he wasn't quite soshed enough for that anymore.

Hawk's looks were about as different from Callum's as a man's might be. Hawk favored his late father's features, his pale skin and wiry frame. Callum's own skin was olive in tone, his hair dark and prone to curling, his body taller and broader. Which was no doubt enhanced by his time spent training for— and serving in—the King's Guard.

Where he'd failed. In the worst possible way, he'd failed.

"I know about what happened. It's no matter. You're not on the payroll." Hawk didn't look up from the stack of papers on his desk. What did they say? Reports full of kingly matters, no doubt. The state of the treasury, perhaps. Reports from the outer districts. Requests for supplies. Lists of princesses hoping to wed. "So if you'd show yourself out, I'm quite bus—"

"Why the fuck aren't I going to Etra?"

Still soshed enough for that, clearly.

Hawk set down his quill with slow, deliberate patience, then dabbed his fingers on the ink rag before turning to Callum. "First, because you are drunk out of your mind."

"I'm fine."

Hawk tapped his fingers on the desk. No doubt he'd much rather be reading from one of those books of his. What did he see in there that was so much more important, so much more engrossing than the world around him?

"I seem to recall dismissing you as captain of the King's Guard. And ex-captains do not lead, or participate in, official delegations."

"You'd dismiss me over a mere fight?" As if Callum didn't know it was much more than that.

"When am I ever less than serious?" Hawk asked.

Never. And he'd told Moore, too—promoted the man to the spot Callum ought to have had—so he meant what he'd said. And yet.

"You continue to hold my failure against me," Callum said. Hawk was already shaking his head, but Callum pushed on. "You've disgraced me."

Hawk stood abruptly, brushing ink-stained fingers through his hair without leaving a mark. "You've disgraced yourself." He didn't sound angry. Merely tired. "Now if you'll excuse me, I have business that must be addressed."

Callum considered disregarding the dismissal, sitting down in Hawk's fireside chair and making the king understand. They'd grown up together, both of them trained to fight under the late king's watchful eye. Callum had helped Hawk out of more scrapes than he could count. Right now, he wanted to recount each one, in detail. He wanted to remind Hawk that though he was Aglye's king, he was still a man. He was still a friend, at least in theory.

But the post-drink headache was beginning to make advances on his temples, and he found he wanted his bed more than he wanted a fight. He merely bowed, his back stiff, his cheekbone throbbing.

By the time he made it to the door, Hawk had already buried himself in the stack of papers. Callum let the door slam on the way out with the petty hope that it would startle the king into making a mistake, forcing him to rewrite a page of notes.

Landon Moore still hadn't graced the courtyard with his presence as Callum made his way into the light, intending to cross to his own accommodations for a day of sleep. A week, perhaps. What else was there?

But as he crossed the courtyard, returning several of the soldiers' greetings—though grizzled old Edmun's came with an eyebrow raise that said the truth had reached his ears, at least—the young soldier who'd nearly collided with him in the courtyard came tearing out once again, this time balancing a cage full of live chickens in his arms.

Whether the chickens were meant to accompany them on the journey, or for some other purpose, Callum didn't know. The kid's boot caught on an uneven cobblestone and the cage went flying out of his arms.

Callum lurched forward, catching the cage before it could smash into the cobblestones. He didn't relish the idea of chasing poultry through the palace all morning. His head was throbbing in earnest now, but it didn't stop him from snatching the cage—barely—and easing it gently to the ground.

When he turned, the kid was staring at him in horror. He was already pale as a moonstone, but now his skin was practically translucent, his freckles popping out like they intended to secede from his face to join a calmer human.

"What's your name, kid?" Callum asked.

The kid swallowed hard. "Godfrey. Sir."

The men who'd first trained Callum to fight would've cuffed the kid for the chicken disaster. And it would've been a disaster, because they wouldn't have caught the cage; they'd have taken joy in letting it drop. And letting the kid face the consequences. They'd probably have banned him from the expedition, or set him to cleaning out the coops for months.

Godfrey clearly expected something along those lines. But he drew his spine up tall, and his lip was barely quivering. He seemed far too young to be serving in the guard. What was he, fifteen? Sixteen? Had he lied about his age so he could join?

"May I give you a word of advice?" Callum asked.

Godfrey hesitated, like he expected Callum to offer the advice without permission. When Callum didn't, he nodded. "Yes, sir?"

Callum set a hand on Godfrey's shoulder and squeezed. "Calm. The fuck. Down."

The kid let out a startled gurgle that might've been a laugh. "Yes, sir. Are you… are you coming with us to Etra, sir?"

Godfrey had no way to know it was the wrong thing to ask, and Callum was not in the habit of punishing young soldiers for their ignorance. He opened his mouth to say no, ready to keep walking to his quarters and fall into his bed for a days-long sleep. That was assuming Hawk hadn't had his things thrown into the street last night while he drank himself into a stupor.

But the soldiers were all ready to go. The horses were saddled, the flag at the ready. And, best of all, Landon Moore was nowhere in sight.

Callum gave Godfrey's shoulder another squeeze before letting go with a grin that actually felt real. "Yes," he said. "In fact, I'm leading the party. And we're leaving now."

CHAPTER 3

*L*aena woke the next morning to a sharp pain in her ear. She sat up, rubbing at it and looking around until Brin came scurrying out of her hair and down the blankets, chirping madly. Laena stared at her in bleary confusion. The little shimmerling had never made such a sound before, had never made *any* sound, and she'd certainly never made her way into the house, preferring to wait for Laena outside. She would have expected the lizard to have done so long ago, if she had any inclination.

"Crazy thing. Did you find a mouse hole to sneak through?" Laena reached out a finger to stroke Brin's back, but Brin skittered away from her touch. Trust her to choose this morning to act strangely. Laena had spent the night tossing and turning, fuming over Katrina's visit and thinking of all the things she wished she'd said. The accusations she should have leveled, the defenses she should have made, the speeches she should have given.

Each of which the Kat of her imagination countered easily. Because even the Kat of her imagination was superior in every way.

Now, her eyes were sandy with lack of sleep, and Brin was here to wake her, as if Laena had slept past her usual waking time. But she wasn't late to her chores. Brin ran down the blanket and spiraled her way down the bedpost, her long tail shining in the blue pre-dawn light. If anything, it was earlier than usual.

Brin paused at the door, skipping back and forth until Laena set her feet on the floor.

"All right, I'm coming. But I can hardly go out there undressed, can I? The villagers already have enough to say about me."

Though it was amusing to imagine the look on old Mrs. Corrigan's face, should she pass by to find Laena working in nothing but her shift. The thought made her chuckle as she tugged on her sturdiest woolen dress. The woman would hurry off to the market with the best gossip of the week. Of the year, even.

When she reached the front porch, though, the laughter died on her lips.

The stench hit her first, so potent that she couldn't fathom why it hadn't leaked into her bedroom. The death and rot was thick enough that every neighbor in the village should be lined up on her street demanding to know what she was doing, and why.

But it wasn't the pungent air that made her choke in a gasp of disbelief as she stared at the yard that had once housed her garden.

The garden was gone. In its place was a stinking mess of rotten mud, with nothing but a few stick-like stalks left to suggest it had ever been anything but a putrid swamp. The few remaining leaves had shriveled, like love letters tossed in a fire. Not a hint of green in the whole place.

Every vegetable she'd spent the spring and summer cultivating was gone. Every zucchini, carrot, tomato, and pumpkin.

Only yesterday, the berry bushes at the far end of the garden had been bursting with green, promising a winter full of jams. Today, they were lumpy husks.

And it was not merely the bushes and the vegetables. The trees that lined the side of her property were peppered with ink-black moss, their leaves beginning to show spots of decay. What would happen if it inched toward the house? Would it stain the walls? Kill everything inside?

Laena pressed her lips together. Queen or commoner, there was one truth life held firm: that standing around would give her no answers or solutions.

She went back inside, ignoring Brin's squeak of dismay, and retrieved a handkerchief from her kitchen drawer, which she tied around her nose and mouth to protect against the smell. She grabbed her gloves from her bucket, trying to calm the shaking of her hand, and stepped back out into the barren wasteland that, only yesterday, had been her beautiful garden and the source of all her sustenance.

Though the summer sun was already warming the skin on her neck, the chill of winter was all too alive in Laena's memory. She would never forget the persistent pain of hunger in her belly, or the way her clothing had hung off her body, her ribs protruding alarmingly. She would never forget how heavy Ben's boots had become as her muscles wasted away.

She'd put them on anyway. She'd taught herself to survive. That had been her second winter here, and the first without Ben; the next had had a full larder and pantries stuffed with provisions she'd provided for herself, as had the following two. All but the flour, which she'd traveled to another village to have ground.

She could not endure another winter like that first one without Ben. She *would* not.

Laena pulled on her gloves and stepped down into the

garden, pausing when Brin once again nipped her on the ear. "I have to investigate. You know I do."

Brin nipped her again, drawing blood, then scurried up to hide in Laena's hair.

Taking care to stay on the path, Laena knelt beside her ruined garden, poking a tentative finger into the soil. She half expected the soup-like soil to dissolve her glove and burn her hand. When the fabric held, she pushed farther, until her whole fist was buried in the stinking pit of earth.

She was wrist-deep in the soil when her fingers closed around a thick root, reminiscent of the icicle-like growth she'd unearthed yesterday. She felt her way along it, noting the ridges and the crystalline material. Its heat radiated through the thickness of her gloves.

Brin ventured back down to her shoulder, peering at the soil before quirking her head back toward Laena, looking at her with those sharp, bead-black eyes. And though Laena could not have said *how*, she understood that Brin wanted her to use her magic.

"I know," Laena said. "I'm just being careful."

Brin lay her head on her shoulder as she, very slowly, called for her power.

The power answered. It tingled through her fingertips, like stretching muscles released after long-held tension. It delved into the soil like an extension of her own body, joyful and curious despite the oily stink of the earth around it.

This was not the bloody sacrifice of a heart-tithe but the unbridled joy of a power that belonged to the Vales, wholly and truly. Laena didn't know how that could be true; in all her studies, she'd never heard so much as a whisper of such a thing. She only knew that it was. That it connected her to this land more fully than any tithe magic could.

Despite what the rest of the Vales might think of magic, it was not fully evil. Not at all. In the years following Ben's abandonment, she'd no longer feared she might hurt someone with her powers. And she'd come to know how gentle her gift could be.

Her hand delved into the earth, and the crystal shuddered in response. Encouraged, Laena pushed deeper, until the crystalline root changed beneath her touch. It loosened, and she found her finger pushing into it rather than against it.

Perhaps this was the key to destroying the blight; perhaps the power would allow her to tear it apart from the inside.

The crystal tore apart beneath her touch, and the next instant she was airborne, flying back as if something had blasted her off the ground. She hit the path hard, catching her head just before it slammed into the brick steps behind her.

Heat seared her cheeks, but unlike natural heat from the sun or a flame, this warmth felt wrong. It penetrated flesh and blood, seeping inward like poison, and made her feel hollow and sick from within. She stumbled to her feet as the *thing* that had blasted her out of the garden rose out of the garden, a blighted shadow made real. A phantom. A wraith.

Brin hissed in her ear, and Laena threw up her hands, calling the power more by instinct than intention. Since the incident that had convinced her of her need to flee palace life, Laena had used her gift with care, to preserve food, cool overly hot tea, and, once or twice, to create intricate frost patterns on a window. Small matters, for a small life. Nothing that would hurt anyone. Nothing that would call attention.

And yet, she knew. She always knew there was more waiting for her, an untapped river that was ready and willing to do more.

Now, icy power pulsed out of her hands, dragging her forward a step as though it was physically wrenching itself out of her body. The wraith gave an unearthly howl, collapsing in on itself, the shadows folding into layers upon layers of infinite darkness. She was hurting it—or at least she thought she was—

yet still it did not disappear. The monster lunged for her, whipping bands of shadows at her legs as if to drag her into the pit of the garden.

Not today, it wouldn't. Laena threw up her hands, and again, the power answered, pushing the monster back, shaving her another inch of margin. She'd fought so hard to use the power for gentle work; and despite the damage she'd seen it do, she'd never imagined a battle.

But the power responded anyway. Though unsteady, it stuttered out around her like a protective wall, batting away the poisonous tentacles of shadow. One of the shadow's whips snaked around her stuttering magic and struck her cheek, but she barely felt it as the power thrummed through her, a cold wash of energy standing against the greedy heat of the shadow creature. If it wasn't quite made of flame, then she wasn't quite made of ice, but the disparate powers clashed nonetheless.

Like a well close to emptying, Laena could feel the power in her core melting away, draining like snowmelt down the mountain in spring.

But if there was one thing she knew about snowmelt, it caused the greatest floods.

Once upon a time, her power had blasted through a palace ceiling, nearly wounding a member of her council as shards of ice came raining into the room. Only the fact that it was winter —and that Riles's position on the coast made the city prone to sudden storms—allowed her to keep her secret.

She'd shattered that room by accident. Surely she could shatter this wraith on purpose.

Throwing her hands up for the third and final time, Laena called the magic. "Don't defend." Her teeth were locked together, the words little more than a breath. She could taste the copper tang of blood as it ran down her cheek, touching her lips. "Attack."

It would be her last chance.

The power responded, raising goosebumps on her arms as it thrummed out of her, pushing one last wall of cold at the monster. Shards of magic coiled from her hands, and the recoil threw her to the ground.

The monster broke against the wave of Laena's power. With one last scream, it dissolved into a foul vapor and disappeared into the wind.

Still lying prone on the path, Laena stared at the steaming garden, blinking at the wisps of remaining smoke until they dissipated. Where the creature had spewed mud into the trees the leaves were already shriveling away.

Her body was trembling, as if from a deep chill, and her cheek stung from the shadow's cut. When she reached a tentative call out for the power, only silence responded. Brin turned a worried circle on her chest, and she gave the shimmerling a comforting stroke on the back.

If she hadn't heard of Vales-born magic, she certainly had never heard of a shadow creature like the one that had just assaulted her. Had it been formed among the mess of the garden? Or had it *infested* the garden?

There was no way to be certain. But as the trembling began to subside, there was one thing she did know.

"Well," she said, her voice scratchy and distant in her ringing ears. "I guess this means we're going to the palace."

WHEN ONE DIDN'T HAVE access to a royal coach, one journeyed to the capital city of Riles via a network of hired stages. It required an exhausting three days of travel and the majority of Laena's meager funds. Saved from her palace days mostly, as the villagers were as loath to purchase vegetables from her as they were to sell.

Mercifully, the other coach passengers didn't appear to

recognize her. The interior was cramped, and Laena hugged her traveling bag to her lap, as did the other passengers. On the first day, a young man with exaggeratedly tall hair felt it necessary to practice a speech he was to give at the university, and despite exchanged looks of dismay, no one moved to silence him. Thankfully, a university coach met the professor at the first evening's stop and whisked him away to practice elsewhere.

In the evenings, the coach stopped at roadside inns, where Laena shared attic accommodations with the other women passengers. The innkeepers had stuffed the rooms with wall-to-wall cots, hoping to capitalize on every possible inch of space. The rooms were stuffy, but clean enough, and the women kept to themselves. Some of them departed on other stages come morning, heading toward the countryside or the mountains, where smaller towns dotted the landscape at intervals. No doubt some would need to walk a distance to reach their destinations.

Every time a new person entered the coach, Laena would tense, certain that this time she'd be recognized. And, if her experience was any indication, thrown bodily from the coach and sneered at. The closer they got to Riles, the more she wanted to bury her face in her cloak.

But it was not until the final leg of the ride, after Laena had spent a blissful two hours riding by herself, that an elderly woman hobbled into the coach, sat directly across from her, and narrowed her eyes.

Laena looked out toward the increasingly familiar roll of the hills, pretending she couldn't feel the old woman's gaze on her. But the moment she turned her head, the woman caught her eye. "You'll forgive me for staring, I hope."

The woman was wearing a woolen cloak pulled over her shoulders, a tarnished broach clipping it shut at the throat. She clutched a bag to her side, no doubt carrying all the coin she had in the world, and though her back was hunched and her entry into the coach suggested some pain in her back or legs, the sharp gleam in her eye said there was not much that passed by without catching her notice.

Laena blinked, affecting the innocent look she had been planning for the entire trip. She would be surprised. She would deny. And she would run, if she had to. "Of course, my lady," she said. "I had not noticed."

The woman laughed. After so many hours of university speeches, polite requests for bench mates to provide more space, and, in several cases, sibling squabbles, it was refreshing to hear someone laugh.

If Laena thought about it, she had not heard another person laugh in her presence—not honestly, not deeply—in some time.

"I'm no lady," the woman clarified. "And you look so much like our queen. I can't help but stare."

Laena swallowed. This close to Riles, she could walk if she had to. It would add time, but not a disastrous amount. "Queen Katrina has golden hair," she said lightly.

But the old woman was already shaking her head. "No, no. I meant Laena. I meant the real queen."

Laena's throat went dry. Of all the conversations and accusations she had imagined, this was not among them. She had never been queen—and officially, Katrina was not yet queen—but that had always been a matter of splitting hairs to the people of Etra. If an Etran queen passed, the heir was spoken of as the new queen. Even if she had yet to complete her tour and be coronated.

"Laena was dethroned," she said carefully.

The old woman leaned in, her expression eager. As if this was a favored subject of hers, whether speaking to a friend or a random stranger who just happened to resemble the abdicated queen. "Have you never wondered why? Laena was so well suited to the role. Well studied. Kind. Smart as a whip when she was a girl, asking questions of everyone she met. She'd walk the streets, and you'd know you were in the presence of greatness."

Greatness. Laena turned the word around in her mind, unsure of how to respond. She would not have known how to respond even when she had been expecting to take the throne. But perhaps she could have at least stopped her cheeks from reddening.

She was so used to the open hatred of the villagers. Their disdain had carved her confidence away in chunks over the last five years until she hardly recognized the confident woman she'd been. She had not imagined anyone in the realm might think otherwise.

Of course, it was possible that this woman knew who she was. But even if she did, there would be no reason to curry favor. Katrina had made it abundantly clear that Laena was out. Unwelcome in Riles, if not officially exiled.

The old woman sat back. "I always wondered why she'd feel she was forced to abdicate over some love affair. Especially when the man was... well. Destined to be fleeting I'd've said. Yes?"

The woman, still craning her neck, leaned forward, as if the subject of their conversation was too juicy to discuss at a distance. Even so close a distance as the interior of a coach. Laena ought to change the subject, to guide it elsewhere, but she found she was interested in what the woman had to say about Ben. Perhaps she represented a thread of opinion in Etra, though she might just as well be an eccentric outlier.

"What makes you say that?" Laena asked.

"I saw him, a time or two." The woman laughed again, and this time it sounded almost girlish. Like a giggle. "I wouldn'a given up a throne to have him between my legs, is all I'm saying. Not saying I would have *minded* him there, just... it always seemed..."

The old woman raised her hand, holding her fingers a short

width apart, and Laena stared at her, taking a moment to understand her meaning. When she did, she coughed, cheeks flushing with heat beneath the bandages. "How could you possibly guess at the size of his..."

The woman reached out and gave her arm a swat. "Small in *character*, I thought. Where was your mind, girl?"

Laena opened her mouth, then shut it as the woman laughed again. "Point is," she continued, "the queen knew what she was about. She spent her life preparing, took the reins with grace after her mother passed so suddenly, poor creature. You could tell the regent was nothing but a formality. And then all of a sudden she was out. Seems like there's much more to the story than we know."

A hard lump of cold energy, roiling at her center, demanded to be set free. Powerful and frightening, a secret that could tear the crown apart and bring so-called allies like Aglye storming in for the attack. The stifling air in that council room, the bead of sweat rolling down her spine as her power had chafed to be set free until she could no longer contain it. Until she'd nearly killed her own advisors over a disagreement.

A fear, so deep and brittle that it had driven her to seek comfort in Ben's arms, to believe the promises he'd whispered in the night. Katrina's wide-eyed shock when she'd walked in on them together, and the way she'd stayed silent as Declan commanded Laena to choose. Choose now. Just as Laena had counted on him to do.

The old woman sat back on the bench, twisting her back with a grimace. "More than you and I will ever know, I suppose."

Laena allowed herself a shaky breath. She might be rusty at controlling a conversation, but she still knew an opening when she heard one. "The regent has things well in hand until Queen Katrina comes of age," she said. "I'm sure."

The old woman snorted. "A small man, if there ever was one.

Character, my dear. I've no need to picture his shriveled old..."
She shuddered.

"Are we still talking about personality?" Laena asked.

The old woman winked. "Of course."

"He's not even that old," Laena said, but the protest sounded weak even to her own ears.

The woman just shrugged and closed her eyes, the ghost of a smile lingering on her lips. And Laena couldn't shake the impression that she knew exactly who she'd been talking to.

CHAPTER 4

$\mathcal{M}$ildly uncomfortable though it was, the stage bumped along without incident until they reached the crossroads that led directly into the city proper. There it stopped, waiting. To the east and down a short rise, the sea sparkled beneath a cerulean sky, the puffed clouds floating like sheep's wool above the waves.

The sight was familiar enough to squeeze Laena's heart with longing. Seated by the window for the first time on the journey, she wished she could open it so she might breathe in the salty-sweet tang of the sea. As the delay stretched, she found herself debating the possible outcomes of opening the window, or perhaps even the door. She was desperate for fresh air, the relief of a sea breeze.

Just as she was considering making the move, the old woman opened her eyes and looked around, then rapped her fist on the ceiling of the coach. "What's the holdup?" she called.

The coachman hopped down from his perch to open the door, letting in a gusty breath of sea air. "Royal procession coming up from the harbor," he said gruffly. "Road's closed till they pass."

The woman rapped on the ceiling again, though the coachman was no longer seated up there. "We could've passed three times since we've been stopped."

The coachman glared at her, clearly just as annoyed at the delay. "If you want to convince the King's Guard to let us pass, be my guest."

The woman got to her feet and heaved herself out of the coach, sending the whole thing rocking on its dubious springs. "At least let us stretch our legs."

"Be my guest." The coachman drew a cigarette out of his pocket and struck a match on the side of the coach. "But I ain't counting heads. If you're not inside, I'm leaving you behind."

The woman snorted a laugh. "There are only two of us, you dolt."

Laena followed the woman gratefully out of the coach, her back popping as she set her bag at her feet and stretched her arms toward the sky. The landscape of her childhood stretched out before her, tall grasses sloping gently down as if running for the loving arms of the sea, interrupted only by occasional knots of boulders. She knew every one of them intimately; during her youth, they'd been fortresses and pirate ships, lookouts and towers.

And indeed, a royal procession was making its way up from the harbor, where an enormous ship was moored just offshore. It was a flagship, if she wasn't mistaken, and not an Etran one; no, that ship flew a flag of cornflower blue set with a royal purple seal. Aglyean colors.

"That little sneak," Laena muttered.

The procession wasn't flying King Hawk's banner, which had to mean they'd come to escort Etra's emissary into Aglye. The countryside with its rocky coastline could be treacherous, and Etra was a small nation. If Silerith really was threatening the realm, they'd need to keep their sparse military here.

But that also meant that Katrina had summoned this delega-

tion before she'd come to speak to Laena. It took a good fortnight to travel here from Vunmore, the capital. And though this
delegation might not include King Hawk, they would not have
sent just any soldiers to escort a royal emissary.

That was the famed King's Guard, and make no mistake.
When Laena squinted toward the head of the procession, it was
not her still-silent magic that sent a chill up her spine, but the
sight of the domineering leader who rode at the head of the
party.

Callum Farrow. The famed Aglyean captain, known for
enforcing Aglye's magic bans with ruthless efficiency. Though
Etra enforced similar laws, they were remote enough, small
enough, that occurrences were fairly rare.

It was said that Callum Farrow could smell a den of magic
from leagues away. It was said he broke down doors with his
fists, and the tight fit of his Aglyean blue uniform suggested he
had the power to do it. It was said he dragged magic users away
from their families, impervious to their repentant pleas.

It was also said that he had murdered magic users out of
hand, on more than one occasion.

They would have been heart-tithers, she reminded herself.
The pain they caused was worthy of imprisonment—though she
could not condone any murder. But Laena did not doubt the
man's famed hatred of magic would extend to any and all such
powers. Including hers.

Although she'd never met him, she'd heard tales of his
massive height, his broad shoulders. His size indeed struck her
now as the stuff of legends, making it a wonder that even his
warhorse could carry him so easily. But it was the curl of his
dark hair that captured her attention, the way it brushed along
the curve of his jaw. It was the ice-blue cut of his gaze as he
looked out over the Etran countryside that made her throat go
dry, and not only out of fear.

As a young woman hearing tales of his exploits, he'd seemed

a hero. But what would he do to her, if he discovered her power?

Nothing good.

"Who's a little sneak?" Laena startled as the old woman from the coach spoke from her elbow. She was looking up at Laena with shrewd dark eyes, her wispy hair stirring in the breeze.

"Oh," Laena said. "No one."

The woman nudged Laena with her elbow. "Come on, darling, I live for the drama. You think I get much drama these days? No. No, I don't. Half the time I have to make it myself!" She cackled at that, eyes glinting.

"Just my sister," Laena said. "It's nothing."

"I have a sister," the woman returned. "She's a wench."

Laena laughed, stifling it quickly, and turned her gaze pointedly back to the procession. They were already disappearing up the road to the city, no doubt ready to enjoy their royal accommodations.

Who, Laena wondered, would Kat be sending in her place? She didn't want to care, but she could admit to curiosity, at least. If only to herself. Kat wouldn't send Declan, would she? The regent would do fine, Laena supposed, but he was needed here. Maybe Lord Graver. Or Cyn Cauthon.

None of them were right. None of them would speak convincingly enough. None of them knew how to sugar their words only to bait their opponent into a bitter bite of their true intentions.

It was no longer Laena's concern. She was only here to inform Katrina of the threat to Etra: the presence of the blight and the shadow monster. Nothing more.

The old woman sighed, clearly disappointed at the lack of gossip, but Laena left it at that.

At length the procession passed, and the coachman ordered them back into the stage.

———✳——

THE COACH DROPPED its only two passengers in the lower city, and Laena shouldered her bag, happy for a chance to stretch her legs. The city folded around her as it so often had in her dreams, the smell of cedar welcoming her back to the streets like a hug. Vendors fried basilnuts and sausage on the corners, and giggling children darted between buildings. Music played, carts rumbled, and shop assistants moved about with packages and pails of waste.

It was a busy place. A prosperous one. And Laena missed it more than she cared to admit.

Brin poked her head out of Laena's bodice to look around, her tongue darting as she took in all the new smells. Laena had thought to leave the shimmerling behind, but in the end, she'd given the lizard a small bed in her satchel. No doubt the pesky creature would have hitched a ride, in any case. Might as well be on Laena's terms.

Besides, she couldn't bear to leave Brin behind in that rotting garden. It wouldn't be safe.

Etra carried a strong tradition of connection to its people and its streets and, as the old woman from the coach remembered so well, Laena had been encouraged to walk into the city from a young age. With protection, certainly, but the guards had kept their distance to allow her as true an experience as possible. From her studies, she understood that Aglye's princess lived a sheltered life. In Etra, they believed in full immersion into their own culture.

Laena had not yet visited the continent, but she couldn't imagine a more beautiful city than this one. It could not exist.

Had she not abdicated the throne, she'd have embarked on her Queen's Journey five years ago, touring the country on her own for a time before visiting the continent. Kat would be undertaking the journey next year, assuming the tradition wouldn't be delayed by war with Silerith.

Laena half expected someone to recognize her, even now. But five years was a long time, and with her hair bound in a kerchief, her skin tanned from days spent in the sun, she blended in with the people more effectively than she ever had. No one even cast a glance her way, except for the shopkeeper who she nearly collided with as she gawked at her own city.

No, it wasn't her city anymore. Even if memories told her that it was.

Forcing herself to focus on the task at hand, Laena made her way up the hill to the palace. The Aglyean delegation was already inside the gates, making official greetings in the plaza as servants scurried about. The delegation might not have sent King Hawk himself, but Callum Farrow's presence suggested that things were indeed as dire as Kat had suggested. Aglye certainly seemed as eager as Kat for the delegation to succeed, if they would lend their famed magic hunter as an escort.

When Laena stopped at the guardhouse, it became clear that her anonymity would be a problem. A rather large one, in fact. People on the street glanced at her as she walked straight up to the palace gates.

Suddenly, she was all too aware of how many days she'd gone without washing her plain woolen skirt. Her satchel felt ratty, her hair wispy and out of place after so many days traveling. The guard eyed her warily as she approached, his gaze lingering on the cut on her cheek. She took pains to hold her spine straight and look him in the eye.

Although if his eyebrows became any more overgrown, they'd obscure his vision.

"I'd like to meet with Princess Katrina, please," she said.

"And I'd like a pet unicorn, miss," he said. "As it is, you'll need to wait for Queen's Day for an audience with the princess and the regent. They'll attend to your concerns then."

He waved her back, gesturing dismissively toward the street, like she was nothing more than a fly. Laena bristled, not only because of her identity but because a palace guard should not be talking to an Etran citizen this way. He should be kind, at least to someone clearly approaching the gates without an attempt to harm.

But it would have been a lie to say his failure to recognize her didn't sting. She wouldn't have expected the people on the street to know who she was; they were busy with their own lives, for starters, and even Kat's appearance would be a mere asterisk to their days. But a member of the palace guard ought to recognize her face.

She shifted her bag on her shoulder. Her back ached after days of travel, and she was longing for a bath. "I… you don't know me?"

He narrowed his eyes. "Should I?"

Yes, she thought. But truly, why should he? If he'd joined the guard any time in the past five years, he'd have had no reason to learn her face. She hadn't returned even once since she'd left the city with Ben. She hadn't been invited, true, but she might have made an effort.

Laena swallowed, trying to piece together a story without angering the guard—so many were angry at what they saw as her betrayal—and without sounding like she considered herself entitled to an audience. She wasn't. She'd ceded that right, along with everything else.

Abruptly, she realized that Captain Farrow had broken away from the greetings and was crossing the courtyard to speak to the guard. To ask for assistance or directions, or perhaps to inform him of some crucial Aglyean protocol.

Instead, he leaned one hand on the iron gate—a posture that was distinctly *not* commander-like—and looked directly at her.

If he had seemed tall from a distance at the cliffs, he was absolutely massive as he stood before her. Laena wasn't a short woman, and he still towered over her. She'd memorized etchings of his face, along with so many others—an essential point in her studies so as to avoid embarrassing important dignitaries from other realms—and though they had portrayed him as much younger, his identity was unmistakable. He loomed over the guard yet somehow managed not to seem frightening. Or at least he didn't appear frightening to Laena.

It was a lie. He ought to be frightening. He ought to be very frightening indeed to a magic user.

"Is there a problem here?" Farrow's voice was deep, though edged with a ragged timbre that might have been the fatigue of a tiring journey from Vunmore. The guard glanced at Captain Farrow, eyebrows raised, as if he'd never expected a visiting King's Guard member to address him and wasn't sure how to interact with an officer from another realm's military.

"No, sir," the guard said. "No problem. It's just that this young woman wants an audience, and I cannot grant it."

Young woman. Laena nearly snorted. She'd stake her lunch on being older than this man.

Scratch that, actually; she hadn't eaten since breaking her fast on hearty porridge at the inn this morning. She'd stake her cloak on it, then. It wasn't overly chilly, after all.

Callum Farrow looked her directly in the eye, and her breath caught in her throat. His portraits showed him with blue eyes, and while that wasn't altogether inaccurate, it certainly wasn't sufficient, either. The blue that had seemed so icy from afar was nearly the shade of the sea, not cold but warm, inviting her to stare into them at length to determine their exact shade.

If she were a fool, that was. But as she wasn't, she averted her gaze back to the guard.

"Do you not recognize this lady, officer?" Captain Farrow asked.

The guard glanced at Laena, then back at the captain. "No," he said. "No... sir?"

Still clearly uncertain about his place in the chain of command here.

"This is Queen Katrina's sister. Princess Laena."

How in all the Vales did he know *that?* She supposed he would have educated himself in the same way she had, to avoid embarrassing situations in other realms. But she would not have expected a foreign soldier, even a high-ranked one, to recognize her with this ratty dress.

His gaze went to her cheek, and he frowned. As if the sight of the cut offended him personally.

"Kat's still a princess, too," Laena said, cheeks burning. It was bad enough not to be recognized by her own family's guard. But to have a representative from another realm speak for her? It was humiliating. "Technically."

Captain Farrow hitched an eyebrow as if to say *I'm trying to assist you, Princess.* He seemed the type to say her title with a hint of disdain, though so far he'd only spoken respectfully. "*Princess Katrina,* then," he said.

And he was trying to help her. She was caught between the desire to thank him and the screaming in her brain that said this man would throw her in prison if he knew her secret. She should be running. Instead, she wanted to step closer. She had the ridiculous urge to reach through the gate and give one of his curls a tug.

The guard swallowed hard. "I... the one who ran off with the...?" He glanced at Laena, then looked back over his shoulder. "I need to find my superior officer."

"That would be best," Captain Farrow agreed. "In the meantime, perhaps we might allow Princess Laena into the plaza? She looks as if she's journeyed a long way."

Instead of waiting for a response, he unlatched the gate and swung it open, inviting Laena back into her own home.

CHAPTER 5

*F*or a woman who'd just been snubbed by a member of her own guard, Princess Laena was remarkably calm as she passed Callum and entered the palace plaza with her head held high and her satchel clutched in her hands. She wore simple wool skirts, a curve-hugging vest laced over the top of a gray blouse, and tall boots that reached almost to her knees. Green eyes sparked with determination beneath the kerchief she'd tied in her brown curls. A delicious mess of brown curls, highlighted with strands of red and gold from days spent in the sun. The kind of curls a man could plunge his fingers into. The kind of curls a man could get lost in.

If that man were a fool. Callum cursed himself, and the fatigue of the road, for even allowing the thought to pass through his mind.

There was no need to lust after the woman, beautiful though she was. Though he did allow himself to entertain a brief notion of throttling whoever was responsible for the nasty cut on her cheek.

He hadn't helped her because of her looks, nor because of

the fresh scent she brought with her. Sea air and fresh soil, with a hint of something floral. Lavender, maybe.

"I'll escort you to your sister in case of another incident," he said. "Though I suppose you'll have to show me the way."

She regarded him coolly. She might be dressed like a farmer, but her bearing was that of a royal. Make no mistake. "What about the guard?"

"We'll get it sorted." Hawk probably wouldn't appreciate him breaking a rule within his first ten minutes in Etra, but then Hawk hadn't wanted to send him on this mission in the first place. He'd have other things to scold Callum about when the party returned.

As for Callum, he didn't much care for idiotic rules. If Etra's palace guards hadn't been trained to recognize their own princess—abdicated from the throne or not—then they ought to learn. Even if their own commanders hadn't bothered to educate them. Not to mention the would-be queen.

Luckily, Princess Laena didn't seem to be much for rules either. She gave a curt nod and shouldered her satchel with a conviction that suggested she would not appreciate an offer to carry it for her.

Callum followed her into the palace entry, where the guards allowed him to pass without comment, darting quick looks at his companion before returning to their posts. They'd been informed of *his* identity, at least. And perhaps some of these *did* recognize her. They ought to educate their colleague at the gates.

She cleared her throat. "I suppose if you know who I am, you're aware of why they don't?"

He wondered if she would prefer for him to pretend he had not heard the story. But gossip was gossip, and the story of the Etran queen's abdication had been the central subject of conversation for months. Bards still sang of it, in the form of love epics and bawdy drinking songs.

He would not have been surprised to learn that Aglye had been more entranced with the story than her home country.

Callum suspected any attempt to deny his knowledge would earn him a scowl. After all, this woman was trained to see straight through a lie. "I pay no heed to rumors," he said.

She let out a laugh, bitter and short. "Rumors, they were not."

"Gossip then. The identity of the man in your bed is no concern of mine, my lady."

Unless it happened to be him. The thought came unbidden, and he shook his head, trying to dispel the notion. He was travel weary; that was all.

She tipped her chin a little higher. "Just Laena, please."

He knew the story, of course. In truth, he'd thought her brave to leave her life in the palace the way she had. What a foolish law, prohibiting princesses from marrying commoners. Callum had often thought a good farmer might make an excellent king. And in a country like Etra, where they claimed to understand and love their people so fully, it seemed particularly hypocritical. Not that he paid much heed to politics, but one couldn't live in the palace without picking up an opinion or five.

She'd left for love. Who could fault her for that?

Then again, he'd always been inclined to cheer for one who balked against the restrictions of a royal existence. If anything, he faulted her only for failing to change the law. As far as anyone knew, she hadn't even bothered to try.

That question was far less common, at least in Aglye. People preferred the romantic story over the practical one.

He'd allowed the silence to stretch for far too long as she led him along corridors lined in salmon-pink and white stones. "I apologize for my fatigue," he said. "I'm Callum Farrow, captain of the Aglyean King's Guard."

"Oh," she said, sounding surprised, "yes, I know who you are. Apologies, Captain Farrow. I appreciate the intervention."

Of course she knew who he was. She could probably recite his family tree—sparse as it was—and Hawk's to boot, which was much more complex. She could probably give him an entire political history of his realm before they reached their destination.

Which, he realized, was one she was leading him toward, rather than the other way around. She was striding through a maze-like collection of corridors, each exactly like the others. Where Vunmore's fortress was made of graying stone and frowning busts, dark corners and candlelit sconces, the Etran palace took every opportunity to allow in the light. The ceiling was made almost entirely of clear glass, showcasing the crystal-blue sky. How did it fare against the seaside storms? He would have expected constant leaks if not breakages.

It was a security risk, too.

His mind truly felt in a fog. The journey had been a long one, true, particularly since he'd pressed the soldiers rather quickly to prevent Moore from catching up with them. He needed a drink—or several, come to that—and a good long rest in a decent bed. Too many nights sleeping beside campfires and trading horses for ships and then horses again.

He'd no doubt missed whatever official welcome had been prepared for the party in the courtyard, though perhaps that was best left for Edmun to handle.

Laena glanced at him, a slight frown on her face, and he realized he still had not answered her thanks.

He cleared his throat. "Of course. I'm happy to help."

Still clutching her satchel, she looked directly at him, keeping a steady pace through the halls without leaving him behind. She'd been gone for five years, if he remembered correctly, but navigating the twists and turns and rhythms of the busy palace certainly seemed to be second nature.

"I'm sorry about the king," she said. "His passing was such a terrible tragedy."

A painful lump dropped into Callum's throat, the same one that materialized whenever someone mentioned the king's death. The man had been gone a year, and still condolences felt like a physical blow.

"A tragedy, yes," he said, unable to keep the growl out of his voice. "At least you didn't say accident."

Laena slowed, giving him a sharp look, and said, "Pardon me, but did I say something out of turn?"

Callum stopped, raking a hand through his hair. He needed to find a swallow of whiskey, as soon as he was able. Perhaps he could bypass the pleasantries of the arrival, beg a headache, and retire to his accommodations with a bottle. Hawk wouldn't like it. But Hawk wasn't here.

Hawk hadn't even *sent* him here, a fact he needed to keep reminding himself of. Though a voice in the back of his mind said that he was blowing his chance to prove himself the worthy and useful captain he'd come here to be. Indispensable.

If he completed this mission with honor, Hawk might decide to reinstate him as captain of the guard. Oh, Callum would have to endure a lecture—a long one, perhaps more than one—on responsibility and deceiving the soldiers and all that. But if he returned triumphant with the Etran emissary, Hawk could hardly admit to the dignitary that he wasn't meant to have led the group at all.

It would buy Callum some time, at the very least.

For now, though, Princess Laena was still looking up at him with wide green eyes. She stood nearer his height than most women, he realized, yet she still tipped her head back to look at him, a question in her eyes. And Callum found, not for the first time, that he couldn't face the conversation. He couldn't face decorum, or a polite response.

He was not one for the rules. And that included the rules of society.

"I believe you'll be capable of finding your way from here."

He gave her a short bow, though he wasn't at all sure that was still an appropriate choice. "My lady."

Before she could object, he turned on his heel and fled down the corridor, doing his best to make it look as if he wasn't fleeing at all.

CHAPTER 6

$\mathcal{I}$f Kat had looked pristinely beautiful in the sitting room at Sunflower Cottage, she was resplendent when surrounded by her own accommodations. Swathed in a forest-green gown with delicate lace cuffs and glittering buttons, she'd entered her waiting parlor in a cloud of lily-scented perfume, with Declan Riennad on her heels, though the regent had taken his place beside the door. Keeping his silence no doubt, to allow Kat to handle the situation.

To say that Kat's expression was smug did not begin to describe the truth of it. Declan might be allowing her to lead, but he needed to teach her to school her reactions. She'd done a decent job in the cottage; now, her triumph was all too clear. She looked as if she'd just won a contentious game of croquet against a particularly brutish opponent. And she didn't even attempt to hide it.

Nor had she bothered to take a closer look at the crystal that Laena had laid upon the table, with a handkerchief underneath it for protection. The rock had shifted in appearance during the journey, and it was now cut through with angry crimson lines. If Laena looked at it for too long, she almost imagined she could see a heartbeat fluttering within. A not-small part of her wished she'd opted to leave it at home. What if the monster *had* been born of it?

But Kat would never listen to her without proof. Even now, her sister wasn't even bothering to inspect the horrid thing. She had not taken a seat on the opposite settee, though Laena didn't know if it was because the corset made it difficult for her to sit, or because she wanted to maintain the power in the conversation. As if this conversation was so unimportant that she would soon be gone.

Laena would have been able to maintain the power, whether sitting or standing or dancing a jig.

Not that it mattered anymore.

"I appreciate you coming all this way, sister," Kat said. "But this appears to be some kind of elaborate prank. Why not alert the village constable?"

First, because the village constable had made it clear upon Laena's arrival that he considered her to be a traitor who ought to be hung. And second, because this was far more than a simple prank. If Katrina was to be the queen of this realm, she needed to protect her people.

But acidic words would not help the situation. Laena drew in a deep breath and met her sister's gaze steadily. "This crystal is but a sample of the blight I discovered in the garden the day before I was attacked."

"Attacked," Kat repeated. "By a shadow monster, you say. But shadows have no form."

Laena curled her fingers into a fist. "Do formless shadows draw blood?"

Kat's eyes flickered over the cut on Laena's cheek. "A wayward branch might have done as much."

"If attached to a blade," Laena shot back. *Or a whip.*

"And how did you defeat such a monster, sister? With sharp words and your few remaining shreds of honor?"

Not dignity. *Honor.* She'd abandoned her country for a man, and that was dishonorable. As if Kat had not been salivating for the job.

For no reason at all, Captain Farrow's face sprang into her head. He'd been kind to her. In fact, he didn't seem to care a whit for her supposed disgrace. Though the mention of the man in her bed had heated her cheeks in ways she wasn't interested in pursuing.

His reaction when she mentioned the king had surprised her. It should be a common enough sentiment; from what she'd heard, the old king had raised Farrow alongside his sons and his daughter.

Perhaps most people gave their sympathies to King Hawk. Or perhaps Farrow hadn't been treated well, somehow.

Laena wanted to believe that if her sister knew the truth, she would understand why Laena had left. She had loved Ben—she sometimes thought she still did—and his betrayal still cut like a knife. But it was the growing power, the rock of icy power growing within her like that poisonous icicle, that had prompted her to abdicate her responsibilities. For the good of the realm.

Callum Farrow's kindness would certainly dry up if he learned of her secret. There would be no interventions, no sharp words to guards. He would haul her to the darkest dungeon, if he allowed her to live at all.

And Kat's last bit of patience with her would be gone, too. Etra might be more lenient than Aglye, but magic was still illegal.

But Laena had anticipated this question. She'd had days to prepare an answer, and had considered everything from cryptic to dismissive to outright lies. Now, looking at Kat's barely concealed anger, the truth on the tip of her tongue, she didn't want to play games. She merely wanted her sister to understand the severity of the situation. "Katrina. It makes me think of—"

"Do not say it," Kat interrupted.

"But it does," Laena pushed. "It makes me think of Mirage."

Declan startled and took half a step forward as if to intervene in the conversation, but Kat was already opening her mouth to speak. "The Miragelands are sealed away," she said airily. "They cannot touch the Vales."

Declan nodded, lips pressed together, and retreated back to his hiding spot. He'd seemed so intimidating to Laena when she'd been the focus of his tutoring. Now, he seemed younger than she remembered, his auburn hair thick, his beard well-trimmed. Hardly worthy of the title she'd given him of dry old goat.

Though the title was really more about one's aura than one's temporal age.

Also, there was something about the way he looked at Katrina, the way his eyes lingered well below her face, that made Laena want to slap him.

"Are you quoting directly from your textbook?" Laena asked. "Or do you have an opinion of your own?"

Kat flushed, the corners of her mouth tightening in annoyance. "I am stating what I know to be true."

A petty part of Laena wanted to flounce out of the room and let Kat discover her mistakes in disastrous fashion. She was not obligated to ensure her sister's success.

But this was not about Kat. This was about Etra. "Please." She hated the pleading note in her tone, hated that she had to beg. But sometimes, a moment came in diplomacy where even the most hated tools needed to be used. "Don't be a fool. Don't refuse to listen just because you hate me. You need to reach out to the farmers and find out if anyone else has discovered this blight. The alchemists can study it, find out if there's an antidote. You can prevent a famine if you just heed the warnings now. Before it's too late."

She felt herself leaning forward, hands on her knees, peering up at her sister. She'd dropped the mask, allowing Kat to see her fear. Anything, everything, if it would break through Kat's frosty exterior.

She cared about Etra, too. Laena knew she did.

Kat's spine stiffened. "I know how to be queen, Laena. Far more than you ever did. I didn't abandon my people."

"Katrina," Declan said softly, and Kat trailed off, though the defiance remained painted across her face.

There was nothing else to say. If Katrina would not listen, then Etra was truly in danger. Laena hadn't truly considered what might happen if her sister rejected every attempt to make her see reason. Laena might go to the farmers guild herself, if she could guarantee she would not be recognized. It wouldn't do if they thought she was causing divisions.

She might well cause an *actual* division, if more people felt the way the old woman in the coach did. If more people believed she should have kept her throne—that she deserved to.

Laena rose. "It was a mistake to come here," she said, keeping her tone even. "I'm sorry for wasting your time."

She would find another solution. She would have to. Unless the blight had stopped with the defeat of the shadow monster, she more than suspected her home would no longer be livable upon her return. The black poison would already be crawling up the walls, eating away everything she'd worked so hard to build.

Kat glanced at Declan, who nodded, his expression grim. Laena nearly rolled her eyes. Kat was the princess, soon to be queen. She shouldn't need Declan's approval to do anything.

Katrina settled herself on the flower-printed chair across the table. "I will look into the matter," she said, "if you agree to serve as emissary to Aglye."

Caught. Well and truly caught. Here Laena had been smugly assessing her sister's poor negotiation, and Kat had been in control of the entire conversation. From the very start, perhaps even from the moment Laena stepped up to the gates. If Kat had watched her long enough to know Ben was gone, she might easily have known when Laena set out for Riles.

Laena should have anticipated it. She'd been long absent from the maneuvers of court life, but Kat had grown up among it, too. And she was not out of practice.

"This is your realm at stake," Laena said. "And you want to make a *deal*? Tell me you weren't the one who planted this poison in my garden, Kat."

Kat's eyes widened. "Certainly not. And making deals is what the role entails, Laena. Or have you forgotten? If there is something you need, then you may have it. For a price."

Of course she hadn't forgotten. Laena's political prowess had been second to none, once upon a time.

She wasn't certain she believed Katrina's protests—the timing of the poison in the garden was far too convenient. But where her sister would have found such a monster to attack her, Laena could not have said.

And unless Kat wanted her dead, Laena didn't want to believe she would have sent such a beast.

Emissary to Aglye. With Callum Farrow as her escort—and no doubt a constant presence even once they arrived in the capitol—it would be a dangerous task indeed. She'd be lying if she didn't admit that the power she'd used against the shadow monster frightened her. It was the kind of incident that had convinced her of the need to abdicate in the first place.

Despite her struggle to learn more about the magic by using it in small increments, she was not convinced she could fully control it.

But if she didn't go, Katrina would ignore the blight. She would not investigate it. And Etra could fall into famine—or far worse, if more of those monsters infested the land.

"Fine," Laena said. "I agree."

Kat popped to her feet, skirts bouncing. "Excellent. I'll go inform the council."

"The council is sitting?"

Kat lifted an eyebrow. "Well, yes. You barged in on us rather unexpectedly. We were attempting to appoint a new emissary. You caused quite a stir." She brushed her hands over her skirt, giving her head a rueful shake. "But then, that is what you prefer, is it not? All eyes on you?"

Laena opened her mouth, then closed it again. Was that truly what Kat thought of her? That she'd abdicated her throne in a bid for *attention*? There had been some, but surely someone with that level of vanity would have wanted to maintain her position, to push for a change in the laws—as the council had begged her to do at the time—and become queen instead of abdicating in favor of her sister's dearest wish.

Otherwise Kat would never have exposed her relationship with Ben after finding them together. And Laena would never have been forced to choose. It all happened five years ago, and Laena could hardly fault a fourteen-year-old for longing to be queen. But her sister had waved goodbye with glee in her eyes, eager to take the throne.

Perhaps if she hadn't reacted with such vicious excitement, Laena would have agreed to the council's demands. Perhaps she would have searched for a confidant, someone to help with the problem of the magic.

Or perhaps there would have been no other course, in any case.

Declan stepped forward to lay a hand on Kat's arm, the first sign of interference he'd shown. Laena could admit, grudgingly, that the regent took his responsibilities seriously. He was preparing Kat to be a great leader.

Kat nodded, but she didn't apologize. As they made their way to the door, Laena heard Declan whisper, "Well done, Your Highness."

———✳︎——

As DUSK SLID INTO EVENING, no one came.

Laena had stood by the window for a time, watching as a parade of lords and ladies meandered the grounds. First the before-supper strolls, then the after-supper ones. A busy place, the palace gardens. Always open to whoever wished to walk there. She took care to hide herself behind the floor-length curtains as best she could, though no one so much as glanced toward the window. Busy with their own affairs, as usual. As she looked down at the gardens, she found herself unable to decide whether or not she missed the palace life.

It had been busy, sometimes to the point of madness, but she'd reveled in the bustle of it all. A stroll with a friend might yield a scheme to build a university in the south; a garden party might give her the opportunity to raise funds for such an endeavor. Every ball, every event, was a chance to hear from the country lords how Etra fared in the south, the west, the central plains. And what might be needed.

As much as she took pride in the life she'd built at Sunflower Cottage, she did miss palace life, and her role in it. She missed it very much.

The lamps had been lit in the full dark of evening, and now the procession had slowed, leaving only a scattering of small groups here and there. Laena's stomach growled pitifully, and she allowed herself to sink onto the settee. No one had even come to light the lanterns. How long would she remain here, waiting like a fool? The council must have finished their meeting hours ago. Perhaps they'd elected not to make her emissary after all. Perhaps they'd learned of her magic and meant to send someone to arrest her.

After they'd had *their* dinners, no doubt. No reason to ruin a good meal with that sort of unpleasantness.

Or perhaps—and this seemed the most likely option—they'd merely forgotten she existed.

Brin, at least, had taken advantage of the quiet, abandoning her perch in Laena's hair to explore each corner of the room. Laena wished her well in finding a meal; the room was spotless, and no doubt scoured of any and all delectable insects.

Laena leaned back on the seat, paying no mind to her posture. What did it matter? Good posture or poor, she would never have her sister's respect.

The curtains stirred, a shadow flinching out of the corner of her eye. Before she could figure out what she'd seen, a pair of hands closed around her neck from behind and squeezed. Her throat worked uselessly, the breath caught in her lungs, as she clawed at the hands, but they were strong. Immovable.

Laena called for the power, but her core still felt hollow. A chill trembled there, like the barest beginning of a frost. After the fight with the monster, she didn't know if it would ever fully return.

Yet even without magic, she was no delicate palace mouse. She remembered her self-defense lessons—and farm life had made her strong. Heaving her legs up over her head, she kicked her attacker in the face and dislodged their hands from her neck as the settee tipped backward. Her head slammed into the floor, sending stars screaming across her vision, and Laena struggled to maintain consciousness.

She'd hoped the couch would pin the attacker—an assassin, it had to be—but the figure moved with lightning quickness, like a shadow flickering in the light. Laena scrambled to her feet and dashed for the door. The attacker caught hold of her wrist, yanking her backward—perhaps they meant to toss her from the window, or stick a knife in her gut—but Laena lunged for the vase in the corner and grabbed it by the lip, then hurled it over her shoulder.

The vase struck flesh—she hoped it was the attacker's evil

head—and the fingers loosened, allowing Laena to dart the rest of the way to the door, where Brin landed on her shoulder with a startled chirp as she escaped into the hall.

Kat had not even posted guards at her door.

Well, why would she, when she herself was not in residence? Few people even knew Laena was here. And if they did, she was hardly worth the trouble of killing.

Laena ran for the first door, twisting the knob, but it was locked. A slam sounded behind her, and she threw herself toward the next without taking the time to look behind her. It opened, and she slipped inside. She shut it quickly and threw her weight against it, breathing hard.

When she looked up, she found herself staring into the startled face of Captain Callum Farrow. He had a bottle in one hand, a mug in the other, his lips parted in surprise.

He was also naked. From the waist up anyway, and that was perfectly sufficient to catch Laena's breath in her throat. Hard lines defined the contours of his arms and the planes of his chest. His tanned skin glowed in the light of the fire. Despite the danger, and the fear tightening around her throat like the assassin's fingers, the sight of him froze her in place. For a moment, faced with that chest, and those shoulders, she forgot what words were. The room smelled of whiskey and woodsmoke, and she didn't know if it was him or the drink or a combination of the two.

"My lady?" he said, the words gruff and the slightest bit slurred, as if the drink had already dulled his tongue.

Already? No, it'd been hours since he'd escorted her to Kat's sitting room. Time for an entire meal's worth of drink. Two meals, even.

"I was attacked." Laena felt lightheaded; the aftermath of the fight had left her trembling. "In the—in Katrina's sitting room."

Captain Farrow's eyes sharpened, and he set the bottle on a sideboard. "Stay here."

He said it like a command, but Laena didn't mind. She wasn't sure she was capable of doing otherwise, in any case. She had just sense enough to move away from the door as he hurried through it. She remained rooted to the spot as the minutes ticked by. Some terror-stricken part of her brain was certain the man would meet his death, and that it would be her fault.

She was too rattled to sit, too rattled do anything but pace as she waited. He'd already strewn his shirt and jacket across the bed, and he'd gone after the assassin without his boots on. They sat by the door, already polished. He'd seen to them before disappearing into his drink.

Laena waited, the shock of the attack wracking her body with shivers, and still she could not keep herself from moving back and forth across the room. Even when Brin scurried out of her pocket to perch on her shoulder.

Laena tsked, offering the creature a hand so she could return her to the deep pocket of the skirt. "When did you leave the bag?" she scolded. "Hurry and hide yourself, before Captain Farrow sees you. There's no telling what he might do to your kind."

At length, he returned.

"I gave chase," he said, "but the imp escaped. The guard is on their way. Was no one stationed outside the room?"

Laena shook her head, her throat stinging as she swallowed hard. "There was a council meeting. I'm sure they were needed elsewhere."

Farrow's expression didn't change, but his gaze dropped to her neck as he stepped closer to her. "Are you hurt?"

She shook her head again, words sticking in her throat. He lifted his thumb, skimming light fingers along her neck and leaving her skin tingling. "This is a nasty mark."

He raised his fingers to her forehead, inspecting the bump that was no doubt rising angrily there. And though he was only checking her for injury, nothing more, she found herself wishing she could close her eyes and lean into his touch. She could feel the heat of him, and she was all too aware of the bareness of his chest. It was all she could do not to lift a hand and run her fingertips over those ridges of muscle, interrupted only by a jagged scar on the collarbone, another on his right bicep.

"I hit my head," she said. "When I knocked the settee over."

"We should call for the physician to inspect your injuries." He brushed the skin alongside the cut on her cheek, as if he felt they should take a look at that, too.

Then he dropped his hand, and she wasn't sure whether to be glad or sorry as he took hold of her elbow and eased her toward a chair by the fire. Dizziness rattled her head, and she swayed, but he didn't let go of her until she'd settled onto the edge of the seat. Where he promptly handed her his glass.

"Knocked the settee over, did you?" The corner of his mouth twitched, just slightly. "Impressive, my lady."

Laena took a swallow, grateful for the comforting burn of the whiskey in her throat. "I had no intention of dying this evening. And I told you, I'm no lady."

Apparently convinced of her safety, at least for the moment, Captain Farrow stepped to the bed, where a pile of clothing lay in a heap. He selected a shirt and shrugged it on over his head. He moved with a fluid kind of grace, despite the drink he'd clearly been taking all evening. Like a wolf, dark and dangerous.

And he was dangerous, she reminded herself. Especially to her.

In this moment, sitting by the fire, she wanted to forget it. But she'd be a fool not to recall that he would imprison her the moment he learned of her power.

"If the King's Guard dragged their feet like this, I'd have their heads," he muttered.

Dangerous, and a bit grumpy, too.

"Are you so used to assassination attempts?" Laena attempted to inject a note of amusement into her voice, but the incident was too near for levity. She could still feel the assassin's fingers around her neck, intent on murder.

"We live in the shadow of Silerith, my lady. We are always on our guard."

She supposed they would need to be. Was that to be Etra's future as well, then? Always looking over their shoulders and watching for assassins? It wasn't their way, and the idea sparked a painful wound in Laena's chest. That was the whole reason for Kat's mission, the reason Aglye had sent an escort headed by Callum Farrow himself. For if Silerith aimed to commit murder, what other choice did they have?

CHAPTER 7

*W*hen Etra's sloth-footed guards finally made their way to the scene of the attempted crime, they came with their queen tucked between their ranks like a porcelain doll wrapped in padding to protect her from bumps and cracks. She swept into the destroyed sitting room with the guards, the regent right behind, and stared at the disheveled room like it was a badly behaving child.

Usually Callum would have been impressed to have the queen—or queen-to-be, whatever she was—give her own inspection. She strode into the room so fearlessly. A family trait, perhaps.

But when he followed, he found her tapping her index finger on her bottom lip, frowning. "Are you sure Laena did not fabricate this situation, Captain?" she asked.

Hot anger boiled into Callum's stomach, conspiring with the whiskey to place an impertinent response on his tongue. But when he caught sight of Laena, who was leaning against the wall —she ought to be resting after her ordeal—he forced himself to speak amicably. As Hawk would want him to.

Laena's brown hair was in disarray, her skin so ghostly pale that it revealed a scatter of freckles along her cheeks he hadn't noticed before. The paleness worried him. That bump on her head might be serious.

Injured or not, he half expected her to bite out her own response to her sister's accusation. But shock had glazed her green eyes with a distant expression, and he wondered if she'd even heard what Katrina said.

"Her injuries are plain enough," Callum said. Angry bruises were already forming on her neck, and that bump on her head was startlingly large. She really ought to see the physician.

To say that he'd been surprised when the woman had come barging into his guest rooms would be an understatement. He'd been in the shallows of a bottle of whiskey and heading for deeper waters when she'd come barreling in, flushed and breathless, as if a demon were on her trail. For a moment, he'd assumed—momentarily—that she was a hallucination. A drink-induced vision. Or that he'd fallen asleep before the fire, prompting what promised to be the world's greatest dream.

But this was no dream, and Laena was injured and frightened, having fought off an attempted murder. And her sister thought she had fabricated it? Callum wanted to give the queen-to-be a shake.

"The former princess has a reputation for attention seeking, you see."

Callum had not yet heard the regent speak, but apparently this situation called for his involvement. The man held his head high, and something about his posture suggested that he would dive in front of Katrina at the slightest hint of danger. Callum recognized coiled muscles when they were ready to strike, like a soldier's. Though this man clearly wasn't one.

A snake, perhaps.

They couldn't truly think Laena would have made this up. Could they? He'd known the woman for a bare few minutes altogether, and unless she was an exceptional actress, her distress was incredibly clear.

He was half inclined to step in front of her himself. Alas, he couldn't protect her from their words. And he had a feeling she wouldn't thank him for trying.

"Be that as it may," Callum said slowly, "I saw the intruder myself. I gave chase. Do I also have a reputation for attention seeking?"

If the words were acidic, so be it. Even Hawk could not object. To speak of Laena—her own sister, disgraced or not—like she wasn't even in the room, after she'd endured such a trial? In Aglye, it would not be tolerated.

Katrina pressed her lips together, as if she wished she might snap back at him. He almost wished that she would.

Unfortunately, one of the guards chose that precise moment to speak. "The window was broken from the outside," he said. "Glass on the floor. Someone was in here."

"By the mages," Laena said sarcastically, "were they *really*?"

Callum suppressed a snort. So she had been listening after all.

Truly, he ought to have heard the disturbance. His room was directly diagonal to Katrina's sitting room. The settee had tipped over and she'd shattered a vase.

He'd nearly allowed a woman to perish while he lazed around in a daze of his own making. It felt so much like a repetition of history that his breath caught in his throat, threatening to drown him.

In truth, he'd not done anything to help Laena at all. He'd merely run fruitlessly after the assassin, whose dark clothing gave nothing away about their origins. Not that he needed to guess; they could only have come from Silerith.

"I think we must assume," the regent said, "that the assassin was after Princess Katrina."

So they were accepting the assassin theory now. Excellent.

"Because we look so much alike." Laena raised her hand as if to prevent the regent from uttering a retort. "No, Declan, that was a jest. You've heard of them? I'm neither dressed like a queen-in-waiting, nor golden-haired like my sister. I cannot believe the attacker mistook me for her, even from behind. Perhaps they meant to kill whomever they found here."

She spoke strongly enough, but she still looked like death had passed over her. Before Callum quite realized what he was doing, he said, "Have you eaten since your arrival, my lady?"

Katrina swiveled slowly in his direction, eyebrows raised, while the regent popped his mouth open like a fish. Almost as if they'd forgotten he was there.

Laena met his gaze, her own expression startled. Or maybe it was... curious. Birdlike, almost. "No, my lord," she said slowly. "I have not."

Callum had never been one for politics or maneuverings, but he could piece the situation together easily enough. He'd met her at the gate in the early afternoon, and the assassin had not come until well after nightfall. Which meant they'd withheld dinner, at the very least. Intentionally.

Callum might not be a royal, but he knew that visitors to palace sitting rooms were typically provided with an unceasing parade of sandwiches and pastries, to say nothing of the teas and coffees and carafes of wine.

It would have to be intentionally withheld, the servants instructed to send nothing.

These roaches had not even given her a guard. Suspicion crawled up his spine, and he found himself leaning toward the sniveling regent, wishing he could wring the man's neck.

Callum didn't know why she'd come back here at all. No wonder her paramour had chosen to remain in the countryside. Callum forced himself to picture the man. He found he needed to remind himself of the fellow's existence, and though he'd never met the famous stablehand, he opted to imagine him with a bulbous nose and knobby knees.

Even in his imaginings, the man was kind. Nothing like these people. And nothing like Callum.

Callum nodded in Laena's direction. "I'm no lord," he said, echoing her protests about him calling her a lady. He jerked his chin at the guard who'd spoken up about the shattered window. He, at least, was not in the regent's pocket. "You. Go to the kitchens and obtain the lady some dinner. She's staying in...?"

He looked to Katrina, who shook her head and—for the first time that he'd noticed—deferred to the regent.

Who cleared his throat. "No rooms have been prepared," he said.

By the black poison, what sort of people *were* these? And Hawk hoped to bargain with them for an alliance? The regent had tipped his chin toward the ceiling, standing by his statement, but the slight shift of weight between his feet gave away a hint of shame. Or at least embarrassment. That was something, at least.

Both he and Princess Katrina were looking at Callum. And he could feel Laena's eyes on him, too. Would she be angry with him for interfering? When he glanced her way, though, she merely looked bemused. As if she wasn't used to someone speaking on her behalf.

In Callum's mind, the stablehand grew a wart in the middle of his forehead. He should be here to defend his lover. His wife? Perhaps they'd wed by now.

"Have the food sent to my rooms, then," he said, the words coming out as a growl. "And be quick about it."

Katrina opened her mouth as if to object to someone else giving orders in her palace. But Callum was finished with propriety. No doubt General Landon Moore would've simpered for the queen-to-be, laughing as she sent her injured sister away in disgrace. But Moore had been too slow, and Callum was here in his place.

He turned on his heel, nodding at Laena to follow, and made for the door. "We mustn't linger any longer," he said. "The king must know of this attack. The delegation leaves at dawn."

CHAPTER 8

*L*aena was too exhausted and sore to overthink the fact that she was back in Callum Farrow's guest chamber, seated by his fire as the palace physician administered treatment. Though the way the captain loomed over the proceedings, it was as if he suspected the physician of sending the assassin.

The physician was a man Laena didn't know. Physician Gale, who'd served her family since her birth, must have retired. She would not have minded seeing the man again. But his replacement was businesslike and gentle, his movements deft as he examined her injuries. He administered cool cloths to her head and neck as well as ointment to her healing cut.

"No intense exertions for the next few days," he said. "A precaution only, you're perfectly fine. But do watch that cut for signs of infection."

Laena nodded, too tired to ask whether 'intense exertions' included traveling to far-flung lands. She would be on a ship. How intense could it possibly be?

The food arrived as the physician took his leave. A servant wheeled in an overflowing cart. Laena didn't know the servant either, which was something of a surprise. She'd always made a point to know everyone, by face at the very least. Many stayed in the palace throughout their careers. It seemed Kat had replaced much of the palace staff. Or perhaps Declan had.

It would be like them—to ensure loyalty by hiring new workers. Laena hoped they had at least arranged new employment for the others, if that was the case; it was hardly their fault they'd worked here when Laena had been heir to the throne.

Captain Farrow shooed the servant away, inspecting the tray of food with a glare she would have expected him to reserve for the most heinous of lawbreakers. Then again, judging by the looks he'd leveled at Kat and Declan back in the queen's sitting room, the man had a whole library of such looks to choose from.

"Any assassins hiding in the pudding?" Laena started to rise from her chair. If she went much longer without eating, especially with the scent of freshly baked bread and savory meat overwhelming her senses, she'd be forced to shove the man bodily out of the way. Though she doubted she was capable of budging him, even if she threw her entire body weight at him.

Farrow grunted as he wheeled the cart over to her, motioning for her to remain seated. "One can never be too certain."

By the mages, she couldn't tell whether or not the man was making a joke. But when he pushed the food closer, she found she didn't much care. They'd brought heaping platters of tenderly roasted meat and crisped vegetables shining with oil, mashed potatoes and cheeses and every kind of sauce she could imagine. There was fruit she hadn't beheld in five years—tangy citrus from the southern islands and the reddest grapes she'd ever seen—as well as a dish of ruby-red apples. The bread alone made her want to weep.

On the corner of the cart was a small plate set with four chocolate cookies. Rolled into balls, they required no baking, only a night spent in the icebox. She'd learned to make them herself as a child, before she'd understood how much it cost to import chocolate from overseas. Her mother had always reserved them for special occasions.

The guards, physicians, and servants might be new. But someone in the kitchen remembered Laena's favorite. The thought brought stinging tears to her eyes, which she blinked away before they could fall and embarrass her.

"They brought the dinner quickly," she commented, grabbing for a piece of bread. She was tired and shaky after the drama of the day, and the long journey. No call for tears, especially where Callum Farrow could see. "They must be frightened of you."

Or they wanted to get a better look at him. Who could blame them?

He splayed one hand across his chest, eyebrows lifting as if in surprise. "Of me? But why?"

Now she *knew* he was making a joke. "No one told me you were funny."

"I'm not. I'm frightening." He knelt beside her chair, brow creased as he inspected her bruises once again. It was all too easy to remember how he'd looked without his shirt, and she found her gaze drifting toward his chest. Chastising herself, she took the opportunity to study his face instead: the rugged cut of his jaw, the crooked tilt of his nose that suggested he'd endured at least one break. Perhaps more. A scar traced up from the corner of his eyebrow to his hairline, light enough that she would not have noticed it at a greater distance.

And those eyes, the ice-chip blue contrasted against the black of his hair. She'd never before seen such a combination.

"I take it you don't trust my sister's physician?" Laena had meant for the words to sound light and airy; instead, they sounded shaky, at least to her own ears. While she knew the palace physician was trustworthy, it was telling that Captain

Farrow, a stranger to Etra, had already seen enough to make him suspicious of both the food and the quality of the medical care.

A foreign captain was taking more interest in protecting her than her own family. It shouldn't sting, not anymore, but Kat was all she had left. She had reason to wish they would one day mend the rift between them and live as sisters again. Perhaps they'd never been particularly close, yet Laena couldn't help wishing for it. If it was a fool's hope, then it was better than not hoping at all.

Farrow lifted his hand, moving her hair aside, and carefully ran his fingers over the bump on the back of her head. His touch was gentle, and she found herself longing to lean into it. "After that display in her lacy little parlor?" he said. "I don't trust her, or anyone she employs."

His attention lingered on the cut, long enough that she thought he might ask about it. Instead, his gaze dropped briefly to her lips—so briefly that she might have imagined it—before he wrenched it away and stood, making his way to the other chair.

Laena swallowed, missing the feel of his fingers in her hair. She took a large bite of bread to cover her discomfort. "Mages, I missed palace bread. Nothing I bake is ever this good." When he didn't respond, she finished her bite and began heaping food onto a plate. "It's all right. The physician. Kat wouldn't hurt me."

His eyes flashed, like a storm brewing on a distant horizon. "She wouldn't help much, either."

Laena shrugged. No use denying it. Though truly, he had no reason to defend her. Part of her felt as if she ought to dress him down, to make it clear that she was capable of fighting her own battles. She had defeated that assassin herself—not to mention a shadow monster, though she could hardly tell him about that part. In comparison, her sister was an easy opponent.

At least, she ought to be.

"You came here alone," Farrow said.

As opposed to what? She couldn't read him, wasn't sure what he meant to imply. Laena slathered butter onto a second slice of bread. "As you see, Captain Farrow."

He waved away the title with a flick of his hand. "Everyone calls me Callum."

"Even your soldiers?"

"That would be inappropriate."

"So not everyone."

She could hear herself teasing him and couldn't stop herself from doing it. This man was the captain of the Aglyean King's Guard. He was famed for his ruthlessness, his cunning ability to hunt down any foe, and yet she found herself wishing she could lighten his burden, smooth out the crease between his eyes. Perhaps even make him smile.

The man before her somehow fulfilled that reputation and also defied it.

And why shouldn't he? People were not the same as their reputations. She should know that better than anyone. Still, it was difficult to reconcile the man before her with the killer she'd heard of.

She couldn't help but be all too aware of the intimacy of their situation. Them sitting together in his chamber, the bed not six feet away, the memory of his bare chest seared into her mind.

"Everyone who is not a soldier calls me Callum," he amended. The corner of his mouth hooked upward, ever so slightly, and it was suddenly all too easy to imagine that mouth pressed to hers. And pressed... elsewhere. "Are *you* a soldier, my lady?"

She raised an eyebrow, grasping for her equanimity. "No. And I'm not a lady, either."

He did not acknowledge the reminder. She wondered if he even accepted it. While it was true that she had never been formally stripped of her titles, and that she was still officially an Etran princess, she was now a commoner in every way that mattered.

Callum leaned an elbow on the arm of the chair, watching her intently. "And did you expect such a reception from your own sister when you decided to return here?"

How was she supposed to respond to *that* question? *Yes, actually I'm used to the disdain of my family and the people I was once responsible for? In fact, I came here to enjoy a helping of hostility, with a side of almost dying.*

What had she expected, truly? That Kat would welcome her arrival with open arms, thrilled to see her accepting the role of emissary after all? That she'd throw a ball in Laena's honor, receive her like some long-lost princess returned to the loving bosom of her family once more?

Perhaps not. But she'd expected a guest room, at the very least. Kat had been the one to come to her after all, not the other way around.

Still. It was not an appropriate question, and he damn well knew it. Callum could act as rough and tumble as he liked, but he'd grown up in his own palace, and he'd been chosen to lead this delegation. He knew how to speak properly, or King Hawk would not have sent him.

She regarded him coolly. "Do you interrogate all members of foreign royal families you meet, or am I receiving special treatment?"

"It might surprise you to learn that I meet very few foreign royal families. This is merely how I make conversation."

"With those manners, it doesn't surprise me at all that you meet very few royals."

"If your family is any indication of the norm, then I count it a very great blessing."

Oh, her family was anything but the norm. Laena looked at

her hands. It should be gratifying, to see him reading Kat's abhorrent behavior so thoroughly. That someone on the outside found it unacceptable. After so many years on her own, and the hatred of the villagers chipping away at what was left of her confidence, it surprised her more deeply than she would have expected.

"I was prepared for a cold reception," she said. She might as well answer the question. "But I admit I did not expect it would be this cold."

"You expected a cold reception, yet you journeyed here anyway. Why?"

It was easy to imagine him questioning a suspected magic user, rather than the sister of a foreign queen. She might put him off with a deflection or a lie, but he would learn the truth when she joined the traveling party at dawn. "I am to be the emissary to Aglye."

The subtle stiffening of his posture was the only indication of his surprise. "Ah." He paused, jaw ticking with an unspoken question. He looked into the fire while she stuffed another bite into her mouth, stifling a moan at the way the roast practically melted on her tongue. She'd save the precious dolloped cookies for last.

He cleared his throat. "What about your... you are free to be away from your own lands? For so long?"

Ah. He wanted to ask her about Ben. She could practically feel it in the air, the famed stablehand's existence hanging between them like a wall, even if he did not know her lover's name. Although he was rough in every way, the words did not leave his mouth.

Best to let him believe Ben was still in her life.

"I am," she said.

He pressed a fingertip to his bottom lip. "Forgive my surprise. It's only that..."

"That judging by my sister's response to the fact that I was almost murdered, it's surprising she would trust me with such a task?"

He inclined his head, ever so slightly.

Laena sighed. "I lost a negotiation."

It didn't answer his question, but he didn't press. He hadn't filled his glass again, though his gaze often strayed toward the bottle he'd left on the sideboard.

When she finished eating, she let her hands fall into her lap. She wanted to ask the obvious question, for no one had returned to escort her to a new room. Somehow, though, she didn't think he would object to her staying.

It was embarrassing, truth be told. She would not have allowed such treatment for any guest, let alone the leader of an important delegation. Kat should have rushed to prepare her a room, to serve her dinner there.

But Laena could not find it in herself to regret her sister's actions. Not when it allowed her a chance to speak with him. Merely because she was curious, of course. Interested in who he really was.

"You know," she said, "nothing about your reputation suggests you'd be like this."

Callum regarded her, head cocked to the side, as if he could not begin to guess what she meant. "What, handsome? Rough around the edges but in a charming sort of way?"

He was those things, and they did surprise her. Or at least the charm surprised her.

"No," she replied. "*Nice.*"

He blinked. "Nice?"

She nodded. "Nice."

He stared at her, lips parted, like he wasn't sure if he should take it as a joke. "I don't suspect any heart-tithers would say the same."

And with that, he dowsed the entire conversation with a bucket of chilly water. Not the welcome frost of her own growing power, but the tugging sensation of a tide beneath beautiful waters, lurking and ready to pull her under.

He might be handsome, and he might be charming—enough that she'd certainly been flirting with him—but it would be a mistake to forget who Callum Farrow was. A scourge upon magic users, the demon in the dark who hunted them down and dragged them from their homes.

Heart-tithers, yes. But she would be a fool to imagine he wouldn't apply the same tactics on anyone he found practicing magic.

The warmth that had been building in Laena's stomach went cold. "You are that harsh toward magic users, then?"

He stared at her, as if confused. "Naturally."

"You would kill them all, given the chance." It wasn't a question.

He sat forward in his chair, eyes intent on hers. "Whatever my reputation may tell you, I'm no executioner." His voice was soft but intense. "I arrest those who break the law. I don't murder them where they stand. If you'd seen some of the things I've seen, my lady, you might well praise that restraint."

She wasn't a lady, hadn't been one for a very long time.

"Forgive my confusion," he went on, "but is magic not illegal in Etra as well as in Aglye?"

It was. He knew that it was. If she kept talking to him, she would reveal her own secret. Her own shame, her own fear.

Laena stood. "If no one is going to escort me to my own room, then I shall have to sleep in this one. *You* may take the chair."

With that, she stomped to the bed, leaving him to stare after her in open-mouthed confusion.

CHAPTER 9

*C*allum suspected that he'd slept more nights on the ground than he had in the warmth of a bed. He'd slept through pelting rain and bone-rattling frost. He'd slept within spitting distance of the Silerith border, where enemy soldiers and dangerous beasts roved in equally frightening measure.

It was no great trial to sleep in a chair by the fire in a palace guest room. He would have offered the bed to Laena even had she not claimed it for herself. He didn't have to be a lord to know what was right.

Though perhaps a lord could have explained the sudden shift in their conversation, and the way her demeanor had shifted from pleasant to angry. Certainly, he was as used to angering people as he was to sleeping on the ground. But he usually knew why.

They'd been speaking of the horrors of magic. She'd known his name from the outset, which meant she'd known his reputation for hunting down magic users and punishing them for their crimes. If she took a softer stance toward magic, then he'd have expected her to hate him from the first moment.

Besides, magic was just as illegal in Etra as it was in Aglye.

No, he must have said something else to offend her. What it might be, he could not begin to fathom.

Now, as the sky began to turn gray, he woke to find the bed empty. Laena was gone, leaving behind only the faint scent of lavender.

Callum dressed quickly and made his way out of the palace.

Though his soldiers had no doubt been looking forward to the reprieve of several days' rest in Riles before starting the return journey to Vunmore, no one was griping as he entered the courtyard. They moved efficiently, loading fresh supplies and preparing the horses for the short ride to the sea.

The horses were Etran animals, sturdy and reliable, if not so fine as Aglyeans. They'd left their own mounts at the stables by the coast; Callum could not justify dragging the horses on a sea journey when the ride from Etra's coast to the palace was little more than an hour.

As he took stock of what still needed doing, Laena strode out of the palace, her skirts brushing his legs as she hurried past him, nose tipped so high she might have been trying to imitate her sister. She'd bullied someone into drawing her a bath; her curls lay damp and thick around the shoulders of her clean gray cloak, and the scent of lavender was even stronger. He wanted to bury his nose in her hair and breathe it in all day.

He swallowed. It'd been too long since he'd had a woman, clearly. "Good morning, my lady," he said.

She paused and looked over her shoulder. "Good morning, Captain Farrow."

She didn't correct him on his use of the title, nor did she use his given name, as he'd invited her to do yesterday. She didn't give him that mischievous hint of a smile he'd seen last night. It felt like a loss.

Before he could ask after the quality of her sleep, she turned her back on him and made for the gate. Not running away from him exactly, but not dawdling. A chilly reception, if he'd ever seen one.

"What'd you do this time, Captain?"

Callum resisted the urge to drop his head back and curse. Of course Edmun would have witnessed that interaction. Of course. The man never missed a beat.

The older soldier was standing a few paces away, arms folded. He'd been in the ranks since Callum had joined. Callum never knew why the man hadn't wanted to rise in the ranks; everything Callum knew, he owed to Edmun. Every time his contract came up, Callum feared he'd announce his retirement. And every time, the old man signed on the line without hesitation. Since Edmun was as fearsome with a blade now as he'd ever been, Callum had never seen reason to argue. In fact, it was a relief.

Edmun was thin and wiry, with only a few streaks of auburn still remaining in his whitening hair. Though Callum stood several inches taller, he often felt the old man was hovering over him. Especially when he had reason to disapprove of his captain's choices.

Callum headed for his waiting mount. "What makes you think I did anything?"

Edmun raised a bushy eyebrow, and Callum sighed. There was no point in trying to hide anything from the man. Ever. "Honestly, I don't know. She seemed perfectly happy last night."

The eyebrow raised higher.

"When I sat with her at dinner," he clarified.

And inspected her injuries, while trying not to think of kissing her. And slept in the same room.

And flirted. He was *sure* she'd been flirting with him. He'd been enjoying her quick wit, and the way she'd called him out on his manners. Not many in Aglye would have dared, but she did it so prettily, sizing him up and proclaiming he was surprisingly... nice. She'd said he was *nice*. It felt like it ought to have been an insult, but from her lips, it sounded like the epitome of high compliments. As if kindness was the pinnacle of greatness to which they should all aspire.

Kindness. No, Callum was anything but that. He simply knew how to exercise common decency, from time to time, when it suited him. And with Laena seated across from him last night, it had absolutely suited him.

The color had been starting to blush back into her cheeks when she'd abruptly shut down their conversation.

"It's just as well," Callum continued, watching her smile her thanks at young Godfrey as the kid handed her up onto a waiting horse. She looked well today, the ghostly paleness banished from her complexion, her rosebud lips curving into a smile. Someone in the palace had provided her with a fresh dress and polished boots. Though he imagined she might well have cleaned the shoes herself.

Edmun cleared his throat, and Callum realized he'd been staring at her. "Just as well, you say?" the old soldier said.

"She's famously taken."

"She is, indeed."

"*Very* famously."

Epic-ballad-level famously.

"Also," Edmun said, "she doesn't like you."

Mages, but he thought she *had*.

Now she was ignoring him. As if he didn't exist at all.

"The captain saved her life," Godfrey said, appearing on Callum's other side as if from nowhere—Edmun must be training the soldiers in the art of sneaking up on their commanding officer—and he reported this bit of news like it was the greatest thing he'd ever heard. No doubt he'd be repeating some other gossip in an hour, and with just as much reverence.

How the blazes did he already know about last night's

attack? That Princess Katrina's palace was leaking, and make no mistake.

Though, Callum supposed, there'd been plenty of guards and more than a couple of servants in the orbit of last night's events. Still. He expected silence from his soldiers on such matters. Absolute silence.

"Did he now?" Edmun said. The old soldier was clearly enjoying this conversation, and Callum's barely concealed annoyance.

Who was he kidding? He wasn't concealing anything. Not from Edmun.

"No, I didn't. She saved herself." Callum ground the words out from between gritted teeth. "I merely investigated the situation."

"*Did* you now?"

Callum glared at Edmun. "Stop it. You're not too old for me to throw you in the stocks for a day."

Edmun snorted. "As if you'd dare."

"I am your superior officer."

"*Are* you?" Edmun's eyes sparkled with amusement, and more than a hint of challenge.

In theory. As far as Edmun and the others should know, anyway.

The courtyard doors swung open, saving Callum the necessity of responding. At least it gave him more time since Edmun was unlikely to let this go. The man had been a soldier since before Callum had been allowed to wield more than a wooden practice blade. Callum might be his superior officer, but Edmun took no shit from anyone.

And it was clear he knew precisely what Callum had done. During the weeks of their journey from Aglye to Etra, he hadn't said a word. But Callum had felt it in the long, knowing looks the old man had leveled at him.

Apparently, he planned to say it outright.

"I wonder that the queen-to-be did not come to see us off," Callum said, shifting the subject before Edmun could speak. "Seems strange."

In fact, aside from the encounter in her waiting room, the queen-to-be had said nothing to him at all. Callum hadn't been lying to Laena when he'd said he rarely talked to royal families. His typical jobs were raids and skirmishes. Battle, not diplomacy.

But he'd have expected the queen-in-waiting to at least make an appearance. Perhaps she'd been planning something—a ball or a feast, or at least an insufferable council meeting with speeches and gaudy gifts—and his insistence at leaving this morning had changed the plan.

He suspected that would be giving her too much credit. Still, she ought to be here, to say a few words or let her regent do the speaking on her behalf. To send the delegation off with the blessing of the crown, or some shit like that.

"I wouldn't know about such things," Edmun said. "Being naught but a simple soldier."

"Stop it."

"My superior officers, *they* know what's best. I wouldn't dare rise above my station."

"Edmun."

Edmun steered his gelding in closer, as close as it was possible to get without entangling the horse's legs. Or so it felt. "What do you suppose the king will do, upon our return?"

Callum shrugged, finding that his gaze had once again drifted to the head of brown curls at the front of the party. She'd taken up the lead, he realized. Without prompting, without asking, and without him. She looked natural there, her back straight, her smile relaxed and easy as she chatted with one of the other soldiers.

"I suppose Hawk will bore the lady with a bookish speech

that she'll probably understand every word of, as clever as she is," Callum said. "Provided that he doesn't put her to sleep. Then he'll hold a party and we'll make an alliance, sign some papers proclaiming our continued peace, and she'll be on her way home."

What were they going to discuss? The question sat heavy in the pit of his stomach. A simple peace treaty between already peaceful nations would make little sense. Hawk couldn't mean to go to war with Silerith—could he?

Edmun rolled his eyes heavenward. "I meant what will the king do about your stealing the delegation."

It was all Callum could do not to reach over and clap a hand over the old man's mouth. Which, aside from drawing attention, would likely unseat him from his horse. "Do not let her hear."

"If you want my advice—"

"I don't." The words came out sounding harsh, but Callum could not afford to be soft. "I want to guide this delegation back to Vunmore in safety. The king will have no objection to that."

Edmun clamped his mouth shut, narrowing his eyes as if considering whether to speak his mind anyway. Before he could, Callum urged his horse forward, cutting around the side of the procession to join Laena and the others at the front of the group.

"My lady," he said, interrupting whatever conversation she'd been having with young Godfrey and another soldier. "I trust you slept well?"

She glanced over at him, her expression shuttering. As though his very presence irritated her so much that she could no longer be cheerful. "Well enough."

"Princess Laena's never played snakes and roses, sir," Godfrey piped up, clearly unaware of the tension between them. "We're gonna teach her."

"Careful playing cards with these rogues, my lady," Callum

said as Godfrey and the others protested. "They'll take you for all you're worth and look innocent while they do it."

She tipped her nose in the air. "I can handle myself, Captain."

CHAPTER 10

*T*he common room belowdecks was more pleasant than Laena would have anticipated, had she given it much thought before first descending to play cards with the soldiers. Cramped, certainly, but pleasant nonetheless. Triple bunks lined the walls, packed together so tightly that it was difficult to imagine how the soldiers on the bottom and the middle could possibly squeeze between the mattresses.

There was a long wooden table bolted to the floorboards in the center of the room, with bench seating on each side and a pair of lanterns overhead. A ladder led to the deck above, and a narrow passage at the end of the room led out to a hall lined with the officers' cabins, including the one the ship's captain had given up for Laena's use.

Callum Farrow had not seen fit to grace them with his presence at the nightly card game. She wondered where he might be laying his head at night. In one of the other private cabins, she assumed, though it was just as possible that he snuck into the common room after her departure each night to take up an unused bunk. It was difficult to picture how a man his size would be able to breathe, wedged into one of those tight spaces.

It was just as well that she saw him only in passing. She did not wish to spend more time with him, to warm to his smiles and forget the danger of spending too much time in his presence.

She spent her days on the deck with Brin, her evenings playing cards with the soldiers. She had the distinct impression that they'd been keeping up a certain level of tidiness for her benefit. No stockings strewn about, all their belongings stored neatly in the bins beneath the bunks. Mages, the place even smelled fresh, as if they propped open the trap door during the day to let the breeze flow through, dispelling any lingering hint of sweat.

It was strange to feel that someone wanted her company enough to do such a thing. In fact, her brain kept trying to protest, insisting that anyone smart enough to think of airing out the room would have done so for their own benefit, not simply because of her presence.

But still, she couldn't shake the feeling.

After three nights of games, the place felt comfortable and familiar. She could admit, if only privately, that part of her wished this would not be the final night. That she could stay on the ship, in the known territory, with people who actually seemed to be enjoying her company.

Though perhaps the tidiness might not last much longer.

Now, she was seated at the large table, a fan of cards spread across her palms. They'd taught her their snakes and roses game, plus a dozen more, though some she'd known by other names—they referred to capture the queen as king's forfeit, for example—but there was no doubt they were the more practiced players. She had yet to win a single hand of any game.

Until now. Laena could barely suppress her grin as she laid her hand out on the table. "I would say the ransom is mine, gentlemen," she said. "Wouldn't you?"

The men gasped, Edmun letting out a groan of disappointment. "Well done, Princess," he said. "I did not anticipate that move."

Laena narrowed her eyes. The soldier beside her, Huck, swallowed hard. And on her other side, young Godfrey looked up from the letter he'd been writing, just a little *too* wide-eyed to be believed.

"You let me win," she said, offended.

The men burst out laughing, Edmun slapping the table while Huck flailed his hands in protest. "It's our final night on the ship, Princess," he said. "You had to leave one game in triumph."

"I see. So it was your scheme."

The men roared with laughter, drowning out Huck's protests. Laena smacked him on the shoulder, then tossed her cards across the table at Edmun. "I expect you to renew the game at the campfire each night between the sea and Vunmore," she said. "I will best you honestly, or not at all."

The old soldier inclined his head. "As you say, Princess Laena. Accept my apologies."

Huck leaned one elbow on the table. "Are you still working on that letter, Godfrey? I'd have thought you could have written twenty letters in the time you've spent on that one."

"He has," Archer put in from the far end of the table. "He keeps crumpling them and tossing them out to sea."

Godfrey twitched his fingers back and forth on the table, pushing the letter about with quiet shushing noises. "The ship's captain says he will deliver it to her when he next returns to Etra. But I cannot decide what I should say."

"Tell her of her beauty," Huck said immediately. "Women love that. Her eyes. Her complexion. Her taste in dresses."

Edmun shook his head, laughing, as the men all tried to speak at once.

"No," Archer said, his voice rising above the others. "Tell of your undying love. My husband loves that."

"None of that."

Laena looked up to see Callum Farrow standing at the entrance to the officers' corridor, his shoulder propped against the frame, arms crossed over his chest. It must be the only way he could stand upright in the tight quarters without ducking.

He brought with him the strong scent of whiskey. How long had he been drinking? He didn't appear unsteady on his feet, though it was difficult to tell with him braced against the doorframe.

Laena met his blue eyes. "What would *you* tell her then, Captain Farrow?"

"Tell her what you wish to say." The captain's words were clear and unslurred, but there was an undercurrent to them, a feeling of something barely contained. "Not what you think she wants to hear."

Laena raised an eyebrow. "And what, Captain Farrow, would *you* tell her?"

Perhaps it was unwise to push him when he had clearly been drinking. But she found that she very much wanted to hear his answer.

"If I were writing to a woman? I would not waste time on her beauty, of which I would assume she was already well aware. Nor my feelings for her, which words would not properly convey in any case."

Laena rolled her eyes. "We can spend all night discussing what you would not write. What *would* you write?"

Callum didn't move, but his eyes flared. Suddenly, it felt as if they were the only two people in the room. No soldiers to overhear and no table separating them. "I would tell her how much I wanted her," he said, holding her gaze. "I would explain the many ways our bodies would fit together. Where I would put my hands when we next met. How I would relieve her of her clothing. And exactly how my tongue would—"

Edmun cleared his throat, shooting an exasperated look at

his captain. Farrow's mouth hooked into a half-smile. "Perhaps it would be best not to continue along that subject."

Laena found she wanted the infernal man to continue. She wanted to know where he would put his hands. And what he would do with his tongue. Her throat went dry and she swallowed, trying to still her thrumming heart. Trying not to imagine his hands roving *her* body.

"Godfrey's known the girl a bare few hours, Captain," Edmun said. "Perhaps a gentler tack would be preferable."

Callum shrugged. As if it were no great matter to him, one way or the other. "As you say, I'm sure. I'm no great romantic."

But he was drunk out of his mind. That much was obvious. "Clearly," Laena said, wrenching her eyes away from the awful man and placing a hand over Godfrey's. "What is your lady's name?"

Godfrey let out a long sigh that might have been tortured, or happy, or perhaps both at once. He did not seem to have noticed his commander's outburst. "Naomi. She is a beautiful maid who works in the palace at Riles. We laughed and talked all night. But our rapid departure wrested me too quickly from her arms."

Huck snorted a laugh, and Laena elbowed him in the ribs, making him cough. Young love was young love, and Godfrey was clearly prone to poetics. Nothing wrong with that. "She sounds lovely," Laena said. "I'm sorry I do not recognize her name."

Godfrey straightened. "You wouldn't, Princess Laena." He sounded almost apologetic. "She and her mother came to Riles after the palace staff quit."

Laena stared at him.

Godfrey licked his lips, nervous. "She said... well, she told me they walked out in protest after you went away from Riles. The entire palace was in an uproar for weeks, with no trained servants. Only a few stayed, saying that when you returned you'd need a friendly face."

Tears prickled Laena's eyes, and she blinked them away. She wished Callum Farrow were not here to watch. The crook of his smile had disappeared into a frown that looked all too much like pity. "The cook?" she asked, remembering the chocolate cookies.

Godfrey nodded. "The cook, yes. A few of the footmen, I think."

It was not often that Laena found herself speechless. She had trained in diplomacy and knew how to handle the twists and turns of a conversation. Oh, she might be rusty—her encounter with Katrina had proved that—but Laena still had something to say.

At this news, she could barely summon any words. Any response. That the palace staff would have walked away from safe, secure employment because of Laena's exile... it was too much to bear. She would have lectured them to do no such thing, had she known of it in advance.

When she got back to Etra, she would ensure they all found employment. A full five years? She hoped they had, that Katrina had not made it impossible for them to secure new positions.

Though... if the servants felt so strongly, and if the woman in the carriage had also felt strongly, perhaps... It was possible, wasn't it, that some of the courtiers and merchants and rich business owners would have felt the same? Perhaps they would have made sure to care for the servants in Laena's absence.

Besides, if this trip went as planned, she would have no reason to investigate anything upon her return to Etra. She held no sway; she could not even provide a reliable reference.

No, when she returned to Etra, she would go home to Sunflower Cottage. She would rebuild her garden. And she would forget she'd ever been anything else.

"Please, Princess," Godfrey said, practically wringing his hands and clearly mistaking her silence for displeasure, "do not judge Naomi and her mother. They needed the work when dear Naomi's father passed from an infection, and—"

Laena patted his hand. "I would never judge anyone for needing employment."

She couldn't believe the palace staff would have done such a thing. She could not see how she would ever make it up to them.

Godfrey's shoulders sagged in relief. "So, what *should* I write?"

—*—

THE NEXT DAY bloomed bright and sunny, the sea sparkling out in every direction like a promise as the Aglyean ship cut a sharp path through the waves. The passage was notoriously rough, more so as it neared the coast; it surged between the continent and Etra's island nation, the iridescent surface belying the violent currents that roiled beneath. Laena had spent her life beside the sea, and though she knew better than to underestimate it, she did not overly fear it, either. Especially with the sky so clear and bright.

She wanted to see the Aglyean coast the moment it appeared on the horizon. Any moment now, the soldiers promised, though even after that it would be many hours until they made landfall.

What would it be like to spy a foreign land for the first time? Probably it would be like watching Etra disappear behind her for the first time, all the while wondering if she was making an enormous mistake. But Etra was rocky, known for its hills, while Aglye's coast was made up of sand and forests. It should look different, especially as they drew nearer.

She'd excused herself shortly after the conversation with Godfrey, needing to be alone after that outburst from Callum.

He'd disappeared ahead of her, no doubt with a plan to drown what was left of his sanity in more whiskey.

Even after she retired to her bed, she lay awake remembering his words. The roughness of his voice, the smell of whiskey and woodsmoke he brought with him. She hadn't been able to keep from imagining the feel of his hands on her, the way he would peel her clothes from her body. No matter how much she reminded herself that she needed to keep her distance —that her magic made him a danger to her—she had imagined it. She had felt it.

And she had not slept particularly well.

Now, as she sat upon one of the long benches that ran alongside the rail, she breathed in the fresh air, begging the cold spray to dispel all ridiculous notions from her head. No matter how handsome he was, no matter how much his presence made her skin ache for his touch, she needed to take care.

To remind herself of the need, Laena withdrew the crystal from the traveling pouch she kept upon her person. She'd found it beneath the overturned settee after the attack in Kat's sitting room, and though she'd pocketed it without secrecy, no one objected.

The sight was enough to sober her. To pull her thoughts away from ice-blue eyes and half-smiles.

Brin scurried from her shoulder to her hair, objecting to the sight of the poisonous icicle. But Laena needed to examine it. To understand it, if she could. Unwrapping the crystal from its handkerchief, she held it in her lap, turning it over in her hand as best she could while preventing it from touching her skin.

And carefully, very carefully, she called for the knot of magic that lived in her core.

If she could have given the magic a physical location, she would have pinpointed it in the space just below her ribcage. At first, she'd feared that the battle with the wraith might have burned it away for good. But with rest, she'd begun to feel it stirring again. A comforting band of cold, like fingers of frost on the window after a long, dry summer.

She wasn't sure whether to be relieved or frightened.

Laena called on the knot of magic, willing it into her fingertips, then funneling it into the crystal.

Dangerous? Perhaps. But necessary. Her power had affected the crystal before. Perhaps she could feel it more deeply. She needed to better understand.

She hoped it wouldn't produce a wraith this time.

"Are you well, my lady?"

Laena jumped, squinting into the sun as Callum Farrow appeared before her. "Of course," she said airily, stuffing the magic back into her core. Once tapped, it did not wish to retreat. But it did so anyway. "Should I not be?"

The corner of his mouth quirked into that almost-smile. It wasn't so wicked this morning; instead, she detected a hint of embarrassment. "I believe someone made a few rather... inappropriate comments in your presence last night."

Inappropriate comments that had left her aching, wanting. Half convinced she ought to rise from her bed to knock on his door.

"Someone did," she agreed, her voice sounding breathless to her own ears. She tried to sharpen it into disapproval. "Most inappropriate."

If he noticed her struggle, he didn't let on. He gestured to the bench beside her. "May I?"

"Can I stop you?"

"Indeed, you can. But the remainder of the journey will be easier to endure if you allow me to apologize."

Easier to endure. As if her very existence were a burden. But she didn't think he meant it that way, not truly. She studied him for any sign of jest, but there was no laughter in his eyes. And she *did* believe in second chances. She nodded. "All right."

He positioned himself on the edge of the bench and kept a

respectful distance. "I allowed myself to get drawn into the soldiers' talk last night," he said, angling his body toward her and meeting her eyes. "I apologize for the uncouth words that left my mouth."

"Your soldiers were being most respectful."

He looked at his hands. "They are good men."

"And you are not?"

He let out a quiet laugh and sat back on the bench, still looking at his hands. His brow was furrowed, cutting deep lines across his forehead, and she had the distinct impression that it was a default expression for the man. He still smelled faintly of whiskey, but it was mixed with woodsmoke, and an undertone of sweet tobacco. There was a nick beside the corner of his mouth, a small red slice interrupting his otherwise smooth skin. A cut from shaving, perhaps.

Which she would not have seen, had she not been staring at his lips. She jerked her gaze up to meet his, but he didn't seem to have noticed.

"No, my lady," he said. "I am not a good man."

She could accept that. Probably should accept that, and end the conversation. Go back to her magic delving, back to watching for the coast.

But he looked so lost, so completely forlorn, that she found herself wondering what could have happened to make him think so. She might fear his hatred of magic, but much of the world saw him as a hero. Could it be that he regretted the pain he had caused?

"Do you want to know what I think?" she asked.

"Is hearing it a condition of my forgiveness?"

"No. I do not set conditions upon forgiveness, beyond that the person be truly contrite."

"And what if that person should betray you again?"

"Then they were not truly contrite."

He studied her, as if looking for a trick behind her words.

When he didn't find one, he said, "All right, I will concede. What *do* you think, my lady?"

She thought that if he kept calling her 'my lady,' she was going to smack him across the face. She could not have said why it bothered her so, when his soldiers called her 'princess' and 'your highness.' Only that it did.

"I don't know if you are a good man or not," she said. "But I do believe it was the bottle speaking to me last night, through you."

He swallowed, his throat constricting. "You may be right. And for what it's worth, I am sorry."

Had he tried to deny that he'd been speaking directly to her, pretending that his words had been for Godfrey's benefit or the men's amusement, she would have stood and walked away. But he didn't. He accepted her accusation, her correct assessment.

As it was, it would be hypocritical of her to refuse his apology when, after all, his words had set her on fire. Still, she felt that her nod was too prim, too proper. "Apology accepted."

He smiled, a real smile this time—a full one, none of that half-smile nonsense—and for a moment she wondered if they might actually have a chance at being friends. Not real friends— she couldn't risk that, with her abilities secreted away—but friendly companions, at least.

And then his gaze dropped to her lap, his eyes widening in shock. "What in the Miragelands are you doing with *that?*"

Laena had forgotten she still held the icicle in her lap. A dangerous thing to forget. She shrugged. "This? I'm taking it to show King Hawk the poison that infiltrated my garden. It might be infiltrating the land."

Callum sat back, propping the heels of his hands on his knees. "Oh? So I'm to understand that your sister wishes you to discuss the pest in your vegetable garden with the king?"

How quickly he went from contrite to judgmental. It was no mere vegetable garden, nor was her fear contained to what happened on her own property. He was a soldier, a guard sent to escort her safely to Aglye. What she discussed with King Hawk should be none of his concern.

Though, was it not his job to root out magic and dispose of its users? And here she had practically waved the magic from her garden in his face.

Warning bells sounded in her head, but she was too annoyed to heed them. "Does this look like a typical pest to you? It spat out a blasted wraith. If my sister does not want me to discuss it with Hawk, then perhaps she's hoping it will invade Aglye."

"Perhaps she's sending it with you to do that very thing," he shot back.

"Then I would hardly display it for you, would I? I would keep it secret."

"I can always smell a heart-tithe."

"It's not a heart-tithe... At least I don't think it is. It's something else."

But she did not know for sure, did she? It might be heart-tithed magic that some villager had planted in her garden.

Strong magic. The heart-tithe would have required a strong sacrifice indeed.

Callum drew in a breath, let it out slowly. She wondered if his head was hurting him after his indulgences last night, if his stomach was roiling. Or if he was so used to the ill effects of the whiskey that he hardly noticed them anymore.

"All right," he said. "I wish you had told me. Could you not have planned to merely *tell* him of this... poison crystal?"

"Would you believe a mere story?"

Callum ran a hand through his hair, clearly conflicted. She clutched the crystal tighter, afraid he would grab it and fling it into the sea. But he was not so foolish. He kept his hands on his knees. "I would believe the story if you told it," he said finally, his words sending a spark of warmth through her chest. "But

Hawk..." he trailed off, eyes distant. "Perhaps you were right to bring it."

The ship dipped suddenly, and Laena pitched headfirst toward the rail, her knees knocking into the bench. She threw her arms out to catch herself, but it was Callum's arms closing around her waist that kept her from tumbling overboard. Still annoyed with him, she shook him off. But a shout went up from the crow's nest, and she looked up just in time to see a bolt of lightning crack out of the sky and strike the center mast, which split with a roaring crack. Callum wrenched Laena toward the bow as it cleaved the deck in half. Rain poured out of the bruised sky with the suddenness of an overturned watering can, drenching Laena's garments in an instant.

She'd been squinting into the sun not five minutes ago. How could the blissful day have turned so quickly to a storm?

A second bolt of lightning came searing out of the sky, filling Laena's nose with singed wood as it struck the deck. Smoke erupted from the fallen mast, the rain doing nothing to quell the flames. If anything, they seemed to lick up toward the drops, as if using them to gather power. The smell of burned hair and sulfur filled the air.

It was unnatural.

Callum was still holding on to her when the third bolt struck. Before the ship could split, he grabbed her hand and pulled her overboard into the sea.

CHAPTER 11

They would die if the lightning struck the water. Part of Callum insisted they ought to already be dead, that the lightning should have knocked the rhythm from their hearts. He'd felt the charge of it in the air, the prickle that raised the hairs on the back of his neck before the first strike on the ship's mast.

Now that they were submerged, the lightning could strike anywhere near them and they would not escape its power. They didn't need to be hit directly to be killed.

But Callum could do nothing about that. As he struggled to the surface to gasp in a breath, pulling Laena up with him, all he could hope was that the princess knew how to swim. The sky looked wounded, dark as it was with red and purple spots. Even the lightning had been laced with lines of crimson, unnatural as it was beautiful.

Behind the scent of briny sea, the air was thick with the smell of a heart-tithe, burned hair and sulfur smoke so thick that the rain itself might have been made of the stuff.

Perhaps it was. That storm had appeared too quickly to be anything but magic. He didn't want to imagine the atrocities that would have allowed for magic of this size. Burned homes. Dead family members. The magic would work no other way.

With his ears still ringing from the triple blows, his nostrils stinging from seawater and smoke, he swam as best he could. Logic said he ought to release Laena's hand to focus on pushing his way through the water, but she seemed as reluctant to let go as he was. A storm like this might well wrench them apart. So he struggled along as best he could, putting a minute's worth of distance between them and the floundering ship, and then another, until Laena tugged on his hand and he paused, wondering if she was having trouble staying above the waves.

He needn't have worried about an Etran woman, princess or no. She was treading water easily, keeping her head above the waves though water streamed down her face, the rain forcing her to squint. Her hair was plastered to her head, the sopping curls flat against her neck, and it was a wonder that dress of hers hadn't dragged her into the depths. But her country was more coast than interior, and if anything, she looked to be the stronger swimmer. With those skirts, she'd have to be.

She was pointing back toward the ship with her free hand.

He couldn't hear what she was saying, but he could guess. She wanted to return, to help the others. It was too dark to see if there were others in the water. The beating rain nearly obscured the remains of the ship behind a curtain of gray. If they could barely make out the ship at this distance, he didn't know how they could hope to see something as small as a person.

Even if they could be certain others had survived, it would be foolish to return. Callum's men would not thank him for risking Laena's life in an attempt to save them. They were trained soldiers, and he hoped to whatever gods might care to listen that they would make it—young Godfrey, the spiller of chickens, and wise Edmun. And Huck and Archer and all the rest.

All he could do now was hope they could swim. And that the lightning would hold off.

"We need to put distance between us and the ship," he shouted, hoping she could hear—or at least understand—over the slosh of the waves and the howling of the wind. Thunder rumbled above, but no more lightning strikes came. Perhaps the storm, and the heart-tither who'd made it, was moving off.

The waves certainly didn't seem to think so. The current grabbed at his feet, attempting to snarl him in its clutches, and it took every ounce of energy to kick hard enough to stay afloat. A second's hesitation, and it would claim him.

Laena nodded reluctantly, and they began swimming again. He couldn't tell which way they were going—no stars or sun to navigate in this violent soup of a day—but every instinct in his body said to keep moving away from the ship.

A particularly large wave lifted them briefly skyward, then they were plunging into the depths of a valley so deep he felt he ought to brush the sea floor. Down and down, the last shadows of the ship lost behind a wall of waves. It was like being at the center of a whirlpool, the sea rising in every direction, with the barest glimmer of that purple-red sky eyeing them from above.

Perhaps the heart-tither hadn't moved off after all. Callum craned his neck, attempting to see something, anything, that might indicate who their enemy was, where they were working from. But there was nothing to see. Only water.

Laena shouted his name, and the current wrenched them apart.

The sea swept him under, and up traded places with down as he fought to kick. Salt stung his eyes, which were no good to him in any case, and his lungs already burned with the surprise of the dive; bubbles swirled in every direction, and the waves gave no hint of which way to turn.

But he'd be damned if he gave up now. Callum kicked. His lungs ached, begging him to suck in a fresh breath, yet still he kicked, ignoring the burn. He would hold his breath until he lost consciousness. He would fight the sea with every last morsel of energy he had in him. Which wasn't much; in a moment, he would lose the battle with his body and draw in seawater. His lungs would fill, and he would sink.

He hoped Laena would have better luck. And Hawk... he hoped Hawk would understand.

Just then, hands closed around his torso and heaved, and as he broke the surface, gasping in a breath that was still half seawater, he coughed and sputtered, but he had breath in his lungs. He was alive.

And Laena was in the water with him once again, her body flush against his back, his head cradled against her shoulder as her hands wrapped around the front of his chest. She'd rescued him. How the demons had she managed that?

"Are you alive?" Her voice sounded muffled behind the water in his ear. But her cheek was nearly flush with his, and he heard her well enough.

"Barely," he said.

Apparently satisfied, she kicked, moving them both through the water until they reached a piece of wood floating nearby. Some leftover hunk of the ship that had made its way here. She shoved him toward it, only letting go of him to pull herself on top of it. He followed, nearly upsetting the thing twice before he managed to balance his weight. But balance he did, until he lay prone on the board.

His chest was sore, his limbs trembling from the effort of the swim, his lungs still spewing seawater, but he was alive. Miraculously alive.

When he'd coughed enough to expel the majority of the water, he turned to look at her, resting his cheek on the wood so he could see her face. She was obviously just as exhausted. Her face, pale as moonlight, was stark against her curls, drenched and matted against her head.

"How did you learn to swim like that?" he gasped.

"I grew up in Etra," she said. "We know how to rescue a drowning man."

"But I'm three times your size."

"Hardly." She twisted her lip. "Perhaps twice."

Even on the brink of death, the woman kept her sense of humor.

She raised her head slightly, glancing over his shoulder. "I can't see anything. It's still too dark."

Callum followed her gaze, fighting a wave of dizziness. His head had been unhappy enough after the amount he'd drank last night. Now, he felt his skull might split open entirely.

But the storm did appear to be calming, though clouds obscured the sky. Even if they could see the stars to navigate, they had no sails or rudder to direct them. "I think we'll be at the mercy of the current," he said.

She sighed, settling her cheek back onto the wood. Was it a piece of a lifeboat, perhaps? A door? Impossible to tell. It might as easily have been a chunk of the hull itself.

"That was no natural storm," she said.

No. No, it was not. He could still smell the putrid tinge of the heart-tithe in the air, the magic still thick and pungent.

Strange, that he had not detected a hint of a heart-tithe in the crystal she carried. He was so well practiced at sniffing out magic that his men sometimes whispered he could detect it from leagues away. Laena's crystal had not reeked of magic. As far as he could tell, it had given off no odor whatsoever.

But if the garden-destroying crystal was not formed from a heart-tithe, then what kind of magic could it be—and how could he hope to help her destroy it?

CHAPTER 12

*F*or a time, Laena feared the storm would carry the door away from Aglye's coast and into the wilds of the open ocean, though she didn't voice it to Callum. He lay draped across their makeshift raft, looking an inch from death. Which he had been.

If she had not been near enough to pull him from the waves, he would have drowned. The thought made her want to reach for his hand, to stare at his chest and ensure he was still breathing.

Only because she didn't want to be alone. And because she would still need a guide to help her reach Vunmore safely.

King Hawk would want to know about the strangeness of that storm, and she would need to send messages to Katrina as well. Her sister might think the plague in Laena's garden was a forgettable occurrence, but she would have to pay heed to a storm like that one. Particularly since Callum was another surviving witness to the incident.

None of that would happen if she and Callum were swept out to sea. But there was little Laena could do beyond holding on to the raft and watching Callum's chest, relieved each time he drew another breath.

She wished she could be as certain of the fates of the other men. She tried to tell herself that they would be watching out for one another, and as trained soldiers they certainly would have secured a lifeboat and known how to make their way in a storm.

If only they could find their way to the coast, they might meet up with the men once again.

Fortunately, the current showed mercy as it washed them toward the shore, allowing Laena and Callum to maneuver themselves onto the beach without much difficulty. The sky was still a starless black, but at least those unnerving red clouds had moved on.

All she could see of the shore was a stretch of sand and beyond that a forest of reedy looking trees. When her feet touched the sand, Laena allowed herself to collapse upon it and said, "If a tiger comes out of those woods to eat me, I'm going to let it."

Callum offered her a hand. "I would object to that, my lady. Who would save me from drowning?"

She accepted his hand reluctantly, and his fingers closed around hers, sending a thrill of warmth tingling across her skin that nearly made her snatch her hand away again. And in her desperation not to do so, she held on perhaps a bit *too* tightly.

Mages, but she was a fool. The man was dangerous. Why was it so impossibly hard to remember that?

"I trust you will avoid such situations in future." She released his hand and brushed at her dress, more to cover her awkwardness than because she had any hope of dislodging the sand that had crusted there. The skirts were thoroughly drenched, and her hair hung in a limp mat around her shoulders, her sleeves clinging to her skin. She shivered. It might be the dip in the ocean, but it felt unnaturally cold for full summer.

"The trees will offer more shelter." Callum started off across the beach toward the forest, which appeared quite threatening. But what choice did they have?

Brin stirred in Laena's hair as she followed Callum across the beach, and she cupped the little shimmerling between her hands for a brief moment, relieved to find Brin was still with them. When she opened her hands, Brin scurried up to her shoulder and craned her neck with an alertness that said she, at least, viewed this as an adventure.

"Mischievous thing," Laena whispered. "I was worried about you."

Brin flicked her tongue out. Probably just hoping for a nice, juicy beetle.

Callum waited at the edge of the forest, and they entered together without comment. The last of the rain had abated, though she could still hear it striking the canopy above. The leaves crunched beneath their feet, dry despite the punishing storm that had passed through.

Though perhaps it had not passed through here with as much... exuberance.

"The underbrush is dry," Laena said. "We could make camp. A fire."

Callum looked around, water streaming from his hair and down his cheeks. "I'm not sure we can do much other than huddle against a trunk and wait for dawn. Without light to see, we'll walk straight into your tiger's den."

Laena raised a hand and stroked Brin's back, eliciting a satisfied squeak out of the newt. "Brin, would you light the way?"

She didn't think the words were necessary, or that Brin understood them. She merely knew that a second stroke down the shimmerling's back—which she administered now—would prompt Brin to start glowing. Which she did, like a large pink firefly, only bright enough to see by.

Only when Callum stepped closer did she realize her mistake. "Magic, my lady?" he asked.

He stood so close that only a few inches separated them as he bent over her shoulder to inspect Brin. Laena stepped back, cupping her hands protectively over the small lizard. "It isn't magic," she said. "It's biology, I'm sure. How else would she hunt at night."

"Cats hunt at night without setting themselves aflame. Bats, too."

"She isn't on fire. She's merely... glowing."

But to her surprise, Callum raised a fist to his heart, bowing gently in Brin's direction.

"Shimmerlings are revered in Aglye," he said softly. "The last remaining magic of the Vales. I have never seen one in person."

Perhaps not the only remaining magic of the Vales, she thought. But she held her tongue. "Why would they be revered?"

"Do you not know the stories?"

She shook her head. She'd heard of shimmerlings of course, but only in the context of fairytales.

"They say shimmerling bones were used to control humans during the time of the mages," he said softly, eyes still trained on Brin. "And they say a shimmerling bone broke the curse at last. Long enough for humans to rise up and banish the mages. But perhaps the creatures felt themselves misused. They disappeared into the wilds, leaving the humans to fend for themselves."

He'd drifted closer again, and without her even noticing. There were drops of water clinging to his eyelashes, each of them shining in the glow of Brin's magic.

"I've never heard that story," she said. Her voice was a mere whisper. She could not have made it louder if she wanted to.

"The mages were not so ensconced in Etra," he said. "Or so they say. Perhaps the shimmerlings fled there."

"How? Did they build little boats?"

He raised his eyebrows and she sighed, forcing herself to move away from him. "The light won't last forever, Captain. Best get gathering."

Together they located a clearing that would be safe for building a fire. No axe to chop wood, but there were fallen branches that snapped easily enough, and they got to work gathering kindling as best they could. Laena withdrew her dagger—still firmly ensconced in its sheath, thank goodness—and struck it upon a stone until sparks ignited the small pile of leaves she'd gathered in the center of the kindling.

It always felt like a puzzle to her, arranging the kindling and logs just so, creating a chimney. There was a deep satisfaction in watching the flames spring to life from just a few strikes of steel and stone. At the cottage, she often broke her spring and fall yard work into several sessions merely so she might have several bonfires instead of just one. True, there were no neighbors to share a hot drink with, no friends to tell stories and jokes. But somehow, the flames were companion enough.

When Callum returned to the clearing, he dropped the firewood he'd collected and sat beside her, gazing appreciatively into the flames. "How did a princess learn the art of starting a campfire?"

"We did not grow up as sheltered doves," Laena said, wrapping her arms around her knees to quell her shivering. "We roamed the countryside around Riles."

He paused, perhaps considering how sheltered Aglye's princess was. Laena didn't really know; the girl was a mystery, rarely seen. "I hope your stablehand appreciates your skill."

Laena frowned, and he shifted an inch closer to the fire. "I said I pay no heed to gossip. I do have ears."

"I suppose that story made it all the way to the Miragelands," Laena said, sighing.

Callum shivered, though she didn't think it had anything to do with the chill in the air. The mention of the mages' lands, after what they'd experienced today... it felt like an ill omen. She wished she could snatch the words back again, to banish the thought of the magic users who had so callously used humans for centuries.

Until they'd been locked away again. Perhaps his legends were right. Perhaps the shimmerlings had played a part in it. As Brin curled up on her shoulder, Laena found she rather liked the idea.

"Don't worry, my lady," Callum said, snatching her out of her thoughts. "I'll get you home safe to him."

For a moment she could only stare at him, confused. Until she realized that he meant Ben. The stories he paid no heed to. The scandal that had crossed all lands.

"It's Laena," she replied, buying herself a moment. "Please. Call me Laena."

He nodded, gazing into the flames, the orange light dancing across his face. She wasn't sure exactly what made her continue. Fatigue perhaps. But despite his reputation for eviscerating magic users, she found she could not help but trust him.

"He's gone," she said. "Ben, that is. The stablehand. He left."

Callum turned his head to look down at her, his expression unreadable in the firelight. And yet... she could tell somehow that he had not already known this. He had not been probing for the truth with his promise to return her to her love. If anything, she thought he looked stricken with shock.

Well, it *had* been rather a shocking day.

"Before you think it, Katrina has nothing to fear from me," she continued. "I'm happy with my cottage life." If the words sounded a bit hollow, even to her own ears, it was only to be expected after the dramatic events of the day.

She could have let him go on thinking that Ben was still in her life. But she didn't feel equal to the deception. Why bother?

The silence stretched on, and she found herself concocting responses he might give. Everything from "Well, what did you expect?" to "It's only what you deserve." She knew, because they were the responses she concocted for herself every day.

And in the back of her mind—that whisper she could never quite quell: "Did you not see it coming?"

She had. Mages, but she most definitely had.

By the time she realized she needed to leave the palace, that her powers would only grow and put her country in danger, her only comfort had been in the fact that Ben would be with her. She had known that Kat went riding every Sunday, and she'd arranged for a tryst at that very time, setting the stage for the discovery.

She could trust her sister to play her part well enough, to grasp for the throne. And still, Laena might have remained. While Ben could not have been her king, there were council members who had begged her to keep him as a lover, stating all too plainly that it had been done before.

It was the magic that had forced her hand and forced her to leave.

It was Kat who had banned her from Riles for five years.

But Laena had truly cared for Ben, and she'd thought she would be able to trust him with so much more. Though she hadn't shared the truth of her magic with him, she'd been on the verge of it when that morning had arrived, and she'd woken to find him gone.

If Callum were to berate her, it would be no more than she deserved.

He shook his head, and she could feel it coming. The judgment. The hatred. He would not try to stand close to her again, not show her the full width of his smile.

It was just as well. She ought to make him keep his distance. She ought to keep hers.

Callum was still shaking his head, as if words could not

adequately express his disdain. "Then he's a fucking fool," he said.

Laena opened her mouth, closed it again. Not disdain for her. Disdain... for *Ben*?

Before she could begin to come up with a response, he said, "The storm was something unnatural."

Laena stared. Was he... had he changed the subject? Why? For her comfort, or because he didn't want to have to state any of the truths that ran through her mind on a daily basis?

But no. He didn't seem the type to say anything he did not mean. If she'd spent her life trading in court politics and deceptions, he was the soldier who said what he meant, and that was that.

"Do you still have the crystal?" he asked.

She nodded but didn't extract the wretched thing from the pouch at her waist. It was there, snug in its pocket, along with her blade.

One dagger, one shimmerling, and one evil crystal. That was what remained. "Do you think the crystal and the storm are related?" she asked.

He shrugged. "Might be. Though the crystal does not smell of heart-tithe, and the storm did."

She nodded slowly, remembering the strange scents on the air after the shipwreck. "I don't recall giving you leave to smell my crystal," she said.

At that, he threw his head back and laughed. The unbridled amusement startled her into silence for a brief moment, and then she couldn't help but smile herself. She hadn't meant to prompt quite that response, though she found herself wondering how she might prompt it again.

"Do you know where we are?" she asked, when he'd finally composed himself.

He rubbed his eyes. "I believe we're in Aglye's coastal forest. At dawn, we should make our way to Inasvale."

Dread curled in Laena's gut like a weight. "To the poison-keepers?"

He stared into the fire, lips taut with tension. She wished she could tell what he was thinking. "I need to speak with the king's brother, Thaddeus. He is a full brother there now."

Laena had not known that the king's younger brother had taken orders as a poisonkeeper. Though when she'd left Riles, he would have been what, sixteen? Seventeen? A spare heir to the throne in any case, and free to follow his inclinations. Provided that the heir remained well.

But Laena had no desire to travel to Inasvale or to meet the order of monks who believed they guarded the passage between the Miragelands and the Vales. If Callum's hatred of magic was well known, the poisonkeepers' hatred of it was the stuff of legend. Should they discover her magic, they would no doubt seek to destroy it. And her.

People in Etra whispered that their religion was a false one, their task purposeless. Some whispered that there was nothing to guard, that the mages were a myth and had never lived in the Vales at all, though Laena could not quite give credence to those theories. She'd studied too many histories to deny the truth.

Callum bit his bottom lip, his expression distant, as though he was rolling the plan around in his head. "Even if Hawk won't take your crystal seriously, Thaddeus will."

So he did doubt his king with respect to the crystal and the poison. Laena had hoped they might be approaching the more reasonable monarch of the Vales. More reasonable than Katrina, anyway. And certainly more reasonable than Silerith's king, locking himself away as he did.

After the assassination attempt and the magical storm, Hawk seemed more likely to turn his eye toward Silerith, as Kat had done. They were the threat; who else would be sending heart-tithers after Etran royalty? And so blatantly, too.

Laena hugged her knees to her chest. If the poisonkeepers

would take the crystal seriously, then she would risk the journey. "Will Thaddeus know what to do?"

Callum looked at his hands. "I'll take the first watch," he said, offering no answer. "Get some rest, my lady."

CHAPTER 13

*A*s a soldier, Callum had endured grueling weeks of training, military campaigns, and all manner of marches, exercises, and drills. Yet he didn't think his body had ever been so sore as when he woke the morning after the shipwreck. His back cracked ominously when he sat up, and he was sure he heard his knees give a creaking groan as he hefted himself to his feet. His arms felt as if someone had set them aflame. If he had access to a bed, he would surely collapse into it and sleep for a fortnight.

Laena was already up and about, dowsing the last embers of their campfire with dirt and stones while her shimmerling skittered through the tall grasses at the edge of the campsite, visible only by the pink licks of its tail. If Laena's muscles were sore, she wasn't showing it; she appeared capable of bending and stretching.

One bend like that, and Callum was sure he'd snap in two. She looked pretty doing it, though. Her figure was a shapely one, and make no mistake. Her arms were strong and well formed, though he admitted her limbs were not the part of her that most engaged his attention.

What had that fool stablehand been thinking, leaving a woman like her? Yesterday's ordeal would have left most people whimpering on the ground. Demons, it had *him* wishing he could whimper on the ground. Yet here she was, finishing off the morning watch without complaint. She almost seemed to be enjoying it.

When she noticed him standing there, she gave him a businesslike nod that reminded him more of the no-nonsense palace housekeeper who ran the grounds at Hawk's palace than any princess he'd yet encountered. If she realized he'd been leering at her like an untried youth, she wouldn't hesitate to heft the largest stone she could find and crack him over the head with it.

"I found a creek nearby," she said. "About fifteen minutes away."

Callum rubbed a hand over his face, trying to dislodge the sleep from his mind. And the lust—might as well be frank about it. "You went traipsing through the woods on your own?"

She gave him an exasperated look. "We needed to find water, and you were dead to the world."

"There are wild creatures in these woods," he said. "And bandits."

Laena cocked an eyebrow at him. "Then perhaps the captain of the King's Guard might work to rectify that problem."

She'd been honest with him last night. The honorable thing would be to tell her that he was no longer the captain of anything, and that he'd stolen this entire expedition out from under its rightful leader. Ass though the man might be.

But she'd woken in good humor, and he didn't wish to spoil it. So he said, "You may have a point."

"Assuming you do still believe we landed in your country, that is." It sounded like a statement, but it was a question. She would not have traveled to the continent herself.

Callum didn't know of anywhere else along the coast that hosted such a thick band of forest. Perhaps northern Silerith.

But they could not have traveled that far, even on such violent tides, and he suspected the cold there would make for very different foliage.

He also suspected they would have been caught and arrested already. It had been some time since the Ruthless King had allowed anyone to cross his borders. Hawk's spies had skimmed the edges, playing with danger, but no one had delved that far into enemy territory without disappearing into Silerith's wilds.

Silerith, on the other hand, seemed intent on sending people out beyond its borders. Though he'd not seen the person responsible for the ship's doom yesterday, it was Silerith he suspected. He'd spent enough time ghosting back and forth across its borders, raiding dens of heart-tithers and getting his hands dirty—breaking accords on King Magnus's orders while knowing the king would deny any involvement, should Callum be caught.

He knew Silerith better than any other Aglyean or Etran could. Their leniency toward heart-tithers gave the magic a chance to grow, to fester into the kind of evil that could cause a storm like the one they'd survived.

"We're in Aglye for certain," he said. "If we follow the coast toward the northeast, we'll reach Inasvale."

"How long will that take?"

"It depends on where we landed. From the southern tip of the forest, I would guess five days walking. And I see no end of the trees in either direction, so the journey ought to be shorter."

"If the sky will cooperate tonight," Laena said, "we might chart our position that way."

She might not know much of the mainland, but he'd be a fool to ignore her knowledge of the sea and stars. He nodded.

They made their way to the creek she'd found. By then his thirst was nearly unbearable, but he forced himself to drink slowly. They washed as best they could—Laena went so far as to dip her head into the water so she could tie her curls back into a plait—and then they began walking, keeping the creek on their left. They should stay with fresh water as long as it ran in the general direction of Inasvale.

As long as the ocean waves sparked occasional glints through the trees to their right, he would know they were headed in the right direction.

What would Hawk say, when he learned their ship had been lost? Callum hoped he'd send soldiers—though that was likely a certainty, given that Callum had stolen his delegation in the first place. Was it too much to hope that he'd have kept General Moore back in Vunmore, so as not to risk outing Callum's insolence to the Etran delegation?

"How long have you served as captain of the King's Guard?" Laena asked, startling him out of his thoughts.

"Since I turned eighteen," he said. "Though for a few years, it was more of a ceremonial title."

He'd been raised with Hawk, Thaddeus, and Emilia, King Magnus treating him like another son. Part of the family. Callum would have stepped aside in favor of Thaddeus, but the prince had never wished to be a soldier.

"And how long ago was that?" Laena asked.

"Ten years ago." Give or take a few weeks of disgrace.

"And how do you like it?"

As they traipsed along through the woods, she stepped easily over logs and rocks, skirting around large sections of ferns. The shimmerling had perched itself on top of her head, its neck extended, tongue darting out every few seconds as if to smell the adventure. It ought to look funny, but somehow it looked right.

It was still quite a thing, to look over and see a creature of legend. He wondered when Aglye had last seen a shimmerling on its shores. Hundreds of years ago, perhaps.

He glanced at Laena, her head quirked to the side. Still waiting on a response.

How did he like being captain? It was not a question he was ready to answer.

"Are you an inquisitor?" he asked, deflecting. "Investigating my past?"

"No," she replied, drawing the word out into one long syllable. "I just figured we ought to have some conversation. Otherwise, you might well die of boredom."

"And you won't?"

She stepped over a tree root. "Not I. Look at these trees. How the light shines through them. I could live here forever."

Callum followed her gaze to the canopy, where the sun did indeed shine through the leaves, making them look like stained glass. They rustled gently in a breeze he couldn't feel through the depth of the forest. But it didn't follow that the place was stuffy; in fact, the shade made it cool and pleasant. Birds skimmed from branch to branch, chasing each other through the foliage.

The place even *smelled* green, each breath filling him with the scents of damp earth and growing things. Alive. It smelled *alive*.

"You underestimate me, I think," he said. "I would not mind living here forever."

When she smiled, the expression lit her entire face. It dimpled her cheeks most enticingly and set her green eyes to dancing, like they wished to join the leaves overhead. "Where would you build, then?" she asked.

He was not well practiced at games or make-believe, but at this moment, he thought he might do anything to keep that smile on her lips. "I think I should build right here," he said. "Near the creek for water. Near the ocean for fishing."

"A cottage?" she asked. "Something modest? With animals to care for and such?"

He wondered if that resembled the life she'd built for herself. A farm, tucked away in the grasslands of Etra. They didn't have forests, not like this one, but rural countryside made up most of the island. She said she'd found the crystal in her garden; he found himself wondering if it had been a large garden. Did she feed herself upon its contents? Keep chickens for eggs, goats for milk? How different from the life she'd been raised in.

Perhaps it suited her. Perhaps she loved it well. But perhaps… perhaps she could have a bit of *both* worlds.

That, he suspected, was not the game.

"Not I," he said. "It will be a palace for me." She opened her mouth to respond, but he held up a finger to stop her. "But I shouldn't want to tear down even a single tree. Livestock means tearing down trees."

"So do palaces, I hear."

"And yet, it must be a palace. Nothing less."

She looked at him, eyebrows raised. "Then how—"

"I would build among the branches themselves, I think. After securing the trees' permission, of course. I'd bring the wood in from elsewhere."

"By what road?" She laughed, and somehow he thought it was something she didn't do very often. Not half as often as she deserved. If he had his way, he'd hear that sound again and again. "You must tear down trees to make a road," Laena said.

"Not I. I should sail the materials in by the sea."

"Why, Callum Farrow," she said, still laughing. "I didn't think you had any whimsy in you."

Neither had he. She unearthed it in him, apparently. "And how long has it been," he said, holding a branch aside so she could pass unhindered, "since you allowed yourself such an indulgence?"

As soon as the words left his mouth, he regretted them. Her smile faded, though it didn't disappear entirely; it merely shifted to a rueful curve, her brow crinkled as if in conflict with itself.

Should he ever meet that stablehand, he'd shake the man. Hard.

"What do you think, Captain?" she asked. "Does Etra have a chance of gaining an alliance with Aglye?"

"Callum," he said, without thinking. He didn't wish to hear his former rank from her anymore. "If you're Laena, then I'm Callum."

"Very well. Callum. Same question."

He was not privy to the king's political plans, but logic said Hawk would not have sent the delegation to Etra without some hope of gaining an alliance. It was an odd choice, though; like his father before him, Hawk stayed largely aloof, preferring distance between Aglye and the other nations.

Yet the borders had been more active lately. Perhaps he did fear attack out of Silerith, a more direct attack than secret assassins. Perhaps Hawk's spies knew more of the Ruthless King's plans.

Instead of answering, Callum stalled. "You're helping your sister, despite how badly she treats you. Why?"

Laena frowned, clearly cataloging his sidestep. He would have to answer her question eventually. For now, however, she allowed it to pass. "I'm here to help Etra, not only my sister. Katrina is... difficult at times, it's true. But she'll be an excellent queen."

"As you would have been." It wasn't his place to say, but he didn't regret it. Someone had to say it, and it was more than clear that no one in Etra planned to do so.

Despite the epic ballads and swirl of romantic gossip around her flight from the palace, Callum could not help but feel that there was more to Laena's abdication than love for a commoner. Especially since that commoner had left her—presumably after realizing he would never be king, nor would he live in a palace.

Though perhaps that was unfair. Perhaps they had merely found their differences too great to overcome. Or that they were not as well matched as they'd initially believed.

But still, it felt as if there was something more. As if relinquishing the crown had been a great sacrifice, one Laena had not wanted to make. Perhaps it was more about Katrina than it was about the stablehand, though Laena must have cared for the man. Again, a spark of anger heated his stomach at the fact that the horse's ass had left her, after all she'd sacrificed for him. And the spark of anger only grew stronger when he thought of the way Katrina treated her. The way she clearly hungered for the throne.

And yet... there was something more to the story. He could feel it.

"Katrina wanted it more," Laena said, after a time. "I believe that will help her to rule."

Callum knew from experience that wanting to rule did not always translate to ruling more effectively. It might be a cynical thought, but he sometimes felt as if the opposite were true. But this was obviously a story Laena was telling herself, and he wasn't sure how hard he should push against it.

He had no desire to anger her. Whatever he'd done to provoke her anger after their first meeting—and there was no doubt he must have done *something*—she seemed to have forgiven him. For now.

So on they walked, in companionable silence, until the sun once again began to sink toward the horizon.

CHAPTER 14

*A*ll day, as they walked, Laena felt the knot of power expanding in her core. How something so cold could expand, or why her body did not shiver in response to its presence, she didn't know. Only that it seemed to be growing back stronger after her encounter with the wraith, like a muscle worked into greater strength.

She'd so missed the comfort of that power, having become accustomed to its presence. She hadn't realized how hollow she'd felt without it until the knot of frost reawakened. Or regrew. Or whatever it was doing in there. She wasn't even sure it was *in there* at all, if it was a physical part of her body or merely a sensation. There was far too much she didn't know.

As they continued on through the woods, she stole occasional glances at Callum Farrow. More than occasional, if she was honest with herself. Of course, the man was huge, and therefore often in her line of sight. It was impossible *not* to look at him.

But it wasn't his size that kept drawing her eye. Nor was it his striking looks, though she couldn't deny that she found him handsome; she tripped over her feet more than once while studying the way his curls brushed the back of his neck. But she'd seen many a handsome man in her life, and she'd see plenty more. It would be foolish to go mooning after this one. Especially this one.

No, her distraction was due more to the way he'd asked her about Kat, how he'd seen straight through to the heart of the situation.

You're helping your sister, despite how badly she treats you. Why?

Simple. Because helping Kat meant helping Etra. Laena would help Etra until her dying breath, even if no one else ever knew it.

And yet, a small voice inside her head insisted that if she cared for Etra, she would stop prodding at her magic. Stop working on it, even in secret. That it would be better for her to have sacrificed her life in the garden to that wraith than to continue practicing magic.

For all his kind words, Callum Farrow would say the same, were he to learn of her power.

But Callum had accepted Brin. Not merely accepted her; he *revered* her. If he felt the shimmerling's magic was good, and different from a heart-tithe, then he might respond the same way to her.

Then again, Laena's power was hardly a gentle glow to light their way. Her magic was a sharp thing. A weapon.

It had never frightened her the way it should. And that, more than stablehands or sisters, was why she had abdicated the throne.

Which was why no matter how handsome she found him, she had to keep her distance from Callum Farrow.

They made camp after a long day of walking in the woods, dining on foraged root vegetables and a hare he'd hunted with his knives. They were lucky not to have lost their knives in the wreck; she found she was ravenous. The vegetables could not roast too quickly. She plucked them out of the coals too eagerly, nearly burning her tongue, while Callum shook his head and grumbled about princesses in the wilderness. She would have snapped at him had she thought he meant it.

Even unsalted, the food was divine. Perhaps the best meal she'd ever tasted.

Laena should have been exhausted. Instead, the food gave her a new energy. She couldn't ignore the knot of ice at her core, the way it begged her to let it free. It wanted to be tested.

She wanted to test it.

When they'd eaten every last morsel, Laena said, "You look exhausted. I should take the first watch."

Callum rolled his shoulders, grimacing. "That is not the kind of compliment a man likes to hear."

"It's not meant to be a compliment. You look like you were shipwrecked and then dragged through a forest. It's not as if I look any better."

He scowled at her. "I beg to differ."

The compliment startled her. He couldn't mean that. Her clothing was dirty and torn, her hair a thick mat around her shoulders. But he certainly didn't seem like the sort of man who was given to flattery.

"All the more reason for me to take the first watch," she said, keeping her tone as airy as possible. She hoped she didn't sound too eager lest he grow suspicious.

Either she succeeded, or he was too fatigued to notice. Instead of arguing, he stretched out on the ground near the other side of the fire, pillowing his hands behind his head. Within seconds, he was snoring softly. Clearly one of those men who could fall asleep anywhere. She supposed it was a helpful quality in a soldier.

Still, she waited several minutes before settling herself a touch farther from the fire, where she could probe at her power without competing with the heat. Her ice could overcome flames—she'd tested that—but it wasn't the easiest feat, and she saw no reason to dampen their only source of warmth.

So she scooted back toward the edge of the ring of firelight. Then—carefully, always so carefully—she called her power forward.

It responded with a jolt, as it often did when forced to lie dormant for a few days, the cold spreading through her chest and down her limbs until frost bloomed from her fingertips. She shaped the magic into snowflakes, marveling at the way they twisted into the summer air.

It could be a practical magic; she always had ice in the summer months, after all. Aside from that, she hadn't let herself think much about the ways it could be useful. It was a pretty magic, fun. Light. Though it felt like a betrayal, she'd sometimes wondered—in the long nights since Ben left—whether it had been worth abdicating the throne for such a magic. If it could truly be as dangerous as she'd feared.

She would always hearken back to that day in the council chambers, force herself to recall the screams of terror, the feel of hands shoving her out of danger. When she'd been the one to cause the danger in the first place.

The battle with the wraith in the garden suggested—no, it damn near proved—that there could be times when she *should* use it to fight.

It ought to frighten her. Instead, she wanted *more*.

Ice crackled from her fingertips, snapping as it flowed from her hands to coat the surrounding underbrush. The sound echoed too loudly in the quiet of the night, and Callum stirred. Laena went still, but he didn't move again. Still asleep. And no wonder, after the taxing day.

But she couldn't risk him hearing her again. After a moment, she rose from her seat on the ground, legs stiff and protesting, and retreated further into the woods. If her magic was going to make strange noises, best to put some distance between her and the captain.

She wanted to do more than coat the ground with ice.

When the fire was no more than a flicker between the branches, Laena drew deeper into her power, exhaling a breath of steam as the air cooled around her. She shaped the cold with her mind until it was sharp, then released it.

Shards of ice flew from her hands, thumping into the trees like oversized darts.

The wraith hadn't been a fluke. She could do this. Laena grinned in spite of herself, reveling in the chill of the power. She didn't tremble with the cold. She *was* the cold.

As she raised her hand to send another volley, a hand clapped over her mouth from behind. She stumbled back with a cry, but her scream was muffled. Strong arms dragged her backward, and she kicked, reaching for her power, for the sharp blast that would bring this person to their knees.

Laena's eyes watered as a distinctive scorching smell filled the air, and her own magic fell away, slipping through her fingertips like melting ice.

And the world fell away.

CHAPTER 15

*J*n his dreams, Callum was trapped in a prison cell with no windows and no doors, so tightly quartered that even his sleeping mind did not understand how he could have arrived here in the first place. Dropped through the ceiling perhaps, though that too was shut fast.

Dripping water. The tap of distant footsteps. And somehow, inexplicably, the crackle of ice on a winter pond. This was what he deserved, where he ought to be. He could not even fault Hawk for dumping him here. If anything, it was long overdue.

Something bit his ear, and he cursed the rats. *How could they get in*, he thought distantly, *with no windows, no drains?*

The bite came again, and Callum sat up, breathing hard.

He wasn't in an Aglyean dungeon, as much as he might deserve that fate. He was in the forest, surrounded by the smell of pine.

Laena's shimmerling companion was on his shoulder, scrambling in a frantic circle as Callum craned his neck to see what she was doing. The creature moved so fast that she was little more than a blur of light and color against the dark fabric of his jacket.

Apparently distressed by his lack of action, Brin scurried to his neck and leapt, clamping her jaws around his earlobe.

Callum cursed, tugging the creature gently into his hands. "What's the matter, silly thing?"

The shimmerling might be worthy of admiration, but it *was* still a silly thing. Brin worked her jaws, straining for his ear like her greatest wish in the world was to bite him again.

Pinning her gently between two fingers, Callum looked around. It was dark, the fire burned to coals. Strange that Laena would not have added a log to it. Stranger still that she had not woken him for his watch. She'd said he looked exhausted, but she seemed too sensible to sacrifice her own sleep for his when she knew days of walking lay ahead of them.

But Laena wasn't sitting by the fire, nor had she propped herself on a tree and drifted off. She was nowhere in sight.

Callum rose. Perhaps she'd gone to relieve herself in the woods. Surely she wouldn't have wandered far.

He opened his mouth to call her name, and the sulfurous burning of a heart-tithe poured into his senses, thick and nausea-inducing. For a heartbeat, memories threatened to pull him under, determined to remind him what a heart-tithe had meant for Hawk's father.

Panic clawed for his chest, like a feral thing locked away for far too long, but Callum pushed it down deep. Panic would save no one. Action might.

Cursing, he crossed the clearing in two strides. "Brin," he said. "Can you light the way?"

He didn't know if the shimmerling would understand, or whether it only responded to Laena's requests. But the little creature scurried down to his elbow and began to glow, giving off a warm pinkish light that allowed him to follow the trail where Laena had left the campsite. He'd spent enough time in the wilderness to have developed a decent skill for tracking, thanks largely to Edmun's training.

The thought of the old soldier squeezed his heart, but he pushed that down, too. There would be time to mourn him later. Edmun would want him to find Laena.

The thickness of the underbrush made it clear enough: broken twigs and crushed fern stems, and here and there a thread of brown cloth that matched her skirts. The scent of the heart-tithe thickened as he followed the trail, the ball of panic working itself into a frenzy as it tried to free itself from its prison.

He could not afford to let it free. He could not afford mistakes.

The trail ended beside a fallen log, and Callum stopped to stare.

The log was covered in a thick layer of frost. Fern fronds brushed up against it, green and hearty, and the branches above were thick with spring leaves. But there was no denying the presence of the frost, the ice that coated the bark.

Beautiful. But full of magic, surely. The smell of the tithe was undeniable, and yet... and yet something about the frost called him forward. Made him want to lean closer. He held back, balling his hands into fists and resisting the urge to touch it.

Brin had no such hesitation. She leapt down onto the log, skittering across the frost as if she hoped to go ice-skating. Callum pressed a hesitant finger to the bark, brushing against the fronds of frost. It didn't feel evil. It felt... fresh. It felt *new*.

There was no denying, though, that the smell of the heart-tithe lingered in the air. And that Laena was nowhere to be seen.

"What happened here?" he asked.

But Brin had no answer to give. She settled into the crook of his elbow, letting out what he interpreted as a worried squeak.

The frost was strange. Stranger still was the complete disappearance of the trail. Callum searched the area, calling Laena's name until the sun had risen well into the sky. Nothing.

She was gone. Vanished into thin air, leaving nothing but a trail of frost behind.

There was one course of action to take, when a company of soldiers became separated. You made for the main road, and you searched for one another. Barring that, for information. As a last resort, you might seek out assistance, if you could find it.

Out here, that seemed all too unlikely.

Callum returned to the campsite to dowse what was left of the fire. He couldn't be sure exactly where they'd landed on the coast, but with the morning sun at his back, he should eventually reach the main road to Inasvale.

He'd avoided it during their first day of walking, fearing the heart-tithers who'd come after Laena on the ship, and the assassin from the palace. There was now no room left for doubt; they had come for Laena. Not for her sister, and not for the Aglyean soldiers. But why? What could Silerith gain from killing her, or capturing her?

It was a conundrum. The bruises on Laena's throat had made it abundantly clear that the palace intruder had indeed intended for her to die. The shipwreck, too, could be interpreted as an attempt at murder. Even the attack she'd described in her garden, strange though it had been, could well have ended in her death. He didn't want to imagine the blight from that crystal she'd shown him, of the magic invading her garden. He wanted to forget it existed at all.

If they wished her dead, why not slit her throat now and be done with it? Why haul her away?

Perhaps he was fooling himself. Perhaps there was no way she could still be alive.

And perhaps it was naive to assume Silerith's involvement. Their king was ruthless, to be sure, but he was also strategic. He would not send assassins in the night without a strong reason. He might want Katrina to rule Etra, for reasons of his own, but he would pull those strings from behind the scenes. Rarely did he make himself known. In fact, it was only through Hawk's network of spies that they even knew he held the throne at all.

Silerith was a complicated country, one given to violence. If anything, they tended to keep to themselves.

Try as he might, Callum could not untangle it. He was desperately short on information, the puzzle pieces so disparate they might belong to entirely different pictures. He needed Hawk's brain to help him sort through it, to ask the questions Callum never thought to ask. To tease out the truth.

But Hawk wasn't here. Even if he had been, the days when he would talk through a puzzle with Callum just for the sake of it had died with his father. Along with his trust in Callum. Though an argument could be made that this particular puzzle involved him, too.

There was no answer to be had, not at the moment. But Callum worried anyway, with Brin perched on his shoulder, her neck craned forward as if she, too, was searching for the road. He wasn't even sure what to do once he arrived there, whether there would be any sign that Laena had passed this way. Or what he would do once he found her. He had raided dozens of criminal dens, faced hundreds of heart-tithers, but he'd always had a crew of soldiers with him. Backup.

He didn't know how he'd get her back. Only that he had to. The panic in his gut had settled into a constant tension, like a pot stuck just before boiling. He needed to get her safely to Vunmore. It was the only option.

Hawk hadn't trusted Callum since he'd been absent on the day of his father's murder. He'd been helping the younger prince, Thaddeus, to reach Inasvale against Hawk's own wishes, worried that Thaddeus would meet with trouble if he attempted to travel alone.

When Callum had returned to Vunmore, he was met with black flags and mourning, and a friend who could not forgive him.

The way Hawk had shut him out, it was as if he believed Callum had intentionally allowed King Magnus's murder. As if he'd had something to do with the attack, the way the heart-tithers had known the inner workings of the palace well enough to spirit themselves straight to the king's own chambers. As if he'd held the knife in his own hands.

He hadn't done any of that. He'd spent the last year rooting out as many heart-tithers as he could find, but he was never sure if he'd captured the king's murderers. No one had confessed to the crime.

So Callum had to fulfill his duty where he'd failed so badly in the past. And he would not allow himself to acknowledge any other reason. The way Princess Laena's eyes shone when she smiled, how he itched to run his fingers through her curls. He would not think about her laugh, or that she'd saved him from drowning after the shipwreck.

And he did not think about any of those things at all, until the sun peaked in the midday sky. Just as Callum was beginning to fear he'd walked in the wrong direction all morning, a flash of movement drew his eyes up into the trees.

Not a bird or an animal. A man. He wore a brown stocking cap pulled over red curls, and he sat perched with his back to Callum, his attention fully focused in the other direction.

Callum slid behind a tree. But the man never turned, never surveyed the forest at his back. Callum crept forward, easing his boots into the underbrush to silence his footsteps.

The man still didn't stir. And after a few minutes of silent stalking, Callum could see that his attention was trained entirely on the road.

He'd made it.

Callum crept closer, until he could see where an enormous tree trunk had been felled just a touch farther down the road. Any carriage that came this way would be forced to stop while the driver cleared the path.

So the man in the tree was a bandit. One of a team. He turned a slow circle, scanning the trees. No one was sneaking up on him. No one was watching from above.

Experienced thieves should know to watch the woods for scouts or random travelers like Callum, not only the road before them. They should know to listen for out-of-place sounds. And they would have picked a better location; few rich caravans ever made their way along the roads in this area. These thieves didn't even know a proper region to hold their stakeout.

And that gave him an idea.

Scanning the woods a final time, Callum crept closer to the road. Now that he knew what he was looking for, it was easy to locate two more of the would-be thieves; even the ones stationed on the other side of the road were so intent on their mark that they did not notice him approach. It was all too easy to see them, though most had at least thought to don green and brown clothing. However, camouflage was useless when you fidgeted constantly, rustling tree branches and silencing the nearby birdcall.

And it was the work of a few minutes to find their leader. From his crouched position at the base of the fallen tree, he frequently reached up to signal his fellow bandits, his white hair flying in every direction as he did. Though Callum could not see what there was to signal about, with no coach on the way. Certainly not his own presence.

Drawing his knife, Callum backtracked, cutting a wide berth behind the first bandit he'd spied. Every second of delay put Laena in more danger, but it would do no good to rush after her unprepared. So he crept through the woods, aiming for the white-haired man.

By the time one of the scouts noticed him and cried a warning, his knife was already pressed to the leader's throat.

The old man flailed, signaling wildly, and Callum leaned in close to the man's ear. With any luck, he would not have to kill anyone today. "If your archer shoots," Callum said, "you'll be dead before I will. Best call them off."

The man swallowed hard, his skin perilously close to the edge of the knife. He held up his fingers in an X that Callum very much hoped meant he was instructing them not to shoot.

He hadn't actually seen any of them with a bow, but surely they couldn't be *that* inexperienced.

"My wife's been abducted from these woods," Callum said.

It would be foolish to admit she was a royal, even to amateurs. He was outnumbered here, and one of them could be targeting his heart. They might agree to his terms, then turn on him and demand a ransom if they thought she would bring in more than he could offer.

"Wasn't us, gent," the man choked. "I swear it."

Callum gave a short laugh. "Oh, I know. You couldn't abduct a willing victim, let alone a fighter like her."

The man bristled. "I take issue with that implica—"

"I'll pay your band to help me retrieve her," Callum interrupted. "You'll make more than you would robbing petty coaches out here."

"How would you know how much I make robbin' coaches?"

"I think you've never robbed a coach before in your life," Callum said. "I think you have no idea that it might be three days until one passes, and that when it does, the only folks who live out here are country mayors and monks. You might make three silvers, and that's if you're lucky. Hardly enough to feed your crew, let alone pay them."

The man swallowed again, and Callum found himself wishing he would just take the deal. He could dispatch this band without issue—though the archer might provide a bit of trouble—but he found he didn't wish to.

These bandits weren't working any magic. He wasn't even convinced they'd managed to rob anyone.

"I think perhaps you'd rather be doing something else," he

said, when the leader remained silent. "Also, I won't kill you if you promise to help me. Win, win."

"How'd you know I won't turn on you?"

"Because you want half my gold now and half of it when we reach Inasvale."

The man hesitated, like he was trying to think of a way around it. Callum squeezed a little tighter, and the man let out a squeak. "All right, gent, all right. You've convinced me."

"Tell them."

"Was getting to it, wasn't I?" The old man held up his hands, palms open. "Change of plan, boys. Highway robbery's done for the day. Today, we're gonna be rescuers."

CHAPTER 16

*L*aena smelled the site of her captivity before she'd fully awakened. Mold, damp and musty. Joined by the sweeter undercurrent of rotting wood. And beneath it all, the persistent odor of burning acid. It itched at the back of her parched throat, threatening to make her cough. But she wasn't ready to open her eyes yet.

Her hands and ankles were bound, the ropes cutting uncomfortably into her flesh. She tried to adjust her position surreptitiously, but her back protested the movement, shoulders shooting pain up her neck after the long night in an unnatural position.

She kept her eyes shut, allowing her senses to take in the situation. They'd dropped her into a corner, her back resting against the wall. She listened for voices, but aside from a consistent drip of water from somewhere in the room and the scrabbling of rodents in the walls, the place was quiet.

She risked opening her eyes a crack and peered around the room from beneath her lashes. She appeared to be in a dank cottage.

Two men sat at a rickety table in the middle of the room,

slurping mouthfuls of something that might have been soup, their mouths to the rims of the bowl. They were both fully clad in black, their boots spotted with mud, tears in their sleeves. No insignia.

The one on the right was large, if not nearly as large as Callum Farrow, with a patch of yellow hair on the top of his head, the sides freshly shaved. His companion was thinner; even just drinking his soup, he moved with a coiled kind of grace. Like he was stronger than he looked.

She had the sense, though she couldn't quite say why, that they were waiting for someone.

"Are you from Silerith?" Laena asked.

The thinner man dropped his bowl in surprise, swearing as the food spilled across the floor, but the bigger one merely narrowed his eyes. "Could be," he said.

"Where are we?" she asked.

"Not far," the man said. "Milla's tithe wasn't enough to get us very far. Just out of your guard's reach, I guess."

Laena's heart dropped into her stomach, and she felt like throwing up. Heart-tithers. That was how they'd spirited her away from the clearing so quickly. Her stomach roiled. How long had she been here? Would Callum be able to find her?

The knot of magic at her core turned over, as if awakening, and stretched tendrils of cold weaving through her ribcage and around her heart. It was soothing. A reminder.

She was not without her own power.

Even if she did manage to escape, she didn't know the way to Inasvale. She might have found it from the original trail she and Callum had traveled; he'd said the religious fortress was situated to the northeast, and her knowledge of geography said they could essentially follow the coast until they reached it.

But she had no idea where her captors had taken her, or in what direction.

Not far, the man had said. And Callum must be searching for

her by now. Though he mentioned having spent more time patrolling the border between Aglye and Silerith, he did have a passing familiarity with these woods.

Laena forced herself to breathe. The tendrils of power stretched. Ready.

The man who'd dropped his food finished mopping up the soup, then kicked the chatty one in the shins. "Shut up, Dane. We're not supposed to talk to her."

Before Laena could ask who'd given them that instruction, the cottage door swung open and a woman stepped into the room. She was similarly clad in black, with no badges or patches to indicate where she'd come from. Of course, that meant little. They could be from Silerith, as she suspected; they could just as easily be from Aglye, whether Callum knew of their existence or not.

They could be working independently, or for a rogue organization. She and the council had been aware of several such groups when she'd been preparing to serve as queen: secret magic users and religious fanatics, mostly. But they could be quite adept at recruiting, and their membership was not contained by borders.

There were too many possibilities to count.

The woman wore her dark hair clipped short against her head. A sprinkle of freckles on her cheeks gave her an innocent look that Laena could say from experience was mere illusion; she was sure, now that she saw the woman, that this was the person who'd snuck up on her in the woods.

"You two were supposed to watch her," the woman snapped. "Not hold a conversation."

"Sorry, Milla," Dane said.

The woman strode across the room and crouched in front of Laena, looking her over as if to check that her goods were undamaged. They were meant to deliver her somewhere else, that much was clear.

Laena met her gaze. She was well practiced at pretending not to be afraid. This woman was no challenge when compared with a stunned council facing the news of her abdication, or a circle of villagers calling her names as they all but chased her from their social gatherings.

This woman was smaller than Laena. Strong, clearly, with wiry muscles and quick reflexes, but dwarfed by the two men. Yet they, too, were looking at her with the wariness of prey. As if one snap of her jaws would result in their demise.

The woman smelled of ash, of burning rot, and Laena knew instinctively that she was the heart-tither. No wonder they were frightened.

It seemed impossible that someone with such a cold stare could love something enough that its pain would result in magic. But even if Dane had not called it 'Milla's heart-tithe,' Laena could not deny her senses.

Or the darkness that crossed the woman's eyes, like a veil of smoke, an occasional flicker. Laena had never been close enough to a heart-tither to know if the stories of those shadows were more than a myth. Clearly they were all true.

Laena swallowed her fear as best she could. If Milla was going to stare at her, she could at least try and get some answers. "I don't understand," she said. "In Riles, you tried to kill me. Now you're taking me alive. It doesn't fit."

Milla's lips curved into a thin smile. She reached forward and patted Laena on the cheek. "Maybe there are multiple people after you. Ever think of that?"

"Not these days, no."

Dane snorted. "There's big plans for you, Princess," he said. "Big plans."

Milla rose, crossing the room with a quickness Laena would not have predicted, even knowing about the tithe. The woman hauled Dane out of his chair by his shirt collar, giving the big man a shake. "Shut up," she hissed. "Don't tell her anything."

Her strength seemed unnatural as she had no trouble lifting the man off the ground, despite her slight stature.

"*You* told her a thing." Dane's voice was strangled, his fear obvious. He should have been able to swipe her aside with a single hit, but he didn't even try. Like a kitten caught by a hawk.

"*I'm* not an imbecile." Milla dropped him, and he missed the chair, falling in a heap on the ground.

"We didn't get her far enough, Mil," the other man said. "What're we gonna do? The King's Guard are sure to come along the road."

Milla paced to the wall. "I'll think of something."

"But you killed—"

"Shut up, Penn," Milla interrupted. "I can do this alone."

Penn wasn't quite as frightened of Milla as Dane appeared to be. Either that or he hid it better. He put a hand on her arm, lowering his voice to a whisper that Laena couldn't make out. Comforting her.

Clearly, Milla had needed to kill, not merely hurt, something —or someone—she loved to work this level of magic. Laena didn't know enough about heart-tithing to guess how much magic that would have given her, or how long it would last. But the way the woman was still moving with that quickness, that unnatural strength, she guessed there was still a trickle of power left.

Perhaps she'd used the majority of it creating that storm. Perhaps she'd drained the rest of the reserves whisking them here to this cabin, leaving her with only the dregs of power.

Silently, cautiously, Laena probed at her own power.

It stretched in response, unfurling against her touch. There was an eagerness there, but also weakness. Her throat throbbed, and she understood: she was too parched to fully access her magic. Ice needed humidity to form, after all.

So Laena started to cough.

Milla whipped around, obviously ready to snap at her, but

Penn rose. "She just needs a drink, Mil." He spoke softly, but Laena noticed the care he took in his movements. As if one sharp word from Milla would send him back to his chair.

When she didn't protest, he brought his glass over to Laena, bending to hold it to her lips.

Laena drank then coughed again, spasming so hard that she knocked the glass from his hands.

"Stupid girl," Milla hissed.

Enough.

Laena called for her power and it responded, freezing the ropes around her wrists into brittle, breakable things. Laena snapped them, slashing at her ankles with the icy blades that formed in her hands, then pushed Penn back with a blast of cold air before he could lunge for her, before he even understood what was happening.

It was easy now, the magic flowing as if from an infinite well. A rush of delicious cold.

And then she was on her feet, blades spinning in her hands as if she'd used them all her life. The magic broke free at last, filling the room with the sharp smell of snow.

CHAPTER 17

$\mathcal{T}$he would-be bandits, it turned out, were far more helpful than Callum had initially anticipated. He'd hoped for strength in numbers, intimidation, whether or not the thieves were good fighters. He'd hoped for backup, covered entrances, and extra pairs of eyes. Even if these particular eyes were not especially well trained.

Instead, their leader—whose name was Maynard—appeared to take the job quite seriously. Thieving he could stomach, while kidnapping was an abhorrence. Or so he declared. Callum couldn't tell if the man was protesting too much and intended to ransom them both at the first opportunity, or if he simply wanted to ingratiate himself with his temporary employer.

It could most definitely be a little bit of both.

Most importantly, Maynard had told Callum of the abandoned cabin they'd passed while scouting for a location to hold up the next passing carriage. "If I needed a place out here to hold a captive," he said, "that's where I'd hold her."

He knew the region better than Callum had assumed. It made him wonder whether Maynard had intentionally chosen a quiet area to make his attempt at robbing coaches. Maybe he'd been hoping that none would come along.

At first, the cabin had seemed as good a place to start looking for Laena as any other. But the closer they got, the more he could smell the heart-tithe in the air, stronger and stronger, until even the thieves were lifting their collars over their noses to block out the smell. Callum had no doubt this was the place where Laena was being held. Part of him wanted to run, to crash forward without thought to allies or enemies, and wrench her away from the danger before the tithers could do her more harm.

He forced himself to take his time. He would not abandon her, nor would he put her in more danger by rushing in without a plan.

When the cabin emerged, a lump of a building hunched within an overgrown grove, goosebumps fluttered over his arms and neck. This had to be the place. Ivy crawled up the walls, snaking into the cracks, and more than a few bricks had crumbled to the ground. The roof was a mess, the half-decayed shingles sure to leak at the first sign of rain, and most of the windows were cracked and broken.

Callum signaled for Maynard to distribute his thieves, one for each window. "And scouts for the woods," he added as the older man hurried away, leaping over fallen branches with surprising spryness as he punched the air, wiggling his thumbs and fingers in what Callum could only guess must be a series of signals to direct his band.

The man was barely out of sight when a crash sounded from inside the cabin, followed by a scream.

Callum's dagger was in his hand before he could think of what to do, instinct combining with a lifetime of training so that his body acted without delay. Abandoning any pretense of subterfuge, he dashed across the grove, the undergrowth grabbing at his boots as if to pull him down.

"Cover the other exits," he shouted, hoping Maynard and the others could hear.

Another scream—definitely Laena's, he was certain of it now —and then his shoulder was against the door. He threw his whole weight into it, which turned out to be unnecessary; the rotting wood splintered, cracking open against the weight of his body and sending him stumbling into the room.

A blast of cold air was his only warning as a storm of icicles volleyed toward him, the sharp ends flying at his face. He threw himself down, his chin slamming against the floor as they lodged themselves into the walls with a sputter of percussive thumps.

One of the men screamed, and Callum looked up in time to see him wrenching an icicle out of his shoulder.

Fighting amongst themselves? Or caught in friendly fire? Either way, it was creative magic for heart-tithers. He'd never seen them use ice before. The room held only the faint whiff of a tithe, like a distant afterburn.

Laena stood at the far end of the room, hands raised as if to shield her face. Her hair was a tangle around her shoulders, her face streaked with dirt, but she appeared to be uninjured.

The panic he'd been holding in his throat dissolved.

In its place, bitter rage poured in.

The injured man staggered forward, blood dripping from his shoulder, icicle raised. Laena pushed her hands out as if they might shield her from whatever he intended. She was wavering on her feet, ever so slightly—but enough for him to notice—and the sight of it made him want to tear this place to the ground.

Perhaps her hands couldn't shield her. But Callum could. He surged forward and grabbed the man's wrist from behind, twisting until the icicle dropped from his fingers. The man screamed as Callum raised his dagger and slashed it across the villain's throat, cutting off his cry with a gurgle.

Rage pulsed across his vision, hot and violent. Rather than

clouding his senses, it made him more aware of his surroundings, aware that a second man was coming at him from the side. He pivoted, blood pooling around his feet as he faced his next opponent.

This man was smaller than the first but quicker. Teeth bared, he dodged Callum's first jab, dancing out of reach. Callum moved for him again, unwilling to give the man any quarter. He needed to reach Laena before they managed to spirit her away again.

The man lunged, his knife aimed at Callum's gut. The point sliced through his shirt, digging into his skin.

Icy air coiled around the hilt and wrenched the blade out of the man's grip, pushing it into Callum's. The man startled in surprise, giving Callum the opening he needed to strike. The man fell with his own knife in his gut, precisely the spot where he'd tried to hit Callum.

Never mind that cold air, or any air, should not be capable of grabbing knives out of the air. He stared at the fallen man, trying to piece it together. Had his own magic failed him?

"Callum!" Laena shouted, a note of warning in her voice. He turned just in time to knock aside a woman who was coming at him from the right, a hammer aimed at his head. She staggered, and the hammer flew across the floor.

Somehow, impossibly, the woman kept her balance, abandoning the weapon as she ran for the door. She, at least, knew when the fight had been lost.

Laena spread her arms wide. Between the rotting doorframe, a curtain of ice hardened. One moment, Callum was looking out at a sliver of the overgrown grove, the next it was obscured behind a window of wavering ice, the edges feathered with frost.

What the blazing kind of magic was *that*? It smelled fresh and sharp, like the morning before the first snow. It was like no magic he'd ever seen, or smelled, or felt.

And it seemed to have come from *Laena*. The princess stood with her back to the corner, her lips pressed into a thin line. The color had bleached from her face and her hands were shaking, her expression distant. As if it was taking all her concentration not to collapse.

The woman hit the ice and bounced back, surprise mixing with fear as she glanced back at the princess. Gritting her teeth, she made another run for the door, this time cracking through the ice with her shoulder.

Shaking himself out of his shock, Callum started after her. But then Laena made a sound behind him—something between a whimper and a sigh—and he turned just in time to see her crumple to the floor, unconscious.

CHAPTER 18

*L*aena cradled a cup of hot tea in her hands, trying to understand how this odd collection of men—and one woman, she noted—had come to be her rescuers. She rested on a fallen log as they milled around the clearing outside the cabin, several of them keeping what seemed like an inordinately careful watch on the woods.

None reentered the cabin. None even glanced toward it, as if by acknowledging the carnage they might cause it to spill out the door and haunt them forever.

She didn't want to think about it, either.

Nor did she much want to think about Callum, though that seemed impossible after he'd come bursting in to rescue her. When he'd crashed through that door, eyes blazing with rage, her own heart had stuttered with fear. For a moment, anyway.

That was the man she'd read about, the scourge of magic users and lawbreakers. He'd dispatched the two men with merciless ease, and she did not doubt he would have done the same to the woman had she given him a chance.

Had he not been distracted by Laena's magic.

It was difficult to reconcile that vicious warrior with the

man who'd been fussing over her for the last fifteen minutes like a worried matron, since she'd fallen unconscious back in the cabin. He hadn't left her side since she'd taken a seat in the clearing, no matter that she was feeling much better. Only a little bit shaky.

All right, he was quite a bit handsomer than a worried matron. His dark hair was damp with exertion from the fight, his eyes roving her face every few minutes as if he thought she might break. Yet despite how much he looked at her, he had yet to meet her gaze directly.

Hanging between them, unspoken, was the magic she'd used in the cabin.

He had to know it had been her. It could not have come from anyone else, and she hadn't done anything to hide it.

Had he taken such pains to rescue her only to arrest her now that he suspected—or knew—what she was? Or would he dispatch her with the same ruthless ease as he had the men in the cabin? It seemed impossible to believe, with the concern drawing lines across his forehead.

She did feel shaky. A burning sensation had taken the place of the cool comfort of her magic, and though it had already begun to fade, it had not eased entirely. It was like she'd inadvertently drawn too close to a fire and stayed there a few seconds too long, allowing the heat to sear her. Only instead of burning the skin, it was burning her inside.

Her hands were still shaking, her breaths a touch too ragged. No wonder Callum was looking at her like she was something fragile.

Or perhaps the concern was for the magic rather than for her safety. Perhaps he only sat next to her now so he could take her by surprise, wrap her wrists in chains, and drag her to the dungeons before her magic had time to revive.

"Don't worry." Laena startled as the white-haired man who'd given her the tea chuckled, easing himself down to sit across from her. "A husband's bound to be worried for his lady now, isn't he? But there's no harm done. You're a courageous one, and that's a fact."

Laena blinked, taking a long sip of tea to hide her surprise. It seemed Captain Farrow had been telling stories. Until she knew why, it would probably be wise to play along. "*My* husband? Worried?"

"Wouldn'a let us rest until you were safe." The man laughed again, then patted Callum's shoulder. "Not been married all that long, have ye? You'll see how husbands are, good lady. You'll see."

Laena looked at Callum, then back at the man. Callum was still avoiding her gaze, his eyes skipping over her face without landing on her eyes. No doubt he'd been concerned for the fate of Aglye's emissary, for the fate of his mission, not for her personally.

Now, with the magic, she wondered if he would allow her to meet King Hawk at all.

"This," Callum said, "is Maynard. He agreed to lend his band of..."

"Traveling performers," Maynard provided.

Callum winced. "He agreed to bring his band of traveling performers when he heard my wife had been taken."

Maynard's allies were traveling performers? Well, that made no sense whatsoever. Laena rested her tea in her lap, savoring the comforting warmth of the cup in her hands. The day wasn't overly cold—it was growing warm, in fact—but she felt the barest shiver of a chill crawling along the inside of her ribcage.

Strange. She rarely felt the cold. Even in that winter of near starvation, it wasn't the cold that had endangered her. And she never felt it from her magic, either. Was it responding to that heat somehow, the feeling of the burn?

Shaking off her unease as best she could, Laena took the opportunity to look more closely at Maynard and his followers.

What would a band of traveling performers be doing out in the woods, with no one to perform for? As long as one didn't count the forest mice and the birds. Perhaps a deer or two.

No, performers kept to the cities. Or at least to roads with frequent villages or manor houses. But Callum *had* said there were thieves in the forest, had he not?

Laena let her jaw drop in open surprise. No need to hide it. "You brought *bandits* to help rescue me?"

Callum winced again.

"We really are traveling performers, good lady," Maynard protested. "It's merely that... well, times are hard and all. Not as many lords are wanting to see a play."

"Not for the prices you charge," the woman bandit—or performer, or both—said from behind him. As far as Laena could tell, she was the only woman in the group. She'd been pacing restlessly between the trees, peering into the woods every few steps as if she expected an attack at any moment.

Of all of them, the woman looked the most like an actual bandit, clothed in black with a bow propped over her shoulder, a quiver of arrows strapped to her back.

"Now, Gretchen," Maynard said, "we have to charge what we're worth, don't we? I was a court bard, after all."

"Fifty years ago," she muttered.

"More like twenty." Maynard's knees cracked loudly as he stood. He brushed the dirt from his trousers with careful swipes, though the pants had been patched and repatched many times over. "We'd best be moving on."

"If you wouldn't mind, Maynard," Laena said, "I need just a moment to talk to my husband."

Maynard bobbed his head and stepped away, shooing the others back as if a few steps would give them true privacy. She supposed it was as much as she could expect, given the circumstances.

She turned her attention to the captain. And still, he did not meet her eye. There was a tick working at the corner of his jaw, his expression so grim she might have thought he'd lost her back there, when in truth he'd saved her life.

Laena ducked her head, forcing Callum to meet her eyes. When he did, the breath caught in her throat. She'd expected him to be guarded with her, careful. Accusatory even.

And truly, a fire did burn behind those ice-chip blue eyes of his. But she did not think it was a fire of accusation. It was a look that seared straight between her ribs, as if to add itself to the band that was creeping its way through her bones.

"Are you well, my lady?" he asked.

She took in his rumpled state, the rip in his shirt where Penn's dagger had nearly sliced into his body. "I might ask you the same."

"And yet I am not the one who collapsed."

"The strain—"

He touched a hand to her wrist, stopping her mid-sentence. His touch was like fire, and her body responded to it, a shiver working its way up her arm, her spine. "That was no strain, my lady. That was magic."

"Are you going to arrest me, Captain?"

He traced his finger toward her elbow, wrapping his hand around her forearm and using the grip to draw her closer. His eyes bored into her like hot coals, as if he could see straight to her heart. "I should arrest you," he said. "If I had any sense, you would be in chains by now."

Laena's throat was dry. "But?"

His gaze dropped to her lips, lingering there. "But you saved my life."

She had. The memory of that dagger poised to dig into his gut was still potent, the panic recent enough to claw at her chest. To save his life, she would have done it again. A hundred times.

She wanted to touch him. She wanted to explain, only she

didn't know where to start. She had no clue what her magic was, only that it existed. Only that she had caused no one pain to procure it.

"It's not a heart-tithe, Captain," she whispered. "I swear it."

"Then what is it?" His voice was low and rough, like a warning.

She swallowed. "I don't know."

She wasn't sure if he would accept that. Would she, in his place?

"It's hurting you."

She blinked, surprised. That was not what she'd expected. Not from the man who was the scourge of heart-tithers, the legendary captain who hated magic above all else. He'd seen her use a power that was unknown in the Vales as far as she'd ever heard. He knew she had lied. Yet his concern was for her well-being?

He said it as if stating a fact, when it had to be a question. Yes, the magic had caused her to lose consciousness, however briefly. And yes, there was still a tender soreness beneath her ribcage. But it was easing by the second, the pain fading to a distant throb. It would soon be gone entirely.

She shook her head. Before she could form a response, Maynard cleared his throat. "Sorry to interrupt the reunion, truly I am. I'd have us camp here for the night if I thought it wise, but..." He darted a glance at the cabin where so much blood had been spilled. "But I think we'd best be on our way."

Callum used his grip on Laena's arm to pull her to her feet, then released her. She forced herself to look away as the bandits rejoined them.

"So, husband," she said, making her tone as light as she could. "Are these fine *performers* to escort us to Inasvale?"

"My brother can pay them there," he said. "So, yes."

At least they could now walk along the road. It was far easier than picking their way through the forest. Callum dispatched two of the bandits to walk a little way into the woods on either side of the road, instructing them to keep a watch in all directions.

The way the rest of them arranged themselves around the party, they did seem to take their new job seriously. Trying to forget the conversation with Callum, and to ignore the way he watched her too closely—whether out of concern or fear, she wasn't sure—she schooled her expression to one of lightness.

The bandits had helped rescue her. It could do only good to get to know them a little.

"How far is it to Inasvale?" she asked as the cabin receded into the woods behind them.

Maynard cast a glance over his shoulder, ducking beneath a low-hanging branch without even looking at it. "Another three days' walk, I'd wager," he said. "Fizz. Get the couple some of those brown bread rolls, will you? The poor lady looks half starved."

Gretchen, who'd positioned herself to Maynard's right, shot them a dark look, though Laena thought that might well be a default expression for her. But another bandit—Fizz, apparently —bounced up merrily enough, handing them each a pair of rolls from the pack he carried on his back. At first, Laena thought he must be one of the younger members of the band, but a closer look revealed lines around his eyes and a deeply receding hair-line. Still, he had a youthful air about him.

Maybe they really were performers.

Or cooks. The roll was hard but good, with an edge of sweetness to it. Different. She found herself devouring it; she hadn't realized how hungry she was. "Molasses?" she asked.

"My best recipe," Fizz said eagerly, and she realized he was watching her with his eyebrows raised in anticipation. Waiting, she thought, for her review of the food.

"It's delicious," Laena said. "I've never had such good traveling bread."

Of course, she hadn't had very much traveling bread. But he didn't need to know that.

Fizz grinned, the smile splitting his face evenly in half. "Isn't it? I said, why should traveling food be so tasteless just because it needs to last? These are hard, they gotta be so they don't get moldy—I baked 'em two days ago, no need to fret—but I could send sailors on a trip for six months and they'd be safe to eat! And happy, too. It's the molasses, sure as anything."

Laena didn't know about the six months, but it did taste good. Or maybe it was just that she was near famished and would have eaten anything they offered.

"Fool," Gretchen muttered. Though she was walking ahead of them, she kept peering back at Laena and Callum with such narrow-eyed focus that Laena wondered how she hadn't tripped over her feet yet. It was as if she expected Laena or Callum to lunge forward and slit Maynard's throat, now that she'd been rescued.

"Perhaps you should open a shop," Laena said.

Beside her, Callum shook his head. She could practically hear him muttering not to encourage Fizz. Which, truth be told, only made her want to encourage him more.

"That's exactly what I'm going to do, soon as we reach Inasvale," Fizz said cheerfully. "Well, except for the shop part."

"So not exactly," Callum said. Laena elbowed him in the arm, and he glanced at her, the ghost of a smile on his lips. At least he didn't leap away from her for fear of her magic.

"I'll sell the bread to the merchants there," Fizz said. "Turn our fates around."

"Fizz, he's not overly happy with our change in fortune," one of the other bandits put in.

"I wouldn't mind a new fortune myself," another added.

Most of them were nodding along, and Laena found herself hoping she could use her influence to help them. What little influence she had, that was. "Forgive me," she said, doing her best to be delicate, "but you don't seem like very *practiced* bandits. How long have you been... without performing jobs?"

Fizz sighed. Before he could speak, Gretchen said, "We robbed a coach last week. How do you think we got the coin to make the bread? Ingredients cost money."

The woman certainly sounded defensive. Not proud of their coach-robbing feat, not exactly, but... not ashamed of it, either. Even though Fizz kept darting glances at his shoes, as if *he* might be a bit ashamed.

One-time performers turned bandits. Who aspired to be bakers. It was... well, it was sweet actually.

"Gretchen," Maynard said, "if you're gonna grouse like your tongue's gone sour, you can take up the rear and watch for anyone who might be following us."

Gretchen shot him a murderous glare, but she did as he said, dropping back to the rear of the group. Though it might have been mainly that she wanted to avoid Fizz, or any further conversation with Laena and Callum.

"Hard times," Maynard said. "Crops withering without reason. Fish have been scarce. We've had to leave the bounds of what we'd usually allow."

Fizz nodded sadly. "And no one wants to pay for a song."

CHAPTER 19

$\mathcal{T}$he bandits' fire was a far cry from the sad little flames Laena had kindled on their first night. Callum might've been impressed with her ability to coax warmth from steel and stone, but they'd had no tools to chop proper firewood, which had necessitated constant maintenance to keep it going.

When the bandits made camp, she set to work helping them collect kindling while Fizz and the others chopped larger fallen branches. Soon the flames were crackling, and Maynard was encouraging Laena and Callum to sit while Fizz tossed savory roots into a pot.

When Laena dipped her hand into her pocket to check on Brin, the little shimmerling licked at her fingertips. Callum had produced Brin from his pocket as soon as they'd stopped, and Laena had barely been able to restrain herself from throwing her arms around his neck.

She wasn't sure he'd thank her for that.

With a silent promise to sneak some food Brin's way, Laena settled on the ground beside Callum, holding her hands out to the flames.

"At odds, are you?" Maynard asked.

Laena blinked at the older man, confused, but he merely chuckled and waved his finger back and forth between herself and Callum. "A married couple, and a young one at that, seated by the fire with nary a touch? After such a frightening adventure? You're at odds, or I'm the King of the Sea."

Laena had nearly forgotten that she and Callum were meant to be married. Though Callum hadn't been able to say as much, she could guess the reason for the ruse. Kindly though Maynard and his 'bandits' were, it might be too great a test to reveal their true identities. The captain of the King's Guard *and* an Etran princess? They'd make more from a ransom than whatever Callum had promised to pay.

Callum scooted closer to her and wrapped an arm around her waist. He kept his fingers loose at her side, where other men would have taken the excuse to sneak a squeeze. It was the bare minimum of decency, certainly, only... Laena found herself wishing he'd try it.

"We're not at odds," Callum said. "We're merely exhausted."

Maynard smiled at them, bobbing his head like he knew better. Laena wondered if she ought to play along, pretend to be angry with him. But exhaustion was starting to fray her ability to play this game. She was longing for a decent meal and a night of uninterrupted sleep.

With Callum's body flush against her side, she might fall asleep right here and now.

Fizz appeared with bowls of stew and a proud smile. And, Laena realized as he hovered over Maynard's shoulder, the expectation of a verdict on the quality of the meal. He was bouncing on the balls of his feet, his hands clasped behind his back.

"Hand it around, Fizz," another of the bandits complained, but the young man waited.

"We've got new tastebuds at the fire," Fizz replied. "I can't waste the opportunity to improve."

Laena spooned a mouthful of stew into her mouth, eyes widening at the medley of flavors that Fizz had somehow mixed into the dish. It was savory and distantly sweet, and she had the feeling he'd created it as a companion to the molasses rolls he'd shared earlier. An herbal note in the background that didn't drown out the natural taste of the roots... it was beyond any stew she'd cooked herself, truly.

"How did you do that?" she asked. "Out here in the woods?"

Fizz grinned. "Practice." He winked. "And a satchel full of spices. I keep it with me at all times."

"You're forgetting the number of failures you've forced us to choke down." Gretchen stomped over and jerked the pot away from Fizz. "Feed the rest of us, will you?"

Maynard ignored his crew's squabbling, intent on his food. "Tell me," he said. "How did you two meet?"

Unbidden, a vision rose to her mind of Callum appearing at the palace gates to insist that her own guards let her in. Truly she was a fool, to think of something so ridiculous—he'd also gone tearing out of his chambers half-naked to chase after an assassin. But it was the image of him staring at that guard, insisting the man respect her, that lodged in her mind.

If I had any sense, you would be in chains by now.

Would he have done the same, had he known about her magic?

"He assisted me," she said softly. "In a... in a matter of some delicacy."

Tucked beneath his shoulder as she was, she could feel him shift to look down at her, and she flushed. No need to let him see how much his intervention had saved her. His numerous interventions, at this point.

No doubt he regretted those now that he knew her secret.

"I'm a seamstress, you see," she continued, "and he was just the right size to model a wedding gown I was sewing. For a horse."

Maynard threw his head back and laughed, and several of the others joined him. But it was Callum's laugh that caught her breath in the back of her throat, the vibration of his chest at her back. "A tall tale," he said.

"It isn't," she insisted, turning to pinch his chin between her fingers. "He looks beautiful in lace."

The reckoning was coming. He might have the decency to be sorry when he clapped her in irons, but she had to believe he might well do it just the same, whether she'd saved his life or not. No matter how tightly his arm was wrapped around her now. No matter how intently he watched her. No matter how pleasant his laugh.

When the dinner was cleared and the laughter had faded into murmurs, Fizz and the others laid out pallets among the trees while Gretchen and Maynard set up to take first watch. Reluctant though they might seem to be, making a home in the woods, the rest of the bandits arranged their bedrolls with efficiency. Fizz showed Laena and Callum to a spot between a more secluded pair of trees, a pallet for the two of them.

A single pallet. For the married couple they were pretending to be.

"One pallet," Laena said, mostly because she couldn't help herself. "Not two?"

Maynard, lingering by the fire, let out a laugh. "You're not still as angry with him as all that, are you, mistress? Nothing a bit of sleep can't cure, I'm sure."

"Sleep," Laena said. "Right."

Callum glanced over his shoulder, the flames flickering warm shadows across his face. "I could offer to take the first watch in their stead," he said softly. "I'm not sure they'd trust me."

But Laena shook her head. "You're as weary as I am."

Clearly he couldn't argue with that. Together, they settled onto the pallet, which, if not entirely comfortable, was surprisingly thick and protective against the bumpy roots of the forest floor. Laena settled onto her back, propping her hands on her stomach, where a knot of tension was slowly building. Callum's elbow brushed hers, sending an electric charge up her arm, and she shivered.

"Why did you have to say we were married?" she whispered.

"I didn't think it through," he replied.

Laena shifted onto her side, propping her head on her hand. "What, you're not going to pretend it was to protect me?"

Callum was already on his side—she'd expected him to lie on his back, more for her—and the size of the pallet meant they were lying scandalously close, mere inches separating his hips from hers. It would be nothing to wrap her leg around his, to invite the touch he'd so carefully withheld at the fire.

"Would you accept such an answer?" he asked.

"Absolutely not. I need no one's protection."

He lifted a hand to her face, brushing a strand of hair away from her cheek and tucking it behind her ear, his finger lingering on the shell of her ear. "Perhaps I am the one who needs protection," he said, a mere undertone in the dark.

Protection from her, he must mean. Protection from her magic. Dread creeped up her throat and lodged itself there, sending pulses of anxiety through her chest. "Will you tell the king?" she asked.

Will you clap me in irons? That half of the question went unspoken, but it was implied. It hung between them like it had the power to push them apart. Whatever he said next, whatever he had decided—or not decided—would define the rest of this journey.

She could escape him, if she needed to. She could run to Silerith, beg for asylum there.

His fingertips trailed down her neck, and her skin came alive at his touch, goosebumps flickering down her spine. "I thought I'd lost you," he said.

For a moment, Laena forgot to breathe.

Not "magic is evil" or "I'll have to report this." Not even "If I had any sense, you would be in chains by now."

I thought I'd lost you.

He smelled of leather and woodsmoke, a delicious combination, and it had been so long since anyone had touched her like this. "They're not watching," she said, her own voice like an exhale. "You don't need to pretend."

He leaned closer. "I'm not pretending." His breath was hot against her lips, his mouth a hair's breadth from hers.

"But the magic..."

"I spent a day and a night fearing you were gone," he said. "I found you held against your will by people who've already tried to spill your blood and damn near succeeded. I spent today pretending to be your husband, and wishing..."

He trailed off, and she found herself aching for him to continue, to hear the words his lips wouldn't form. "Damn the magic, Laena. If you say it's not a heart-tithe, I believe you."

She couldn't be hearing him correctly. It wasn't possible.

Only he was looking at her with that blue-eyed intensity, all seriousness. All truth. Callum Farrow was all blunt force. He might have a talent for subterfuge, should he try it, but she knew enough of him by now to know that he preferred his words to be taken at face value.

And he said he *believed* her. How long had it been since someone had believed her? She'd had to extract a rotting crystal from her garden to convince Katrina of the danger facing Etra.

Callum believed her, trusted her, with no evidence or proof, only her word against what he'd seen in the cabin. And in fact, the evidence pointed harshly against her; he could not be blamed for attributing the lingering scent of the heart-tithe to her magic rather than Milla's.

Yet Callum believed her. He trusted her.

Tears stung her eyes, rising quick and fierce, and she blinked them away, hoping he would attribute them to the dryness of the fire, the exhaustion of the day.

Callum must have interpreted her silence as a denial, her tears as fear, because he let out a breath. "But I'll stop, if you ask me to."

As if to demonstrate the truth of it, he drew back, allowing the coldest air she'd ever felt to drift between them. This was a cold she did feel, hollow in a way she couldn't explain.

Laena brought a hand to his face, drawing him back toward her, tipping her face to meet his.

And yet before their lips could touch, a horse screamed at the edge of camp. Torches flared throughout the woods, and the startled figures of the bandits scrambled up from their pallets.

"Up with you, criminals," a man's voice commanded. Callum cursed, releasing Laena as he leapt to his feet.

"Demons," he said. "It's the King's Guard."

CHAPTER 20

*T*hey were lucky that Landon Moore hadn't sent his soldiers roaring into the camp on horseback, or half the bandits would've been trampled.

It hurt to think of them as Landon Moore's soldiers when they should be Callum's. But there was no use in denying it to himself. Soon, he would have to admit it to Laena, too.

But first, he needed to save their allies. He owed them a debt.

He made his way to the center of the camp, where Moore was lording over Maynard, his chest puffed like a pheasant's, sword primed as if he planned to dispatch the man without a trial. His gods-damned hair was arranged into a golden swoop that hardly even moved, as if he hoped the bards would sing of it with as much awe as they did of his deeds.

When Callum inserted himself between the two men, the look on Moore's face would have captured the bards' attention, for certain. His eyes went wide as moons, his lips parted in shock. He actually dropped his sword, the fool.

"*You,*" the general breathed. "We thought you'd been lost at sea."

Another soldier coughed in the background, and Callum

found Edmun in the crowd, his sword half-heartedly raised in Fizz's direction. Young Godfrey stood beside him, looking bedraggled but alive. Huck and Archer, Reggie and Bertrand. His men were *alive*. Callum could have cheered.

Instead, he leveled his most hardened glare at Landon Moore. "Don't sound so disappointed, General. And tell your men to unhand Mr. Maynard." Callum wasn't entirely sure whether Maynard was the man's given name or his surname, but at the moment, it didn't matter. "He and his fellows are helping us to Inasvale."

"Us?" Moore glanced around, his lips already starting to curl into an insolent response when his gaze landed on Laena.

She was standing beside the sleeping pallet, her hands propped on her hips. Callum thought his own glare was a hardened one? Hers would have shattered diamonds.

And if Moore had held off his attack for one more minute, another blessed minute, he'd have been kissing her. Yet another reason to curse the man.

Though perhaps Callum ought to thank him instead. Laena didn't yet know what he was, and she was about to find out. Better that Callum did not give in to temptation, kissing her before he was even sure it was what she wanted.

She'd seemed sure enough herself, truth be told.

"The Etran emissary," Callum said.

Gretchen swore. "I *knew* they were important."

Maynard was frowning. He hadn't guessed it, and Callum didn't think he'd have used it against them anyway. If anything, the man was probably insulted that Callum had lied to him.

"Lower your weapons," Callum said, "or King Hawk will know why."

Edmun and Godfrey followed the order, along with Huck and Archer. All the soldiers who'd accompanied him to Etra, in fact.

The rest waited for Moore's nod before stowing their swords.

Callum didn't want to look Laena's way as Moore turned to her, but honor said he owed it to her to meet her eye. Whereas he'd avoided it after the incident in the cabin, afraid of what she must think of him, after seeing him shed so much blood, this time she met his gaze straight on.

And she was not happy with him.

Moore stepped between them, offering her a bow and dipping his head with almost regal grace. "I trust you are unaware, ma'am, that you've been taken captive by an imposter."

Callum had the distinct sense that Landon Moore didn't know who Laena was, and that he was covering his ignorance by avoiding her name. Well, she'd only just agreed to serve as emissary, had she not? It stood to reason that Katrina would not have named her to Hawk. And Moore had the sense to pretend he knew her.

He had access to the same records that Callum did. Why the mages had Hawk named him general if he hadn't bothered to study?

Laena raised an eyebrow. "An imposter? Is this man not Callum Farrow?"

Moore, who had yet to sheath his own sword, though he held it casually at his side—as casually as one could hold such a thing—gave an ugly laugh. "He is, my lady. He is. But he's no longer the captain of the King's Guard, nor was he given charge over the expedition."

Laena narrowed her eyes, as if she didn't quite believe what Moore was telling her. "And yet he arrived in Etra with the delegation."

"Well, my lady," Moore said, "I'm sorry to say that he stole it."

---*---

IF THE STEW the bandits carried was excellent, the whiskey they carried decidedly was not. It was the type of stuff they only carried at Callum's third-favorite pub in Vunmore, a place where he hesitated to even darken the door. It wasn't typically necessary; the first two served him just fine.

Most places wouldn't even use this stuff for medicinal purposes, unless pressed. Yet it did the job well enough, and Callum always found that if he sat with the bottle for an hour or more, its contents would begin to taste just fine indeed.

There'd been moments on this journey when Callum had nearly forgotten the mission didn't belong to him at all. He'd nearly convinced himself that was the case. That Hawk owed it to him, that he'd declare all forgiven as soon as he saw how much Callum had achieved. How well he'd done.

Assassins. Shipwrecks. Kidnappers. That was how well he'd done.

And now Laena knew it all.

When Callum had taken up the bottle, she'd taken up a conversation with Moore, then with Edmun and Godfrey, working her way down the line and checking in with each of the men, as Callum ought to be doing. But he'd failed them, as Hawk had known he would. He'd lied to them, betrayed them, left them to drown.

It didn't matter that Edmun had known from the beginning. It was a betrayal nonetheless.

No doubt General Moore would have found a way to keep the ship from sinking. The way the man was strutting around the camp's perimeter, nudging the nervous bandits in the ribs by turns and earning himself a hard stare from Gretchen—who, given a chance, would surely skewer the man through his own ribs—he would no doubt be spinning this tale to make himself the hero who'd intentionally discovered Callum, rather than by pure accident.

What was he doing, raiding random camps in the forest, anyway?

"Is this seat taken?"

Callum was tipped just far enough toward drunk not to jump at the sound of Laena's voice. A bit drunker and he'd have fallen off the log. Luckily, he maintained his dignity. "Not sure why you'd want to sit on it, but it's free for the taking if you care to."

Laena sat down beside him so her side was flush against his. As close as they'd been on the pallet. Closer even, though thigh to thigh was not quite as desirable as their previous position.

"I'm surprised you don't wish to avoid me," he said. "I lied to you."

"Please." She plucked the bottle from his hands and took a swallow, grimacing before handing it back. "I can hardly be angry at a fellow outcast. One, I think, who did what he did with good intentions?"

Callum couldn't help it; he stared at her. "Perhaps," he said carefully, half afraid she'd stand up and laugh, call him a fool, and head off to make friends with Moore.

Instead, she leaned in closer, her arm flush with his. It took a concerted effort not to tuck her in closer and resume the activities Landon Moore had so rudely interrupted.

"You could have arrested me the moment you saw the way I..." She trailed off, but he noted the way she twisted her hands, fluttering her fingers. A mild approximation of the movements she'd made back in that cabin. The movements that had sent deadly icicles flying into walls, and men's shoulders. That had barred the doorway.

Again, the liquor saved him. Without it, he would have startled. He would have flinched.

If Hawk discovered that Callum had been escorting a woman who could do magic, and without clapping her in chains… well, he'd add it to the growing list of Callum's crimes. What was one more.

"Arrest you for what?" he said, trying to keep his voice light. "Unprovoked teasing?"

She held his gaze, obviously not buying the casual act. "You put your trust in me, Captain. It's only fair I return the favor."

Did he trust her? He wasn't sure. He'd never seen magic such as hers, had not even heard of such a thing.

But he knew this: she smelled of crisp winter mornings, of sweet spices baking over a fire. She did not smell of evil. The opposite, in fact.

Callum had seen too much to believe that everything was black and white. Magic or no magic. Evil or not. It was never that simple.

"Also," she whispered, leaning in closer to his ear, "Landon Moore is a bullheaded fool. I'm relieved not to have been stuck surviving a shipwreck with him."

Callum swallowed, trying to ignore the way his body responded to the heat of her breath against his skin. "And pretending to be married to him?"

Laena grimaced, as if the idea were worse than the whiskey. "I'd rather be robbed."

Mages, but the woman was beautiful. With the firelight flickering across her face, she looked like a promise out of the depths of his dreams. He'd kiss her right now, if Moore weren't here to be his audience.

But who was he kidding? He wanted to do more than kiss her. He wanted to bury his nose in her hair, run his hands over her body. He wanted to feel her writhing beneath him, to savor every gasp of pleasure as he touched her.

Once again, it was a good thing that Moore was here.

If he kept repeating it, he might even begin to believe it.

"Why did you lie?" Laena asked.

Callum drew in a deep breath, steadying himself. A cold shower would have done better, but he doubted she'd appreciate him abandoning the conversation for a dip in the stream. The whiskey was putting improper thoughts into his head, and he owed her an answer. Truly, he did. "Hawk relieved me of my post," he said.

"And you thought you'd prove your way back into his good graces."

Callum took another swallow of whiskey. The stuff was beginning to grow on him. "Something like that."

"By stealing the job?"

"In my defense," he said, "I wasn't entirely sober."

She studied him for a long moment, her expression unreadable in the dark. "Yes," she said. "We might want to work on that."

Damn the reasons he'd concocted for not kissing her. If she kept looking at him like that, kept pressing her side to his, kept smelling like snowy days and cinnamon... he was going to pull her into his arms. To the Miragelands with Landon Moore, and whatever he'd think of it.

Unfortunately—or fortunately, depending on which of Callum's body parts was making the argument—Landon Moore chose that moment to sit down on Laena's other side. "Nice friends you've made, Farrow," he said. "They do match the descriptions of the band of robbers that ambushed Lord Finneas's coach not two days ago."

"Funny," Callum said. "You match the description of a dung-eating weasel, but I'm polite enough not to mention it. Until now, I suppose."

Laena raised her hand to her mouth, coughing, and he'd bet the last of this deceptively fine whiskey that she was covering a laugh.

"Quip all you like, Farrow." Demons, but the man's voice was smug. How could Hawk not see it? "You know what the king will have to say when we reach Vunmore. You'll be lucky if he doesn't throw you in a cell."

Hawk was his friend, close enough to be a brother to him—or he had been, once—but he was King of Aglye first and foremost.

Landon Moore was a fool and an ass, but he might very well be correct.

"We're not going directly to Vunmore," Laena said. "I have reason to stop at Inasvale first."

To Callum's surprise, Moore inclined his head in agreement. "Some of the soldiers you abandoned after the shipwreck—excuse me, my lady, that was meant for ex-captain Farrow over there—require medical attention." He stood, offering her another bow. "For now, I must suggest you take your rest. We ride at dawn."

CHAPTER 21

*G*eneral Moore talked a great deal. Which wouldn't have been a problem in itself—Fizz also talked a great deal, and Laena didn't find herself wanting to slam him over the head with a cook pot—except that every word out of Moore's mouth was a boast. He and his soldiers had reached the coast in a day and a night, the fastest ever attempted with such a host of men. King Hawk had sent him specifically to retrieve the wayward former captain. The way the man talked, she'd hardly be surprised to hear him say he'd personally installed a hook in the sky to hang the sun.

And he insisted on walking beside her, too. There weren't enough horses for everyone to ride, and the exhausted soldiers had taken up the saddles. Laena was grateful for the walk, not least because she had no idea what would happen when they reached Inasvale. Moore had sent messengers out to assure both Hawk and Katrina of the party's discovery. What their instructions would be after this point, Laena could not guess.

Through the day, they traveled, and Landon Moore talked incessantly. And before she slid into sleep that night, she allowed herself to wish she could return to sharing a pallet with

Callum. Ridiculous though it was, she thought ... from the way he kept catching her gaze from across the fire, from across the camp, she was sure he wanted the same thing.

Not that Moore's incessant chattering gave them so much as a moment to talk together, or revisit the topic of magic, or stolen armies, or—it should not have numbered among her concerns, but it did—that almost-kiss.

By the time they reached Inasvale, Laena's nerves felt as if they'd been rubbed raw against a washing board. It took a concerted effort not to cringe each time Moore opened that foolish mouth of his.

The forest ended with an abrupt shift, a single step carrying her from dense vegetation to rolling fields. The sea, ever their companion, sparkled to the right beneath a clear sky. And ahead, the city sat perched upon the side of a cliff, its multi-tiered walls giving it the look of a rather drab wedding cake. A golden flag fluttered from the highest layer: the monastery of the poisonkeepers.

The monks came from throughout the Vales, called to their vocation from across Etra and Aglye, and even parts of Silerith. Or so the textbooks had taught her. The books never mentioned the murmur of waves in the background, or the salty spray as they split upon the rocky cliffs. Nor had they described the perfume of wild roses that grew along those same cliffs, or the singular joy of breathing their scent combined with the brine of the sea.

When she looked to Callum he actually seemed... relaxed. He would have seen this place before, of course. "How long has it been?" she asked, as Moore busied himself instructing his soldiers. "Since you last saw Thaddeus?"

"One year and two months," he said. "I escorted him here myself, against King Magnus's wishes."

That surprised her, the idea of King Magnus's famously trusted captain escorting the younger prince to join the monks.

What had Callum's relationship with Magnus been like? It was said that he was treated like another son. "Was the king angry?" she asked.

A shadow fell across Callum's face, and she wished she could snatch back the words. One year and two months. Was that not the precise time when King Magnus had been killed? *Careless, Laena*, she scolded herself. She'd not been living in the palace when he'd died, but even she could not avoid hearing such news.

"I'm sorry," she said. "I should have realized. The timing..."

Callum gave his head a shake, as if extracting himself from a memory. "Don't trouble yourself. It is my fault that I wasn't there."

Laena frowned. "I don't think you ought to blame yourself for—"

"Pick up the pace!" Moore called from the front of the group. "No need to dawdle now."

Except for the rockiness of the path, Laena thought. But as Callum took the excuse to hurry ahead and check on his soldiers, she found she wanted to hurry herself, to make for the city gates and meet the younger prince whose desire to live as a poisonkeeper had so angered his father... and prompted Callum's defiance.

Was this the reason, too, for his demotion? His removal from the captaincy? Truly, he could not be blamed for his absence. He likely would have been killed along with the host of guards rumored to have been massacred along with the king by a heart-tither. One who'd never yet been caught, unless she'd failed to hear the news.

If Callum had been relentless about pursuing heart-tithers before the king's death, what had he done since?

The road shifted to cobblestones just before the gates to the city. No guards were stationed at the wall, though she supposed they could see threats approaching from the watchtower in the city's center.

Inasvale's streets were quiet, at least compared to the bustling city of Riles. Where the Etran city was all bustle and cheer, Inasvale was calm, as though every shopkeeper, fisherman, and street sweeper aimed to live with the same serenity as did the monks who oversaw the city.

Children, she noted, were still children. They chased one another down side streets, giggling wildly, if a bit more furtively than they might have done in Riles.

The city's hilltop position, paired with its twist of a fortress, made it appear large and imposing from the outside. Within the walls, the streets closed in tightly, each overlooked by the guardian walls to either side. The streets were surprisingly bright, the indigo sky shining down on neatly arranged cobblestones.

And once they were within the walls, it was barely a few minutes' walk before they found themselves at the peak of the hill, standing before the gates of the Inasvale Monastery. Wrought in a lacework of twisted iron, these inner gates appeared both beautiful and unbreachable. Bereft of decoration, the gates stood without shining paint or gargoyles or carvings, yet they gave off a distinct feeling of elegance.

Someone, she noticed, had planted a bed of marigolds at the foot of each surrounding wall.

There ought to be some kind of protocol for approaching the monastery, likely one that involved Landon Moore puffing out his chest and demanding to be seen on order of the king. Which, to be fair, he already seemed primed to do; he was striding toward the gate, and in a moment, he would certainly open his mouth and start talking. She found herself wishing a bug would catch in his throat as soon as he did.

Before Moore could demand entrance, or whatever he planned to do, a man in long black robes approached from inside, withdrew an impressively large iron ring from within his abundant sleeves, and unlocked the gates.

"You are welcome here," he said. "Please, come in."

General Moore nodded, as if entrance to the poisonkeepers' monastery were his due, and strode past the man without a comment for the wounded soldiers who were supposedly his entire reason for stopping here.

It was Callum who paused, giving the keeper an appraising look. "Still at it, I see."

The man pushed a rickety set of spectacles up his nose and met Callum's gaze, fingers twitching around the key ring, and Laena had the distinct impression he was stopping himself from running a hand through his dusty brown hair. "Someone needs to keep the poison at bay."

The two men stared at one another for a good long moment. And even though the monk gave the impression that he was half ready to dart away, he held his ground until—to Laena's incredible surprise—Callum broke into a wide grin and embraced him, jangling the keys as he did. "Thaddeus," he said. "Did you see us coming?"

"Hours ago," Thaddeus choked out, clapping Callum awkwardly on the back. "We keep watch from the outer bulwarks."

Callum released the younger man, and Thaddeus stepped aside, allowing the party to pass into a neat entry courtyard. Which, like the rest of the fortress, was surrounded by neat stone walls. These walls protected a simple wooden structure, short and squat, with pillars to hold up the far-reaching corners of a slanted roof. Pink-flowered trees bloomed in the corner, their fallen petals leaving splashes of color along the cobblestone paths that meandered back and around the main building, suggesting that it was one of several.

"We have soldiers in need of medicine, but it is not the sole reason we've stopped here," Callum said as they entered. He, at least, was not gawking like a youth.

It was too easy to forget that Laena ought to have seen this place years ago, during the traditional tour that would have marked her ascension to the throne. In Etra, the queen was no distant student of the world; she was an active participant in it, expected to grow up in the streets of her own city and visit the continent before her coronation.

She'd know the significance of the trees—were they native, or had they been transplanted?—and the owl carving on the main building's windowsill. She'd know what the main building was called, and the name of their most treasured feast days, and how to address their leader without stumbling.

She'd spent so much time studying kings and queens and the intricacies of their families and customs, yet so little on the other cultures in the Vales. Even the poisonkeepers, and they were as important as any family in the realm. More so, perhaps. Why had her upbringing not included more details about them? Why could she not name their ranks, their titles, their prayers and customs? Now that she was here, it seemed a massive oversight.

While she mused, Thaddeus studied Callum as if trying to read the true purpose for their visit in his expression. At length, he nodded. "The master has ordered the physicians to the guest cabins. You may bring your wounded there."

Callum hitched his chin toward Edmun and Godfrey, who began helping the injured soldiers along the cobblestone path. They certainly seemed to know their way around. Had they assisted Callum in escorting Thaddeus here? Had they come to check on him since them, at Callum's request—or King Hawk's?

As for General Moore, the man was reaching into the boughs of a flowering tree beside the wall, his motives unclear. Though not, Laena noted with disapproval, focused on the health of his injured soldiers.

"It is good to see you, Callum," Thaddeus said, and Laena thought he meant it, though he spoke in a low tone, casting a significant look toward General Moore as he did. "You must know that the king has been in touch. I'm sure he will be relieved to learn that you live."

Callum raised an eyebrow. "There's a 'but' in that sentence, isn't there?"

Thaddeus inclined his head, fingers twitching like he'd very much have liked to grab a fistful of his hair and pull. "He knows you led the delegation without authorization and will expect you to involve your entire party in any discussion we might have."

The poisonkeeper said this last bit with just the barest lift of his eyebrow, and Laena got the impression Thaddeus very much wanted to know the story.

"Then perhaps," Laena stepped in, "you might be allowed a private reunion. Callum is as a brother to you, is he not?"

Thaddeus blinked, looking at her in surprise, as if he hadn't realized she was there. As his gaze landed on her, Brin scurried deeper into the folds of her pockets, like she thought he might pierce through the cloth with his eyes—and perhaps singe her to a crisp. Laena had trouble imagining this kindly looking man causing hurt to any creature, but she'd learned to trust Brin's instincts.

"Very well," Thaddeus said slowly. "But if the master calls for me, I must answer."

Callum pressed his lips together, and she thought he might object, but he only nodded. "Of course."

What did Callum think of the younger prince's choices, then? He said he'd escorted Thaddeus here, but he hadn't told her whether he'd done that in support. Perhaps he'd been attempting to bring Thaddeus home. Had Callum objected to the younger man's decision to join the poisonkeepers and live an isolated life here in Inasvale? Rumor said Thaddeus had not even left the monastery to attend his father's funeral.

Whatever Callum's feelings on the matter, they were not evident. He'd scrubbed all telling expressions from his face, as if he'd come to visit a stranger rather than a man who he'd been raised alongside like a younger brother.

Thaddeus led them directly into the main building and down a wide entry hall bordered by wooden benches. A waiting area, she supposed, for the pair of tightly shut doors straight ahead. Light streamed in from the lofted windows, and the place smelled like freshly cut cedar. Pleasant and bright.

A pair of boys were sweeping the floor as the party entered, and they bowed deeply to Thaddeus before continuing their work. Thaddeus nodded to them, smiling faintly, then gestured for Laena and Callum to follow him up a tight staircase to the left.

From the outside, she would not have thought this building had a second floor at all. But the staircase spilled them into yet another hall, this one narrower, the walls stained with oil from the burning of lamps.

"The master keeps his study below," Thaddeus explained. "Full poisonkeepers work in our study chambers. The students share a space at the end of the hall."

"And you're advanced enough to merit a study chamber of your own?" Callum asked. "You've not yet been here two years."

Thaddeus merely opened one of the doors and ushered them inside. "After you."

The room was small and spare, furnished with a round table, a shelf piled high with books, and a curtained area that contained a bed and dresser. More piles of books graced each corner, and there were several open on the foot of the bed. What was Thaddeus studying so feverishly? Or was this merely the life of any new poisonkeeper, to spend his days learning?

"I may owe a few returns to the library." Thaddeus was gripping his hair openly now, and Laena half expected him to rush around and tidy the space. "If you need to speak with me privately, we'd best not tarry. The master will call for me soon, I'm sure."

Laena saw no reason to delay. Careful not to dislodge Brin from her hiding spot, she withdrew the crystal from her pocket, set it on the table, and flicked the covering away to reveal the hateful thing. Thaddeus adjusted his spectacles and leaned closer as Laena told her tale, though he had the sense not to touch it.

Callum picked up the story from the assassination attempt, then told of the unnatural storm, the lightning, and the shipwreck. Followed by the kidnappers. Their different goal—to capture rather than to kill—had not escaped him, either.

When Callum had finished, Thaddeus sat in silence, tapping his fingertips against his knee and scrunching his nose every few seconds, as though he simply couldn't get his spectacles to sit right.

"I believe there's a simple explanation for all of this," he said finally, his chin so low it was practically propped upon the table.

Callum crossed his arms. "Don't tell me you think we're mad."

Thaddeus straightened, giving his head a vigorous shake. "Unfortunately, no." He drew in a deep breath. "I believe the barrier between the Vales and the Miragelands is thinning. And I think very likely it will soon break."

CHAPTER 22

*T*hroughout his childhood, Thaddeus had been a serious child. Fidgety, nervous, soft-spoken, and never prone to exaggeration. Which was why, when he'd come to Callum with his plan to join the poisonkeepers at Inasvale, Callum had escorted him there personally.

Rarely did Thaddeus say anything in jest. And when he did, it was more likely to be a play on words that nobody got—including Callum.

"Thinning," Laena repeated. "Thinning how exactly?"

The fear in her voice was evident, and no wonder. The mages had ruled the Vales for hundreds of years, leaving generations of wreckage in their wake. After ruining their own world —the Miragelands, it was called—they'd stormed the Vales like avenging demons, enthralling humans to do their will.

A group of rebels had finally risen to oppose them, and they'd been locked back behind the barrier ever since. How the rebels had managed it was a mystery. Nobody knew how it had been done, except for the few who'd been there. Callum had often suspected the secret might unveil a way to free the mages once more.

Only a fool would want to. But then, there were fools aplenty in the Vales. Heart-tithed magic was a remnant of the mages, a way to access their power. Had Callum not objected to the premise of the magic—that the pain of a loved one bought it—he still would have objected to the idea of accessing anything the mages would offer.

Anything they offered would be a trick. He'd no doubt of it.

"I can take you to the pool," Thaddeus said. "Perhaps—"

The door burst open, interrupting Thaddeus' suggestion as a tall, rail-thin man flowed into the room, black robes swirling around his body like a mist. Thaddeus dropped to his knees, crossing his hands over his chest, and bowed his head.

Callum had met the poisonkeepers' master once before. He hadn't been impressed then—he had, in fact, been near convinced the man had recruited Thaddeus through manipulations and lies—nor was he impressed now. The man's head was completely bald, his beard black as ink and cropped close around his chin. And though he was certainly not the only man to wear a beard alongside a bald head, the arrangement gave the master a distinct air of being upside down.

Landon Moore strode into the room on the master's heels, looking as smug as a man possibly could. Like he'd just slain a dragon and devoured its tender heart. Callum would have wagered he'd been paying attention to their conversation in the courtyard, and that he'd been the one to summon the master for the sake of shortening their meeting. Possibly with the simple aim of annoying Callum until he snapped.

Moore stopped in the doorway, crossing his arms and leaning against it as though looking forward to the show.

"Brother Thaddeus." The master's voice was deep and resonant. "What is the meaning of this secret conversation?"

"It is no secret, Poison Master," Thaddeus said. "They were merely telling me of their journey."

The truth, yet not the truth. Thaddeus was as a brother to

him, but Callum had no illusions that he would keep their secrets. He belonged to the poisonkeepers first and foremost—his loyalties were theirs.

Though he hadn't spilled the entire story yet, either. Interesting.

The master scanned the room, his gaze catching first on the crystal laid out on the table, then flickering past Callum as though he were invisible. When he reached Laena, however, his eyes narrowed. "Traitors," he said, "are not welcome in our halls. *Princess* Laena will need to find somewhere else to stay."

Thaddeus's mouth tightened, but he said nothing. He, at least, had known Laena's identity from the first.

Landon Moore certainly had not. He straightened, his jaw falling open in a way that would have been most satisfying had he not then taken a step into the room. "I thought you were a random courtier. A member of the council." He laughed, delight and disbelief playing across his face in turns. "Did the queen of Etra truly send a whore to treat with King Hawk?"

The implication being that she, too, had stolen the delegation.

Laena's face turned white, and Thaddeus's head snapped up, as if he could not have imagined this reaction. Thaddeus had always been the kindest of them. He would not have expected this reaction.

"Maybe she'll take up with me," Moore said, taking another step into the room. "Or am I not common enough for your tastes? Do I not smell enough like horsesh—"

Callum stepped in front of Moore, blocking his path to Laena. And his view of her, too. "Princess Laena is the Etran queen's emissary, and a member of the royal family," he said. "You'll speak to her with respect."

The corner of Moore's mouth turned up in a definite sneer, the kind Callum had always thought belonged to puppet-show villains. "King Hawk will not agree to treat with her. He'll send her to a brothel, where she belongs."

Rage exploded on the edges of his vision, and suddenly Callum's hands were around Moore's neck. He shoved the man back against the wall as the general clawed at his fingers, struggling to draw breath. But Callum was bigger than Moore, and stronger—and much more dedicated to training, or so he once had been—and it was a simple matter to hold the man in place. Black anger throbbed at his skull, tunneling his vision into this one man, this one villain.

Thaddeus reached him first, dragging him away from Moore with a good deal more strength than Callum would have expected from him.

"Apologize to her," Callum spat as Moore gasped for breath, doubling over and clutching at his throat. There would be bruises tomorrow, and Callum could not be sorry for it.

"She's gone," Thaddeus said softly.

"Fled, like the traitor she is," the master said.

Thaddeus held Callum for another beat, and then, apparently satisfied that his brother no longer intended to murder General Moore, he let go and turned toward the master. "We have a tradition of housing every lost soul in the Vales who appeals to our door," he said. "No matter who they are. Is it not so?"

The master flushed, eyes flashing, but Thaddeus held his ground, merely meeting the man's gaze with calm patience. Maybe he wasn't as naive as Callum assumed.

"It is so," the master said grudgingly. "The Book requires it."

Moore gestured to Callum, his face red. "But he *attacked* me."

Whiny, for a general. What in all the worlds had Hawk been *thinking?*

The master, who had regained his composure, drew up taller. "And that is a matter for your king to address. And to punish, as I'm sure he will. Our healers will see to your injuries."

He glared at Callum. "And you will be gone in the morning, or I'll know the why of it."

And with an imperious flap of his robes, he swept out of the room.

———✳︎———

BY THE TIME Callum made it out to the courtyard, Laena was gone. He shaded his eyes against the bands of red sunset, which were setting the pink-petaled trees alight with blazing glory. He walked behind the main building, in the direction his soldiers— Moore's soldiers—had headed earlier, where he found Godfrey and Edmun leaning together against the trunk of a well-placed tree.

Edmun looked up at him with a frown. "Captain?"

Callum grimaced. "I believe you know it by now, if you did not know it before, but that title is no longer in use." Edmun lifted an eyebrow, and Callum sighed. "And I apologize for the deception."

"Young brute." Edmun shook his head, though the news could have been no surprise to him.

It was the hurt on Godfrey's face that made Callum want to cringe. The young man was frowning, as if he could not believe Callum would have lied. But he had. Completely and thoroughly. He'd lied, he'd led them into danger, and he'd failed them. Multiple times.

At the moment, all he cared about was finding Laena.

"I can't deny it." Callum glanced around the yard again, barely seeing the neat row of guest cabins lined up there. "Have you seen Princess Laena?"

Edmun shook his head, but Godfrey cleared his throat. "She went running out the main gates," he said. "Into the city."

Godfrey might be angry with Callum, but he adored Laena.

199

They all did. Callum nodded his thanks, and Godfrey looked away, swallowing hard.

He'd make it up to the young soldier later, if he could. He'd make it up to all of them. For now, he had to find Laena.

He didn't know where a disgraced princess would choose to go when distressed. But he knew well enough where a disgraced captain would go, and he'd spent enough time with Laena by now to learn that it might very well be the same place.

Inasvale held a surprising number of taverns for a city run by holy men. Not that holiness necessarily translated to sobriety —the poisonkeepers were known to age their own wine, after all—but the size of the population hardly seemed fit to support the number of drinking houses he now walked past.

He fully expected to find Laena in the first pub, where cheerful flute music emanated out into the streets, or perhaps the second, where a splash of stained glass decorated the front door. Almost ostentatious by Inasvale standards, that amount of decoration.

By the time he reached the eighth tavern, he was beginning to think he'd miscalculated. Perhaps disgraced princesses visited seamstresses or bookshops or a blacksmith's forge. Though at this hour, those options were limited at best. The sunset had given way to a milky dusk, and stars were beginning to shine boldly through the heavens. Lantern-bearing travelers made their way through the streets, their straight-backed daytime postures relaxed into smiles and even laughter.

Callum found Laena in the ninth tavern, which bore a painted sign dubbing it the Playful Otter. Did everything in Inasvale have to be so damned... well, cute? For a place that protected the known world from the threat of evil banished mages, it was too charming for its own good. Could do with a few more mercenaries or a hardhearted pirate or two.

Perhaps the master provided enough unpleasantness for an entire city.

Laena sat at the end of the bar, with such an impressive distance between her and the next customer that he had to assume she'd violently rebuffed any attempts at conversation. He only hoped she'd done so without her ice magic. If the master heard of it, she'd be clapped in irons before the sun rose.

One elbow on the bar, a half-empty bottle of wine, and a glass at her side, she'd certainly wasted no time. Her complexion was no longer ghostly pale—in fact, she appeared rather flushed—and she'd found a ribbon somewhere to secure her hair at the nape of her neck.

"Mages," she said when he eased onto the stool beside her. "I thought I'd be unfindable here. Un-find-able? Is that a word?"

"Is it not a word simply because you said it and I understood it?" he asked.

"That's preposterous. You'll understand what I mean if I say I'm plimping down to the store, but that doesn't make it a word."

"You're making assumptions," he said. "If you say you're plimping down to the store, I have no idea if you're skipping or walking or riding, or if the word simply means you're going without specifying the manner in which you plan to achieve it."

She snorted. "I don't think I've ever heard you say so many words."

"What are you doing here, Laena?"

She reached for the bottle, adding another generous pour to her glass. "I should think that was obvious. I thought I'd give your problem-solving method a whirl, Captain Farrow."

"Not a captain. How's it working?"

She raised her glass, lips twisted in a poor imitation of a smile. "Delightfully well." She tipped her head back and drained half the glass.

"Come morning, you may have a different opinion," he said.

She set down the glass and leaned toward him, placing a

hand on his shoulder. "P'rhaps not. But I like it now." Her hand slipped, and he caught her before she could topple off her stool.

She laughed, but there was no mirth in it. And when he settled her back on the stool, she held onto his arm. "He called me a whore."

A fresh surge of rage spiked through his chest. "I heard, my lady."

"Not a lady. I'm a whore. Remember?" She released his arm and leaned back on the bar, swirling her wine hard enough to slosh several drops out onto the counter. "I know people think it. The traitor. The whore. But they don't often say it out loud."

"They shouldn't think it, and they shouldn't say it."

"Kat wanted me to do it." Laena leaned her chin on her wrist, eyes locked on the swishing liquid. "She wanted me to fuck him and leave so she could be queen, and now she acts like I'm less than a worm in the garden. Worms have value. Good for the soil."

The way Callum heard it told, it'd been a surprise to the entire country. Laena and Katrina's parents had died of fever, years back, but there were always talking heads to deal with, or so he'd learned from spending years in the palace. The regent and the council, and all the lords and ladies that'd been prancing through those pretty gardens.

He didn't think anyone had known enough about the fool stablehand to want Laena to do anything. Supposedly, she'd merely appeared one morning in her riding skirts, her beau at her side, and announced her abdication. Simple as that.

But he'd seen how Katrina treated her. More importantly, he'd seen how she used her magic. There were layers to this that no one else understood, layers that Laena had kept from everyone.

Now she leaned closer, her lips brushing his ear. "Can I tell you a secret?"

His heart hammered in his chest, begging for her to go on.

Begging for her to stop. He wasn't sure he wanted to hear more about the fool stablehand who'd left her. Or what Katrina had caught them doing together. "Can I stop you?"

"I didn't leave for him."

There was more to the story, but he didn't want Laena telling him when she was too drunk to be sure she wanted to. He stood, taking her gently by the arm. "Come, Princess. Let's get you to bed."

The yard with the guest cabins was quiet by the time they made their way to it, with only the gentle whisper of the salty wind through the trees. The stars watched from above, diamonds in a moonless night, as he helped Laena toward the door that'd been marked with a slip of paper bearing her name. Written, Callum noted, in Thaddeus's hand.

When they reached the steps, however, Laena stopped him with a hand on his arm. "Thank you for finding me."

He swallowed, all too aware of her nearness. "I thought you wanted to be unfindable."

She ran her hand up his arm and across his shoulders until her fingers met the skin of his neck. It was all he could do not to shut his eyes and lean into her touch. "Princess—"

She rose on her toes and pressed her mouth to his, and mages but she tasted good, the tartness of the wine she'd been drinking mixed with hints of sweet honey, of fresh apples from a tree. That cinnamon spice, always that, threaded with the apple's sharpness. But she was anything but cold; she was warm, as soft as a rose petal, and for a moment he was so surprised that he returned the kiss, his mouth moving on hers before he could quite stop himself.

She made a sound like a whimper, pulling him in closer, but he forced himself to break the kiss. Even so, she lingered close, her breath tickling his upper lip and nearly stealing his will away entirely.

"You do not have your wits about you, my lady," he whispered, his voice a husk in the dark.

"I had my wits about me the other night, when we nearly kissed."

He reached behind his neck and took her fingers gently in his, sliding them away from his skin. "And yet we did *not* kiss. Even if we had, wits then do not translate to wits now. Let me get you to bed."

"Come with me," she said. "You want to bed me, do you not?"

Oh, he wanted to. He could practically feel that silken hair tumbling around him, her naked hips settling against his. His cock stiffened just thinking of her like that, draped above him, giving herself to him fully.

But he should not have even let her kiss him in this state. Indeed, had she not surprised him, he'd have broken it off sooner.

Gently, he put another inch between them, reluctantly letting a breath of cool air between their bodies. Which he very much needed right now, though admittedly it was doing little to quell his very obviously growing need. Demons, she was beautiful, gazing up at him in the starlight.

She swayed on her feet, and he shook himself, forcing his brain to take the lead so he could help her up the first step and open the door.

The room was outfitted much like Thaddeus's, though with fewer books strewn about. A narrow bed in the corner, a bureau, a table, a shelf. That was it. Callum assisted Laena into the bed. But as he stepped away, she locked her fingers around his.

"Stay," she said. "I won't try to kiss you, I promise. Just... just stay with me. Please."

He nodded, his throat tight. As if he could deny her anything she wished. She sighed with relief, and he would have lost his mind entirely had it not sounded like a sob. Callum lay on the bed, the mattress creaking under his weight, and held her in her arms as she wept.

CHAPTER 23

*T*he sun had absolutely no business being as bright as it was. It beamed harsh rays across Laena's face, and when she cracked an eye open, she could see there were no curtains to pull, no shutters to clap shut. The morning of a monk, up with the dawn.

She felt as if a monstrous serpent had seized her head between its coils, squeezing mercilessly. Demons, but it hurt. Her throat was dry, and the aftertaste of wine lingered on her tongue.

She rubbed her eyes, half hoping Callum had slipped out in the night. She'd been drunk—very drunk, obscenely drunk—but she remembered every last wanton detail of their encounter. Had she truly asked him to *bed* her?

The shame of the memory brought heat to her cheeks. It was almost worse that she'd asked him to stay and comfort her. She would not blame him if he'd left. The door cracked open and Callum appeared, juggling a carafe of water and a fistful of herbs in one hand, a packet of sausages in the other. At least she thought that's what they were, judging by the smell—and judging by the fact that Brin had come racing out of her hiding place at the foot of the bed and skittered up to the tabletop, where she ran in eager circles like a miniature dog awaiting a treat.

Callum nodded, giving her a hint of that half-smile he liked so much. It didn't quite touch his eyes, though. Maybe he was afraid she might throw herself across the room and attempt to drag him into bed with her. Again.

She'd spent the night in his arms. She'd *kissed* the man, for demons' sake.

Of course, he *had* kissed her back. For a moment, before his honor had stepped between them. So perhaps she needn't be quite so mortified. Maybe.

"I brought sausages from the town," he said. "Turns out the monks are vegetarians, and you need grease in your stomach if you're to ride today without falling ill."

She ran a self-conscious hand through her hair, then made herself get up and go to the table, inspecting his gifts. The water was self-explanatory—she could have guzzled the entire jug, had she not been afraid her stomach would revolt and throw it back up—and she took a moment to study the herbs.

"Byflower leaves," he said. "Should ease the pain in your head."

She raised her eyebrows. "I didn't know that."

"Thaddeus's suggestion." He raised a hand, as though anticipating her objection. "I told him they were for me."

Brin hopped onto Laena's fingers, running a loop around her wrist, then leaping back onto the table. "All right, greedy thing," she said, laughing as she opened the packet. Her stomach turned at the smell of it, delicious though it was, and she broke off a piece for Brin. "I hope you didn't have to endure a lecture."

Callum grunted, taking the seat across from her. The wooden chair looked reluctant to hold his weight. "Thaddeus knows I'm a hopeless case."

A hopeless case who'd risen before the sun to procure breakfast and herbs to ease her pain. Her head was murky with the aftereffects of the wine, and her stomach was most displeased with her, yet she couldn't help wishing she could kiss him again. The feel of his lips against hers, strong and sure—and all too brief—warmed a pool of desire beneath her belly. One she'd thought, quite honestly, she might never feel again.

Her wits might be foggy, but they knew what they wanted.

"Drink some water," Callum said. "It'll do you good."

Laena shook herself and obeyed, taking slow sips. "I want to apologize," she said, setting the jug down. "For propositioning you last night."

What a sentence. She very much wished to crawl beneath the table and disappear forever. Embarrassment and lust were a strange combination, but here she was.

"Nothing to be sorry for," he said. "You were upset."

"And drunk."

"And that."

When she met his gaze, there was no judgment in it. Just those ice-blue eyes, a touch of a crinkle at the brow that she thought might be concern. Or—he *had* returned her kiss last night, for the barest moment—was it desire?

Having finished her breakfast, Brin leapt onto the back of Laena's hand and skittered up her arm, startling her out of a most inappropriate thought of what they might do with the time they had before taking to the road.

Callum cleared his throat. "The poisonkeepers sent a change of garments," he said. "Gretchen insisted on trousers, and I was able to procure some for you as well."

Clean clothing, herbs, and breakfast. The man was nothing less than a hero. "The bandits are traveling with us?" she asked.

"The poisonkeepers have agreed to house them in Inasvale for a few weeks. Perhaps they're hoping to perform."

So the master had no trouble offering accommodations to thieves, then. It was only disgraced princesses he objected to.

Laena had difficulty imagining the man enjoying any kind of performance from Maynard and his crew. Perhaps a very pious one. Or an angry one.

Callum rose. "We ought to be going."

Before Landon Moore had figured out her identity, before the master had tried to—before the humiliation and the wine and the kiss, gods that *kiss*—Thaddeus had revealed his suspicions about the barrier, the Vales, and the Miragelands. He suspected it might be thinning.

Which meant he must suspect that the mages intended to return.

And she'd spent her evening drowning her sorrows over personal trials. She was as selfish as Kat always said she was, self-absorbed in a way a queen should never be. Could never be.

She'd been tired, a voice in the back of her head reminded her. Tired and sad, and so very sorry for everything. She might be able to work magic, but she was still only human. And so was Katrina.

"What of the thinning barrier?" Laena asked. "What of the crystal?"

Callum ran a hand through his hair, reminding her of Thaddeus for a moment. "Thaddeus has agreed to keep it here and study it." He raised a hand, as if anticipating her objection. "And we will discuss it with King Hawk, as you planned."

In truth, Laena had no objection to the plan. The crystal had been growing ever heavier, a burden she wanted to be rid of. It seemed to burn in opposition to her magic, and so she would not protest its absence.

Her instinct said Thaddeus could be trusted. She hoped she was right. Thinking of Ben, she supposed she had room for improvement when it came to character judgment, but there wasn't much to be done in any case. She doubted the master would let her steal the crystal back, even if she demanded it.

Laena gathered Brin into her pocket and took one last bite

of sausage. Her stomach protested, but Callum was right; it would help.

Unfortunately, they opened the door to find a courtyard full of soldiers preparing to take to the road. An audience. Including General Moore.

"Her taste turns to disgraced captains." Moore's laugh was ugly, his mouth stretched wide as he looked around, clearly hoping to share smiles and snickers with his men.

The other soldiers, however, did not join him in his mirth. Not a single one of them, even those Moore had brought with him directly from Vunmore. In fact, they were looking to Callum with such identical frowns that the expression might have been part of the King's Guard uniform.

Callum walked over to Moore. "I will remind you a final time that Princess Laena is a designated emissary to Aglye, and will be afforded the respect she deserves. Or King Hawk will know why."

Moore's lip twisted. He stepped away from Callum, gave Laena a shallow bow, and mounted his horse, taking off into the city without another word.

"Well," Laena said, "this is going to be a fun journey."

"Don't worry. If he bothers you, Edmun and the men will set him straight."

"Oh? And what about you?"

Callum grinned. "I'll set him crooked, my lady."

"I'm not sure I want to know what that means."

Inasvale didn't have enough fresh mounts for the entire company, but Laena didn't mind walking. There were still injured and exhausted soldiers, and she couldn't shake the restless urge to move, to walk. To do something with herself, even if it was just a matter of moving arms and legs. Thaddeus's herbs had eased the headache, with a gentle aftertaste of mint and basil that she was certain continued to soothe her stomach. Byflower leaves. She would have to research that later.

She kept thinking about 'later' as if it would involve her returning to her cabin, her garden, her life on the outskirts of the village. But the more this journey progressed, the more she thought that was unlikely to be the case.

Laena would not have been surprised if Thaddeus was kept too busy with his duties to see them off. Nor would she have been surprised to learn that the master had intentionally assigned extra tasks to prevent it. To her surprise, though, Thaddeus caught up with them as they neared the city's outer gates.

He was breathing hard, his dark hair springing in every direction, and he gripped his robes in his fists.

"What's the matter?" Callum asked. "Are you coming with us?"

Thaddeus gave him an odd look. "No, I'm here to warn you."

Callum's gaze sharpened, and Laena could practically feel his fingers itching to reach for his dagger. "About?"

"Hawk." Thaddeus's chest still heaved with the effort of his run. "Hawk is here."

— * —

THE LAST LIKENESS Laena had seen of King Hawk had been a freshly painted portrait of him at seventeen. Her age at the time, in fact. She could remember the way Katrina had run fingertips along the side of the picture upon its addition to the collection, remarking on the strength of his jaw, the straightness of his nose, the laughter in his gaze. "He looks like he would play a good prank on Declan," she had said at the time. And Laena had agreed.

Now, as both parties returned to the monastery courtyard to greet one another, Laena was not sure she would have recognized King Hawk of Aglye. He was handsome, certainly, with that sun-blond hair falling across his forehead just so. But shadows darkened the skin beneath his eyes, and he looked pale enough to have spent the summer in a cave rather than a palace.

There was no laughter in his gaze now.

He dismounted smoothly, and to his credit, he approached her first. While the rest of the assembly bowed to him, he came straight to her. "The princess of a foreign nation needn't curtsy to me," he said. "Well met, Princess Laena. Though I wish it were under better circumstances."

His voice was low, with a rasp that hinted at bone-deep fatigue. She could feel Callum stiffen at her side as Hawk took her hand in greeting.

And she nearly gasped at the contact as her magic stirred in her gut, as if drawn toward the young king. She held it back, trying to coil it, but she could feel its response.

It felt like how the magic had leapt to investigate the crystal in her garden.

It seemed impossible that he would not feel it, too. She glanced at Callum, and though the captain's gaze was locked on where her hand met the king's, he didn't look alarmed. He didn't see anything amiss.

She shook away the sensation as Hawk dropped his hand. He didn't bring the aura of a heart-tithe with him, or that overwhelming smell of rot and ruin that had overtaken her garden. He didn't look at her strangely, or demand that she be dragged away to the dungeons. If Inasvale had such a place.

And yet, she couldn't quite convince herself that she'd imagined the sensation.

"I trust you are well, after the trials of the journey?" Hawk asked. She thought she discerned true concern in his gaze, though certainly the king would be well practiced at arranging his face into appropriate expressions just as she was.

"Well enough," Laena said. "Thank you."

He inclined his head. "I'm glad to hear it. We will meet formally in Vunmore, as planned." He glanced at Callum, and his eyes darkened. "You've had a trying journey, to put it mildly. You should take your rest. It is but a few days' trip to the capital. We will talk there."

The resonance of magic aside, she found herself returning his smile, though the one that curved his lips could barely be classified as such. And though she typically withheld her judgment on the character of foreign dignitaries and monarchs, she found herself inclined to like him.

And she found herself wanting to insist that the king meet with her now, that he examine the crystal she'd left in Thaddeus's possession and hear what she had to say about the threat to Etra. To all their lands. Surely he would have some idea of how to deal with the assassins, the kidnappers, the strange storms. The rotting gardens.

But no monarch would respond well to being pushed in front of such an audience. So Laena repressed her impatience. "There is much to discuss."

He gave her a short bow. "If you'll excuse me, I need a word with Callum Farrow."

Judging by the roughness of his tone, and the way Callum shifted his weight, his energy alive with tension, it would not be a gentle word.

Before she could stop herself, Laena stepped forward and lay a hand on King Hawk's arm. "Your Majesty?"

He turned back to her, tilting his head in surprise. "Yes?"

Laena lowered her voice. "Just remember that he has had a trying journey, too. I owe him my life many times over."

Hawk blinked, then gave a curt nod. With that, he turned on his heel, gesturing for Callum to follow.

CHAPTER 24

*C*allum hadn't been fooled by Hawk's restraint in the courtyard. The king was nothing if not patient, and as Thaddeus showed them through the halls of the monastery, Callum could feel the anger in the snap of the king's boots against the stone floor, see it in the way he balled his fists at his sides. As if he wanted nothing more than to wheel around and punch Callum in the jaw.

Hawk waited until Thaddeus had ushered them into the master's own sitting room and his guards had searched the place and declared it safe. He waited until they had disappeared back into the hall, taking up their stations outside the door, until Thaddeus had seated himself on a trunk in the corner of the room—not too close, but not too far either, as though he expected this conversation to require intervention at some point.

And then, just for good measure, he waited more. He just stood there, arms folded across his chest, the point of his crown glinting among his light hair.

There was no point in saying anything. Hawk would speak when he was ready to speak.

In the meantime, Callum decided to pour himself a drink. Surely the master kept decent wine in here. He made it himself, didn't he? Callum did his best to saunter, to take his time, pretending he couldn't feel Hawk's eyes boring into his back as he swirled the wine in its decanter, then splashed a good amount into a cup.

He supposed it was decent wine. A more discerning taste would take the time to pick apart the threads of cherry and oak, the sweetness, the tart aftertaste.

Callum swallowed it down too quickly for any of that. Then he poured a second cup, turning in time to catch Thaddeus rolling his eyes in exasperation.

"What the blazes were you thinking?"

Hawk had the quiet voice going, the one that could frighten his advisors into pretending they agreed with his worst ideas.

Callum held up a finger. "Hold on. If we're talking now, I need to drink this." He drained the second goblet, holding Hawk's gaze as long as he could. He wasn't sure exactly what he expected or wanted. In some distant part of his mind, he knew that drinking himself into a daze would not help him face this conversation.

Yet he couldn't bring himself to stop, either.

When he was done, he set the goblet on the nearest bookshelf. "All right. I'm ready."

The king was standing so still he might have been made of marble. Callum had seen it before. It was the calm before the storm. "You stole my soldiers."

"Technically, they were my—"

"No." Hawk slammed a fist down on the desk, scattering a pile of papers to the floor. "*Technically*, they are mine. I'm the king, so *technically*, everything is mine. The soldiers. The cities. Even your sorry ass, distasteful though that fact may be."

Callum knew he should take this seriously, that Hawk could have him dragged away at any moment. But he couldn't stop himself as he tilted his head, adopting his best bemused expression. It was a cover for the anger, like a lid set on a pot to keep the boiling water from spilling across the range. "Really?" he said, drawing the word into a long, mocking drawl. "*Everything?*"

"Callum," Thaddeus said, a warning in his tone.

But Callum was done pretending the king was the reasonable person in this room, that his anger didn't stem from his desire to punish him.

He'd spent his childhood chasing after Hawk, making sure the heir to the throne didn't fall from a tree and break his royal head. It had been a job, yes, assigned to him by King Magnus. But it had also been a calling, one he'd taken very seriously.

And they'd been friends, damn it. No, they'd been *brothers*. The first time they lost their heads with drink, it had been together. The first time they'd ridden into a border skirmish, hands clenching their swords in fear, it had been together.

"Are the birds in the sky yours, then?" Callum felt his chest growing warm, the suppressed anger rising to the surface. "What about the Etrans? Do they belong to you?"

"You know very well what I meant." Despite his desk-punching outburst, the king was disturbingly calm.

Callum poured another goblet of wine, hands shaking. "*Your* General Moore called *your* emissary a whore. Is that truly the man you want as captain? As *general?*"

Hawk's lips thinned, his disapproval evident. He was a lot of things, but a judgmental snipe wasn't one of them. He'd never liked the way Laena had been chased from her own capital, shunned for supposed love. "I will deal with Moore," he said. "At the moment, I'm dealing with you."

Callum set the goblet back on the shelf, untouched. Mages, but he wanted it. But he needed his wits about him for this conversation. "What of the attacks?" he asked. "The assassins? Silerith is stirring, and you're wasting time lecturing me."

Hawk glanced at Thaddeus, then back to Callum, as if he was

not sure how much he wanted to reveal. He drew in a deep breath, as if to calm himself.

A pity. He was easier to deal with when he shouted.

After King Magnus's death, Hawk had shut him out entirely. He might have blamed Thaddeus, too, for defying his orders and running off to join the poisonkeepers. Instead, he blamed Callum, who hadn't wanted the younger prince to risk himself riding alone through bandit-infested woods. The King's Guard had been so intent on stopping heart-tithers that they hadn't been paying enough attention to the rest of their country.

None of that mattered. It only mattered that Callum had been absent from the capital. That King Magnus had died. And that Hawk would not forgive him.

He hadn't shouted. He hadn't lectured. But he'd made it abundantly clear, in every way possible, that the friendship they had cultivated since childhood had died along with his father.

Now, he was glaring at Callum like he thought anything he said here might be repeated. Like Callum's disloyalty ran deeper than one mistake.

Perhaps he couldn't be faulted for that. Callum had ignored Hawk's wishes, had taken the delegation to Etra. And it had turned into enough of a disaster that Hawk had felt it necessary to leave the capital and come to Inasvale himself.

"I'm no traitor," Callum said, and though he softened his tone as best he could, the words still came out as a growl.

Again, Hawk glanced at Thaddeus. Brothers in reality, even if Thaddeus's status as a poisonkeeper should mean that he no longer considered himself part of the family. It was never that simple.

"My spies have reported no indication that Silerith is stirring," Hawk finally said.

A retort sprang to the tip of Callum's tongue, but for once he managed to suppress it. Hawk was opening a door, inviting

Callum into a conversation that, if his silent exchange with Thaddeus was any indication, had been going on for some time.

He wondered what the king had seen in his brother's face that convinced him it was safe to speak.

"The crystal—" Callum began, but Thaddeus shook his head.

"It isn't a Sil crystal," he said. His voice was soft, as though he were attempting to talk down a pair of unruly horses. Or hounds. "It's from the Miragelands. We cannot know who planted it there."

Without realizing what he was doing, Callum reached for the wine. More for something to hold onto than anything else, as if the goblet could tether him to this world. It was one thing to suspect the thing was evidence of the Miragelands. For Thaddeus to confirm it had come directly from that place? He shuddered, wishing he could banish the thought.

Demons, he wished Laena were here. Should they not be holding this conversation with her? She was the one who had discovered the crystal.

She was the one who'd discovered the crystal. And her country claimed increased activity out of Silerith was a threat. Callum's head snapped up, suspicion sending renewed sparks of anger through his chest. "You cannot be implying that Princess Laena is in league with the mages."

Thaddeus looked at his hands. "We don't have enough information to determine who planted it," he said carefully.

They didn't know of Laena's magic. They *couldn't* know of it. Her magic was not a heart-tithe. It was born of the Vales, not mage-made poison. Even had he not trusted her to tell him the truth—and demons, he *did*—he knew what a heart-tithe felt like. And her magic wasn't it.

Aside from the physical proof, the smell and the feeling of it, he had never seen a heart-tither rendered unconscious by their own magic.

His fingers tightened around the stem of the goblet. "But you cannot rule out her involvement, either?"

"That's not how evidence works, brother." Thaddeus's eyes were sympathetic, as if he knew far more than he was saying, even more than Callum would admit to himself. As if it were no great task at all to reach into his very heart and examine his feelings.

The thought was disconcerting. Callum wasn't entirely sure he wanted to know what Thaddeus would see there.

Hawk only sighed. Clearly, they'd been in communication about all of this, while Callum had been left in the dark. "You'd best show me," the king said.

—*—

THEY DID NOT TRY to prevent Callum from accompanying them to the magepool. He'd never seen it; he didn't want to see it, even now. It was a place for poisonkeepers and kings, not disgraced captains. Not commoners. The guards taking up the rear of the group kept casting anxious glances at one another, and Callum had to suppress the urge to give them a few words of encouragement.

They would not want to hear it from him.

Thaddeus led them deeper into the monastery, down narrow staircases where Callum's shoulders brushed both walls and into the ancient part of the keep. It was damp here, musty, and Thaddeus sneezed several times before they'd reached the bottom.

At which point he unlocked a door that led to the longest passageway Callum had ever seen. The ceiling was low enough that he had to duck, the walls pressing in on either side. They walked for long enough that he thought they must have exited the outer walls of the city. The only sound was the shuffling of their footsteps, and the occasional drop of water splashing to the stone floor.

Not even the rats wanted to hang out here.

At length—great length, during which Callum remembered how late he had been up searching the bars for Laena, how late it had been when he'd finally laid his head down and how he'd stayed awake even longer, afraid to move lest he disturb her sleep—the passage finally opened onto a forest.

This was not like the forest where they'd met the bandits, with young trees and great amounts of underbrush. This forest was old, the trunks wide, with so many leafy vines snaking up them that it was difficult to tell one tree from another. The canopy was so thick, the clearing so dark, that for a moment he wondered whether they'd spent the day in the tunnel and emerged into evening. But the occasional pocket of blue sky told him the afternoon was still young.

This forest did not feel like it was in Aglye at all. A deep, frightened part of Callum's mind wondered if it was in the Vales at all.

The forest floor here was paved in well-kept stone. No weeds poking up from between the cracks, no vines snaking along the ground.

And straight ahead, up a shallow set of steps, the pool.

It was the size of a small pond, the water too black, too still. It seemed impossible that no branches could have fallen to the surface, no seeds, not even a yellow streak of pollen. The surface didn't even reflect the trees above; it was a block of uninterrupted obsidian, more like stone than water.

At the far end, a single torch burned, its flame an unnatural purple. It looked so much like Laena's crystal that Callum could not help but shudder.

"The magepool," Thaddeus said, his voice little more than a whisper. There was awe in his tone, but it was the kind of frightened awe that promised even the poisonkeeper—the supposed protector of this place, and of all the Vales—would rather have been somewhere else. Anywhere else.

This was the place where the mages had entered the Vales. Many centuries ago, they'd been driven back by a band of rebellious humans who'd found a way to break their enthrallment just long enough to drive the mages back into the Miragelands.

This was the place, both holy and corrupt, that the poison-keepers guarded. To prevent the mages from rising again.

At least, if one believed the legends. And standing here, facing the stillness of the water, the ancient aura of the trees, Callum did believe them. It would be impossible not to.

He wondered whether the master knew they were here. Even he could not gainsay the king himself, surely. Hawk was not entirely wrong when he said that everything belonged to him—this place included—though he'd never been one to say it out loud before.

Hawk let out a breath, then made for the stairs.

"What are you doing?" Callum asked.

The king ignored the question as he knelt on the top step and reached for the pool. Callum started forward, ready to intervene in whatever this foolishness was, but Thaddeus moved first, skirting past Callum and hurrying up the stairs.

The poisonkeeper would prevent the king from touching the poisonous pool. He would talk sense into Hawk, whose eyes looked nearly as dark as the water itself.

But Thaddeus didn't put a hand on Hawk. Instead, he withdrew a pouch from deep within his robes and held it out to his brother. Hawk nodded in thanks, plucking something out of it and pressing it into his mouth as Thaddeus retreated down the stairs, coming to stand beside Callum. He was all nervous energy; he kept fidgeting with his robes and adjusting his spectacles. His attention did not leave his brother.

Callum felt like he'd been dropped into a story he did not understand.

Closing his eyes, Hawk touched a fingertip to the surface of the pool. The water should have rippled, if only slightly. But the only indication that this was water, that the pool wasn't made of pure stone, was the fact that Hawk's fingernail disappeared into its depths.

Callum started forward, but Thaddeus laid a hand on his elbow. "Just watch."

Callum watched. There was nothing else to do. The king crouched before the pool, half his hand now submerged in its depths. His eyes were still closed, lips pressed tight, and his skin had gone so pale it seemed impossible he could still be conscious. The shadows beneath his eyes seemed to darken.

Finally, the king lifted his hand from the pool, allowing a stream of water to drip from his fingertips. It fell too quickly, the drops landing heavily, leaving no ripples. As if they'd simply been called back home to rejoin the rest of the water.

At the side of the pool, the purple lantern flickered.

"Thad is right," Hawk said, his voice raw. "The barrier is thinning."

Thaddeus released Callum's arm. He hurried to Hawk's side and handed him the pouch once more. Hawk withdrew several leaves, shoving them into his mouth without examining them. A breath, then another, and he opened his eyes. The king rose, breathing hard, and turned to Callum. "Take the delegation to Vunmore. I'll follow in a few days."

Questions poured into Callum's mind, insistent. "But—"

Hawk stepped down from the pool. "Take the delegation to Vunmore, Farrow," he said, his hands visibly shaking. "And if you disobey me again, I will banish you from Aglye for good."

CHAPTER 25

They finally left Inasvale the next day, with enough horses for everyone in the party and an expanded entourage to escort them to Vunmore in safety. No one discussed the king's absence; it was as if everyone but Laena had been informed of his reasoning for remaining behind. It seemed to her that the entire party might have waited on him—he *was* the king—yet he'd opted to send them on ahead.

Whatever had passed between Callum and Hawk yesterday, it couldn't have been pleasant. He'd disappeared for the rest of the day. Judging by the grayness of his complexion this morning, he'd spent much of that time in his cups. He rode beside her, near the middle of the group, his expression distant. When she asked why the king would not be accompanying them, he'd muttered something about stubborn idiot children. Even though the king could not have been more than a few years younger than him.

At least the soldiers appeared to be deferring to him again, and not subtly. He barked orders at them, and they complied, while Landon Moore sulked at the back of the party.

She would have expected that to at least bring a smile to

Callum's face. But when she mentioned it, his expression grew even darker. "Hawk dislikes traitors. Calling his emissary a whore amounts to a betrayal."

Laena huffed out a breath of annoyance. "If not even Landon Moore's fall from grace can bring you out of your bad humor, then I must admit myself defeated."

"Apologies, my lady. I've been lost in my thoughts."

Clearly. Even her mention of it was not enough to pull him out, or to lighten his expression. He rode on, back straight, eyes trained on the road ahead until she thought he might be trying to sear a hole in the hills with his gaze alone.

Laena decided to ignore him, opting instead to take in the beauty of the countryside. After Inasvale's cliffs, the land had smoothed out into a vista of gentle hills. The road cut around them, which minimized the difficulty of the trek. The hills, thick with green grass, were interrupted only by white and yellow flowers, the buzz of bees, the occasional flash of a butterfly's wing. Here and there, a lone tree stood upon the top of a hill.

They passed a fork in the road. Rooftops in the distance announced a village. She would have liked to stop, to wander the streets and meet with the people, but the entourage moved forward without so much as acknowledging the place's existence. It was just as well. There was business to attend to in Vunmore.

They rode in silence for so long she nearly jumped out of her saddle when Callum spoke again.

"Why did Katrina send you to Aglye?"

Laena patted her horse's main, though the animal didn't seem overly worried about its jumpy rider. "And here I was thinking you'd been paying attention, Captain. She sent me to speak to King Hawk as emissary."

If her lighthearted response affected him, he didn't show it.

"But why *you*? She is surrounded by councilors and courtiers and regents—"

"One regent," Laena corrected, but Callum kept going as if he hadn't heard.

"—and yet she insisted it be you. That you abandon the life you've made for yourself, that you leave your village and face insult and disdain at every turn."

"Not every turn," she murmured. But he just shook his head.

And what kind of a life had it been, truly? Her only friend was a lizard, for goodness' sake. She'd gone so long without admitting how much that hurt that she certainly couldn't do it now. And there had been reasons for Katrina's request. Reasons she'd at first rejected, true, but reasons nonetheless.

Perhaps he was embarrassed by yesterday's forwardness. Only... only, he'd stayed with her. He'd brought breakfast. And he did not seem the kind of man to be embarrassed by a kiss. Especially one he'd returned, if briefly.

"Are you sure," he said, "that Katrina does not know of your magic?"

The magic. That was what this was about? She thought he had accepted it, that he trusted her. Laena glanced behind her, hoping the nearest riders were yet too distant to hear their conversation. "She couldn't possibly know. I'm here to help Etra."

"I know why you want to be here, my lady. What I cannot discern is why your sister would send you, specifically."

Laena straightened. If he kept repeating that, she was going to find a way to kick him in the shins. As soon as she wasn't seated on the back of a horse. "I'm a skilled negotiator, Captain Farrow. I still hold a title equal to meeting with a king, and I have spent much of my life studying the intricacies of court life."

If nothing else, it was odd that Katrina would admit this. Declan might have convinced her of it.

"No doubt," he replied. "But the queen has other well-trained negotiators at her disposal, does she not?"

Laena shook her head. "Katrina believes Silerith is stirring. For all her faults, my sister does care about Etra. Perhaps she merely sent the person she knew would care as much as she does. I trust her to do what's right."

"Hawk claims Silerith isn't stirring at all," he said. "Hawk claims that the Ruthless King keeps to himself, as he ever has."

"Perhaps Hawk is wrong." Or perhaps he had reason to keep them from seeing what was happening in Silerith. She thought of the strange resonance she'd felt when the king touched her hand.

"Callum, when King Hawk shook my hand, I felt..." He looked at her expectantly, and she swallowed. "It felt as if he might have been using magic. Like..." She lowered her voice, glancing around. No one was riding close enough to hear, or so she hoped. "... like mine recognized his somehow. The way it did the crystal."

Callum snapped his head toward her, eyes glittering. "You think Hawk is working a heart-tithe?"

She hesitated. "It didn't have the signature—"

"Exactly. Magic is forbidden in Aglye." He said it like a warning, and she sucked in a breath, suddenly frightened. He would not use his knowledge of her power against her. Surely he would not.

What had the king said to him, to put him in such a humor? What did he know that he was keeping from her?

Before she could say anything more, he dipped his head. "Excuse me, my lady. I need to check in with my men."

And with that, he rode off and left her alone.

———✳———

LAENA COULDN'T HELP but be impressed by the efficiency of the King's Guard as they erected their camp for the night. In traveling with the bandits, they'd had no shelter to assemble; now they had a field full of tents. Some had peaked roofs that she suspected would provide ample space for the king's bed, while others looked as if they would barely fit two men.

Callum was nowhere in sight. And it was just as well—she had no wish to renew their earlier conversation.

It was Edmun who came forward to help her from her horse. She might have managed it herself, though she wasn't certain she could trust her legs to hold her after the long ride. Another day ahead, and another after that. She would sleep well tonight.

Or she would lay awake replaying the conversation with Callum and wondering what she had done to offend him so.

"Never mind the captain, Princess," he said. "He's out of sorts more often than not."

Not with me, she thought.

"He'll apologize before the morning," Edmun added. "Take my word on that."

"If he tries, I may slap him for his trouble."

Edmun grinned. "I'll relay the message."

The old soldier led her to a larger tent near the center of the camp. Her legs were sore from riding and the discomfort stiffened her lower back. When he lifted the flap to usher her inside, she paused at the entrance, unable to suppress a gasp.

It seemed impossible. It *was* impossible, but there it stood: a bathtub, in the middle of the tent, the water still steaming.

Edmun chuckled. "There's a village right over the hill there, to the west. King Hawk pays a good sum for people to attend the camp for the night."

"Wise of him," Laena murmured, her head throbbing. All she wanted was to submerge herself in that water for as long as it would stay hot. And perhaps sometime after. "I imagine he takes a different route each way, to spread the coin around."

"That he does," Edmun replied. "I'll station two guards outside. You call out if you need anything."

As Laena lowered her aching body into the tub, she thought she would never need anything ever again. Her muscles loosened in the heat of the water, allowing her to stretch, and she let her head rest against the side of the tub. She might have wept from the comfort of it.

When the water grew lukewarm, she washed her hair with the pat of soap someone had left—it smelled of roses—and scrubbed her skin until it ached pleasantly.

Someone had left her a clean shift, which she slipped on. She wrapped herself in one of the soft blankets from the bed. This town clearly had a lot of experience serving the king and his soldiers. She wanted to thank each of them personally.

As she was considering that, one of the guards rapped on the pole outside the tent. "Captain's here," the guard said. "Only, Edmun says I'm to send him away if you don't want to see him."

Laena hid a smile and said, "It's all right. I'll call for you if he acts out of turn."

Callum ducked into the tent, and her heart stuttered. He'd managed to procure a bath, too, or perhaps Edmun had dumped a bucket of water over his fool head. He'd attempted to smooth his dark curls away from his face, but they were as unruly as ever, falling across his forehead and over his ears.

"My lady," he said. "I owe you an apology."

"And I owe you a slap," she replied.

He had the grace to look ashamed. "Edmun warned me you'd say that. It would be no more than I deserve. Shall I position myself here by the wall? I'll face my punishment without complaint."

Laena slid off the bed, the blanket still wrapped around her. She approached him slowly, unsure of what she planned to do until she got there.

"Do you trust me?" she asked.

He swallowed, drawing in a long breath. "I trust you."

She raised her hand, and he didn't flinch as she gently touched his cheek. His skin was warm beneath her fingers. "I felt magic when I touched the king."

"That," he said, "is a sentence I never want to hear you say again."

"Tell me why."

He leaned into her touch, ice-blue eyes boring into her as though he could see to her very soul. Instead of answering the question, he leaned forward until he was a breath away. Less than a breath—the width of a coin, the width of a hair, his lips so close that the slightest quiver would bring them together, until she thought she would go mad. This sliver of distance would be her very undoing.

"Because, my lady"—his lips skimmed along hers as he spoke —"you belong to me."

He tilted his head, and then he was kissing her, capturing her lips between his with a hunger that made her gasp. He made a sound in the back of his throat, sweeping his tongue into her mouth with an urgency that made her dizzy with need. Wrapped in his smell of woodsmoke and leather, and the barest hints of whiskey, she dropped her hands to his neck, running her fingers through his curls as he kissed her.

The blanket slipped from her shoulders, landing in a heap on the floor. His hands were already on her hips, drawing her closer to his obviously growing need. She pushed her body closer to his, reveling in the feel of his hands. He lifted her off her feet and carried her to the bed.

When he laid her down, it was with a reverence that made her breath catch in her throat.

As he pressed his lips to her neck, she arched into his touch, throwing her head back to allow him full access to her throat. His fingers played at the laces of her shift, freeing her chest, and she gasped as he flicked a thumb over her nipple then worked it between his fingers. His body, now flush against her, radiated heat even through the layers of their clothing. Their legs tangled together, her shift riding ever higher as his hands skimmed along her sides.

He took her breast into his mouth, swirling his tongue around the nipple before taking it into his mouth. Ripples of pleasure pulsed out across her ribs and down through her core, her magic rising to join with her desire.

When she moaned, he pressed his knee between her legs. "Ride," he commanded, his teeth grazing her nipple, and she was all too eager to comply. She jerked her hips against his leg, rubbing her sex against his thigh. He pressed a thumb to her breast, freeing the second one for his hungry mouth as she dragged her body against him, the fabric of her underthings rubbing against her, bringing her ever closer to her climax. She could feel the swell of his own desire against her belly, and it emboldened her to ride harder.

"Come for me, Laena," he said, his fingers skimming beneath the waist of her trousers as she rode him. When he pressed his thumb to the sensitive nub above her sex, she exploded, pleasure expanding out from her core in exquisite waves. He muffled her moans with a deep kiss as her pleasure subsided, leaving her limp with its aftereffects.

Still, she could not resist touching him. She reached between them, tracing the outline of his straining cock, and he groaned into her mouth. Smiling against his lips, she unfastened the ties of his trousers and freed him from the stays. Demons, but he was large. Part of her wanted to straddle him now, offer herself fully to him. Instead, she let her fingers explore his body, taking in the massive length of him, the combination of soft skin and rock-hard want.

"You needn't—" he began, but she traced the tip of her finger around the head of his cock, wetting it with the bead of his own desire, and he groaned. "Mages, Laena, you drive me wild."

She wrapped her fingers around him and stroked, reveling in the rhythm of his hips, his clear desire for her. Her hips moved in time with his as he fucked her hand, panting and moaning into her mouth while her own climax built a second time. She'd never felt so powerful, the instrument of his pleasure, and the maker, at least in part, of her own.

When he spilled his seed, she came again, and they cried out together in shared pleasure.

As she fell back onto the bed, she imagined the entire camp must have heard them. And yet for the first time in a long while, she cared nothing for their opinions.

CHAPTER 26

*C*allum had barely allowed himself to imagine he might
be fortunate enough to hold Laena in his arms. The
attraction between them had been clear enough, certainly, but
attraction certainly did not always turn to... well, what had just
occurred between them.

Now, with Laena nestled against him, her body flush against
his and filling his head with the sweet scent of snow and sea
salt, her lips curved into a satisfied smile. She was a woman who
knew what she wanted, and that much was plain. He stroked the
soft tresses of her hair, wishing they'd removed more of their
clothing. He wanted to feel her skin against his, warm and alive.

The sounds of the camp, the clanking of pots and murmurs
of conversation just outside, reminded him that there was but a
thin barrier between them and the soldiers. A guard might enter
at any moment—though perhaps they could be trusted to know
better—yet he found he was too languid to move. Too
comfortable.

"Callum." Laena's voice was soft in the fading dusk. The tent
was dark, the lanterns not yet lit, though orbs of light flickered
through the fabric. "May I ask you a question?"

He kissed her hair, inhaling that sweet scent of hers. "Anything."

"Why did Hawk dismiss you as captain?"

Callum stilled, his fingers still grazing her bare shoulder. She looked up at him, her eyes shining in the darkness. He allowed his fingers to trace down her skin. Mages, but she was soft.

"King Magnus's death was my fault." Callum had never spoken the words out loud before, nor had Hawk said them. They'd lived in his heart for more than a year now, wedged there like a splinter. He told himself all the drinking dulled the pain of it, but in truth, it only increased the hurt.

Laena propped herself on her elbow, resting her head upon her palm. She would leave him now, Callum realized. He was confessing the truth to her, and it was too awful. Her expression would turn to horror, when she understood. Just like Hawk's had.

And yet now that he'd begun, he couldn't stop the story from spilling out.

"Thaddeus wanted to go to Inasvale. He had the right, as a second son, though tradition... usually the second son remains in Vunmore."

"But they also have a sister."

Callum inclined his head. "King Magnus changed the rule of inheritance when he took the throne. What used to be father to son became parent to child. Queens. Kings. Anyone."

"Like Etra."

"Indeed. And with Emilia there, Thaddeus felt the freedom to follow his heart. Only..." He paused, running his thumb along her arm. She shivered. "Only Magnus left the choice to Hawk, and Hawk refused. He said Thaddeus only wanted to run away."

"From what?"

Callum shook his head. "He still won't say. But Thaddeus came to me in the night, his bags packed, already wearing the

robes of the poisonkeepers. He begged me to take him to Inasvale."

"And you agreed."

Callum wanted to put off this part of the story. He wanted to leap out of the bed, if his injured shoulder would allow it, and insist they seek out something to eat. Someone was frying bacon out there; he could smell it.

But there was no stopping the story now. "I escorted Thaddeus to Inasvale against Hawk's wishes. While I was gone, a band of assassins crossed the border from Silerith. They used a heart-tithe to enter the palace, murdering one of their own so they could reappear within the walls. It takes a strong tithe to travel through walls or over great distances."

He didn't want to bring this story into their midst. The darkness would invade the small bit of safety they'd carved out. And yet, it felt right that she should know. That he should tell it all.

"They killed the king's personal guards, Silas and Dom. And then they killed him." He swallowed, picturing the scene as he so often had: the guards dying, their blood running rivulets between the stones. Hawk's cry—Hawk had been the one to find him—and his mother's screams.

By the time Callum had returned, the floors had been scrubbed clean. But the smell of the heart-tithe, that had remained. Sometimes it felt as if that night had infused it into the stones of the palace itself.

Laena waited. Her eyebrows raised as if she expected more to the story. "And?" she prompted.

He frowned, confused. "That's the end of the story."

She reached a hand to his face, smoothing the wrinkle from between his eyes. "You left out the part where the king's death was your fault."

"I wasn't there," he said. "I left the castle unprotected."

"I don't think Edmun would see it that way," she said softly.

"Or even Silas and Dom. Were they not trained under your command?"

"Partially, but—"

"As the king's personal guards, I would expect they were among his best."

"I still have no soldiers as fast as Dom, nor as dextrous as Silas."

Their loss had been devastating. Not only for their skills, but for their place among the guard. Dom's jokes and Silas's quiet dedication. The men had marked the anniversary of their deaths with a visit to the gravesite and a night of stories, their grief still fresh.

Laena traced her finger down his cheek, cupping his jaw. "If you had been there, you would be dead, too."

Callum opened his mouth to argue, then closed it. He had never considered the possibility, not once. If he had been there, surely there would have been something he could have done.

But the thought vanished. She was right. If Dom and Silas could not win against the assassins—there was reason to believe, in fact, that the two guards had not even seen the attackers' approach—then what hope would Callum have had?

"Hawk blames me," he said. "He blames the drinking for my removal from the King's Guard, but he wants me gone from Vunmore altogether. He holds me responsible for his father's death. He cannot forgive it."

"Then Hawk is a fool." Laena twined her hands around his neck, drawing him into a kiss that set his head to spinning.

He allowed his hands to travel to the hem of her shift, dragging it up over her knees, caressing the sensitive skin on the inside of her thighs. This night would just have to go on, forever.

"Callum," she breathed, and he dropped his lips to her neck, sucking gently on the patch of skin where her throat curved toward the collarbone.

But when she said his name again, it was with alarm rather than desire. He sat up, alarm bells ringing as the tent flooded with the unmistakable scent of a heart-tithe.

CHAPTER 27

*T*he sky was boiling.

Night air whisked around Laena's legs, the wind pulling at her thin shift, but she hardly noticed the chill. She was distantly aware of it, like she was distantly aware of the clanging alarms, the shouts of the soldiers, the *shing* of metal swords leaving sheaths, the camp roused from its after-travel rest to face some as-yet-unseen attacker. The smell of the tithe was thick in the air, each breath of it filling her lungs with a searing heat, but that, too, was little more than a vague sensation.

It might have been a dream. *She* might have been a dream, a ghost, leaving the comfort of her tent—of Callum's arms—to wander into the midst of these frantic battle preparations.

Callum. He was calling her name, his voice nearly lost behind the clamor of activity. But the sky was boiling, the clouds undulating with red and purple lightning, and there was no time to hear.

As she reached the edge of the camp, her body felt as if it were not entirely her own. She walked as if in a trance, the knot of ice at her core pulling her forward like a tether as thin as a fishing line, her magic reaching for whatever was coming.

Ready, like a sword not yet drawn. She was *there*, and yet she was also *here*, counting each grain of dirt beneath her bare feet, each whisper of wind in her hair.

Steel clashed behind her, and she thought she heard Callum call her name again, but his voice was immediately lost in the din of the fight.

But this, her magic said, was not the real threat.

This was the distraction.

A band of shadows materialized out of the darkness, and in her core, Laena's magic unfurled. She threw up her hands, pushing out a wave of frigid air to meet the oncoming threat, the pulse so strong she could almost see it as the surge of cold air met the warmth of the summer night.

The first wave of shadows dissolved, crystalizing into snowflakes that swirled in the breeze, finally falling to coat the green grass like a swath of spilled paint. She could hear each hushed landing, feel the blades of grass bending beneath the gentle weight, taste the sharpness of the cold on the tip of her tongue.

Behind her, the shouts intensified. A dagger escaped the fight, whistling toward the back of her head, but she felt it coming—she felt *everything*—or her magic did, and she batted the blade aside with an icicle.

As a fresh wave of shadows thickened over the hills, Laena readied another wave of magic. It was coming easier now, flowing from her center like it would keep coming forever.

A woman materialized at the center of the shadows, her slight form cutting a sharp outline amid the smoke.

"Milla," Laena said. "I didn't think you had anything left to care about."

Not when her last heart-tithe had failed to whisk Laena more than a few leagues from where she'd stolen her. Not when she'd had to run from the cabin, her magic drained.

Milla sneered. "Your Aglyean troll left Penn for dead, but I was the one to end his misery. I have nothing left."

Why, then, did she seem so smug?

"I do hope the Ruthless King appreciates all the sacrifices you're making," Laena said.

The woman smiled. It looked like a challenge. "You still think this is about Silerith. How adorable." She bore no weapons in her hands, yet she stared at Laena like she'd already won this battle. Like she had won the war. "The Ruthless King is a fool. But he is not the only monarch in the Vales. You should know that better than anyone. Perhaps you would do well to join us. Where the real power lives."

"Is that an invitation?"

The woman tilted her head. "Would you like it to be? They claimed you would not... but with your powers added to ours, we would be unstoppable. A deal might be brokered."

Her words were not her own, as if some other voice were using her as a mouthpiece.

The magic in Laena's core writhed, as if disgusted by the suggestion of an alliance. But the negotiator in her had seen an opening, the barest gleam of what Milla might want and what Laena might be able to offer. "I cannot join you," she said, "without knowing who sent you."

Milla laughed, an ugly sound. "Nice try, Princess. I admit, I'd rather hurt you than ally with you. But they would have wanted me to try."

Laena would have pushed her for information—if not Silerith, then who?—but Milla threw her head back, and the shadows behind her hardened, taking the shape of men.

No, these were not men. These were *monsters*. They loomed alongside their maker. Their edges melted into clouds of black smoke and remaking themselves again, joining with one another until she could hardly tell if they were dozens of monsters or just one.

Laena pushed a wave of cold air at them. She drew deeper into her well of magic, turning them into nothing but a thick band of snow, but they kept coming, undeterred. Gritting her teeth, she called on her magic to try again, and again, yet they were nothing but shells, shadows given form. Milla's heart-tithe could not be that strong. It couldn't.

She didn't know if she said it out loud, or if Milla could hear her thoughts—or read them on her face, somehow—but the woman threw out her arms to the sides as if welcoming her monsters. "I gave everything I had." Milla's voice echoed with unnatural strength, booming over the camp-turned-battlefield. "I sacrificed every friend, every lover, every ally to their cause. Did you not think the mages would reward me? I will kill your army, and then I'll take you. And there won't be a thing anyone can do."

Laena didn't have a chance to ask why Milla wouldn't kill her, too, because the first shadow monster reached her, and she tapped her magic again, forming a dagger of ice in each hand. She slashed, and the shadow man fell in a cyclone of snowflakes. Again she slashed, and again. Again.

A tendril of heat unspooled through her core, like a hot wire dropped into a frozen pond. A trickle of discomfort, a warning sign, but she could not stop. There were too many monsters, and they kept coming. Shells they might be, but they were shells with weapons. They were shells that would tear apart everything she knew, everything she had left. And she would not allow it.

She pulled on her magic, reaching to the bottom of the well and ignoring the heat searing the bottom of her ribcage.

The battle had moved toward her, and it surrounded her now as the soldiers came from the shadows, bringing with them the smell of blood and sweat and fear. Landon Moore's voice cut across the din, calling orders, and when she spared a glance behind her, she saw him fighting back-to-back with Callum, the men trying to make their way to her. Fear spiked through her awareness, brash and painful, and she blinked, taking stock of the situation for the first time.

To her right, Edmun clashed with a human soldier, his movements precise despite his clear exhaustion. Beside him, Godfrey and Archer were fighting a single shadow monster, slashing and slashing while the beast re-formed and re-formed again. Callum and Moore were merely defending at this point, pushing back those who came near.

Many had fallen, too many to count. She didn't want to look at their faces, didn't want to know who she had lost.

The fight would not end until Milla saw every last one of them dead. There were far too many shadow monsters—and just as many humans come to fight on Milla's side. Laena would never best them with individual slashes, one-on-one battles. Milla would keep creating monsters until she drained the mages dry. And Laena didn't know if that was even a true possibility.

But Milla had not seen all that Laena could do.

Risking another glance behind her, Laena caught Callum's gaze. Ice-blue, desperate. And sorry. He was sorry for failing her, as he saw it.

She would not fail him. She turned away.

"Laena, no!" His voice was just beside her, yet it was far away to heed.

Laena raised her hands again, delving deep into the well of her magic, and pain answered.

She stumbled, a gasp wrenching her body with a jolt, but still she reached, like she had delved the crystal, like she had delved her garden, only now she was reaching deep within herself at the last layer of her power.

The dregs were the most potent.

Magic flowed from her outstretched hands, answering her call, eager to do her bidding. It hit the closest shadow monster, coating it in a wave of ice. She pushed, painting the monsters with cold, and the camp filled with the sound of cracking ice. They were too thin to stay—shells only—and they crumbled into a thousand heaps of ice, oblivious to Milla's screams of rage.

But there were people here, too, enemy soldiers who had attacked the camp from the rear to create the distraction. Clothed in black, they still fought, but Laena's magic knew how to distinguish them from her allies. She weaved it through the battle like a needle, arms raised, pain radiating from her center as she burned from the inside out.

No one on the battlefield felt the heat. Only the cold, unleashed from the depths of her soul.

When the magic hit the enemy soldiers, they did not crumble. They froze fully, fingers and faces turned ice-white, their black clothing crusted with frost. Too quick for frostbite, too quick to blacken the skin, the magic froze them with swords raised, ice dripping from the blades.

Milla was last to freeze, in motion to her final moment. She frozen with her arms outstretched, her mouth open in a cry of despair.

And then, silence.

Laena was on her knees. She wasn't sure when she'd fallen; she knew only the buzzing in her head, the heat at her center, like someone had set her insides on fire. The agony of a sunburn times a thousand, only her skin was unmarred. Whatever the magic had done to her, it was burning her from within.

Landon Moore's voice, no longer distant but close. Too close. "Arrest the whore."

No one moved. She could see the sky now, feel the blades of grass beneath her head. When had she fallen? Something hot dribbled down her face, and she realized she was bleeding from her nose.

"She saved us, General," one of the men said. She didn't know which one. Only that it wasn't Callum. Where was he?

"She used *magic*." Moore's disbelief, his disgust, was palpable, and she was glad she couldn't see his face.

"She did more than use it. I'd say she conquered it."

That. *That* was Callum's voice. And then, finally, his face. He appeared above her like a damn angel out of a story, his face wreathed in moonlight. He was *alive*.

The world blinked, and she was in his arms, her head cradled against his elbow. "Do you trust me?" he asked.

Her lips parted to say yes, she trusted him—she always had, she always would, even if her *always* was doomed to last only another minute—but her throat was made of fire, her voice lost to the raging pain in her body.

Again, Landon Moore called for her arrest. Callum said something she did not hear, and she wanted to tell him not to sacrifice himself for her. Whatever consequences Moore had in mind for a magic user, one who could freeze entire armies to a standstill, she did not have enough time left in this world to face it. Callum needed to think of himself.

She would not pretend she felt no fear. But she would face her death with courage. As much of it as she could muster.

But none of the words would come.

CHAPTER 28

*M*oore was the only one to protest when Callum took his horse. It was the strongest one, the horse master told him. The one capable of carrying Callum with Laena in his arms. So Callum took it, weaving around the frozen figures of the soldiers and calling out final orders to keep them under guard and send word to Vunmore for backup. There was no way to know whether they were corpses, or if they were enemies yet to awaken.

He didn't care. He needed to get Laena back to Inasvale.

He thought his men would physically hold Moore back, if they had to. But the general was a coward at heart, and he let them go, still muttering about the famed magic hunter rescuing a whore of a witch instead of letting her die in the dirt.

There was no time to reply, no time to argue with the fool. There was only time to ride, with Laena gathered in his arms. Her breaths were so shallow, so infrequent, that he found himself lowering his ear to her mouth so he could reassure himself she did still breathe, that she had not slipped away. She felt too warm, the blood from her nose soaking the patch of cloth he'd ripped from his shirt to stanch the blood.

Brin lay nestled beneath Laena's chin, her pink scales shining in the light of the setting moon. The sight made Callum swallow, his throat too dry. "Can you help her?" he whispered.

The shimmerling made no reply.

Yesterday, they'd ridden a full day from Inasvale to reach the meadow where they'd camped. Callum could not hope to reach the city quickly. But that knowledge didn't stop him from seeking the sight of it over every hill, around every bend, searching, searching for any glint of the sea against the moonlight. As if his panicked need could break through the hills and will the city to slide closer.

Yesterday, they'd traveled with a full company of soldiers. Yesterday, they'd taken their time. Callum should be able to get there in a matter of hours.

But he would not be able to do it if he pushed the horse too hard. The poor beast was bearing an extra load as it was. Yet he could not stop himself from urging the creature forward.

"Why Inasvale?" Edmun had asked as Callum mounted with Laena, bleeding and unconscious, in his arms. "Why not the nearest village? Why not a healer?"

Callum hadn't been able to voice it. Hadn't *wanted* to voice it. But Laena's suspicions about Hawk... he'd watched the king as he dipped his hand into that magepool. He'd seen the look on his face, like he was reaching deep within himself and outward at the same time. And he'd known the truth then, even if he hadn't been able to put words to it.

There could no longer be any doubt. Hawk had magic, too. And Thaddeus had given him something to help with it.

Thaddeus knew how to help.

The fact that Laena may well have suspected more than Hawk's magic, that she had stopped short of suggesting he could be involved in all of it—the assassination attempts, the kidnapping—did not stop him. Hawk had not smelled of a heart-tithe, nor had Callum seen him hurt anyone to work his magic. He had to believe the king was like Laena. That his magic was benign.

At this point, he had no choice.

An hour he rode, and another, and yet another, and as he skirted around the hundredth hill—it felt like the thousandth—finally, finally Inasvale came into view. Distant still, its shape little more than an elevated smudge against the horizon, but in view. In reach.

Callum felt for Laena's breath. It was as shallow as ever, her skin hot to the touch, but at least he did not think she was any worse. "Hold on," he said. "You have to hold on."

He refused to entertain the possibility of losing her.

Inasvale disappeared around the next bend in the road, and Callum rode harder, as though keeping the city in his sight would bring him to it faster.

When he rounded the next bend, the road was blocked.

A carriage, a dozen soldiers, a pair of horses. And a queen.

Laena's sister stood in the road, her soldiers fanned out around her, more like a decoration than a shield. The regent hovered a few steps behind her, his expression cold.

She would have traveled a long way to get here, likely directly from a ship, no doubt from Etra itself. Yet her pink gown looked crisp and fresh, her golden curls smooth as they brushed against her shoulders. She'd taken the time to see to her toilet, clearly; the scent of her perfume reached him even from this distance.

They must have missed her arrival by mere hours.

"My sister may not be queen, but she still cannot be arrested by a foreign kingdom," Katrina said as his horse approached her. "Even for the working of magic."

Callum stopped, his heart thrumming in his chest. "How do you know she—"

"I have spies among your people. As your king does among mine, I assume."

He could not deny it. Hawk had recently spoken of his spies and their certainty that Silerith was keeping to itself, as it always did. If he had ears in Silerith, he certainly had them in Etra, too.

There was no way Callum could make it past all these men without unseating himself. Not while protecting Laena. And he had to protect Laena. It was the only thought he could muster.

"Your Highness," he said, his voice rough. "I do not mean to arrest your sister. Only to bring her to safety. Please. I'm sure you must have questions. But you must allow me to pass."

Katrina looked to Declan. But if the regent had an opinion on this interaction, he didn't offer it. Callum wanted to shake the man, to demand that he speak so Callum could be on his way. Katrina turned back to him, concern in her eyes. "Leave her here and ride ahead. It will be faster."

Callum hesitated. He had no wish to leave Laena. He didn't believe Katrina would keep her safe.

But Laena did, he realized. Laena trusted her sister enough to accept her fool's errand of a mission. Enough to leave the life she'd built for herself and reenter the lion's den.

Katrina raised an eyebrow. "Do you not trust me to care for her until your return?"

Callum cleared his throat. He did not. But Laena would. Laena *would*. "I do not think anyone can care for her, Your Highness. Save perhaps for my brother."

Katrina gave a pointed look at her sister. "Then I think you had best hurry."

—❈—

CALLUM SHOVED the door to Thaddeus's room so hard that it crashed into a table, knocking several books to the floor. Hawk was seated in a chair by the window, a book open on the table before him and another in his lap. For once, his hair was as disheveled as his brother's, and his blinking surprise channeled Thaddeus so strongly that, in another context, Callum might have laughed. The poisonkeeper was on the floor with three volumes spread before him.

And in another context, the sight of the brothers working together might have squeezed something in Callum's chest. With affection, with loneliness. He'd been included in their number once.

Today, in this moment, only Laena mattered.

Hawk rose, snapping his book shut. He was arranging his face into an expression of official rage, the angry king replacing the relaxed brother. "Callum. What—"

"You," Callum said. "You have magic."

And there it was: *fear*. Now that Callum knew to look for it, he wondered that he'd never seen it in the frozen expression before: the tightening around the eyes, the way the color bleached from Hawk's face, his lips parting just slightly to allow a shaky breath to enter. As if he thought Callum would produce cuffs and haul him away to the dungeons.

Hawk was the king. And he feared Callum? Callum was no one. He led at the king's favor only. He'd been demoted. Disgraced.

And yet. And yet, Callum had been able to steal the Etran delegation by his word alone. Edmun had known from the beginning that Callum had no authority to lead the mission, and he'd come along anyway. How many more of them would have done the same?

Hawk thought Callum might stage a coup. Worse, he thought it might actually work. All this time, maybe even since Magnus's death, the king had been playing a game, when all Callum had wanted was to prove himself.

He didn't have time for this.

"Did you kill King Magnus?" Callum asked. "Did you kill your father?"

He knew the answer. He had to hear it, anyway.

Hawk set the book down, the fear on his face stark now. His eyes were flashing with it. But he faced Callum anyway. "No."

"Hawk wanted you at the pool," Thaddeus said, ignoring Hawk's warning glare. "He wanted you to see the tru—"

"You have to help her." Callum rounded on the younger prince. Thaddeus was still sitting on the floor, robes pooled around him like a black puddle of fabric. Thaddeus could play peacekeeper later and fabricate as many stories of Hawk's wish to reconcile as he pleased. Now, there was no time.

Thaddeus blinked up at him over the rims of his spectacles. "Help who?"

"Laena." Callum practically choked out her name. Was she still breathing? Was Katrina keeping her alive? Could her voice call her sister back from the depths, or was it too late?

It would do no good to panic. He took a breath, painful as it was. "She has... she used magic. Not a heart-tithe. Something else."

Part of him expected Hawk to deny any knowledge of such a thing. Instead, the king straightened.

"How much did she use?" His voice was sharp now.

Callum shook his head. "Everything. All she had, I think. She froze an entire army into statues."

Hawk looked to Thaddeus, who shook his head. "It took us weeks to learn the little we do know. It would take months to research the effects of fully depleting one's magic. If the information survives at all."

That explained the stacks of books, the obsession they both had with studying.

It might even explain why Thaddeus had joined the poison-keepers in the first place. He'd wanted to access their archives, their knowledge. And Hawk hadn't wanted to let him make the sacrifice. Puzzle pieces drifted together, the pieces clicking into place.

And none of it mattered. Not compared with the sorrow in Thaddeus's expression. "I can't help her. I'm sorry."

Callum refused to accept it. He *wouldn't* accept it. He pointed at Hawk, though his attention was still focused on Thaddeus. "You gave him something. At the pool."

Thaddeus rose, finally, and stepped over the books on the floor to come nearer. "I gave him herbs, for grounding. It's like a tether. The theory is that the magic brings your mind and body partially to another realm—not the Miragelands, this is Vales magic, so—"

"I don't need the full history of the herb." Callum could practically feel Laena's life leeching away while they talked. "I need the *cure*."

Thaddeus rolled his eyes. "I gave you the same herbs for your hangover. But they won't help her if she's never had them. The books say—"

"It was her hangover," Callum interrupted. "Get them."

Thaddeus and Hawk shared a look. "Callum," Thaddeus said, "it's not as if we don't know your weakness. They could cause her more harm than good. You need to believe me."

As if he'd ever felt the need to hide his vices. Callum wanted to shake them until their teeth rattled. "By the mages, it *was*. Your general called her a whore, and she drank an entire city's worth of wine. Now are you going to help me, or am I going to have to make you?"

Alarm bells rang out as if in answer to his question. The bright noise cut through the silence of the monastery and vibrated the very walls around them. Mages, but they were loud. Callum supposed they would have to be, but still.

He repressed the urge to demand the herbs from Thaddeus and run. There was no time for interruptions. Laena had no time.

"The watchtowers," Thaddeus said.

Hawk was already at the door. Together, they ran, Hawk's

guards falling into step behind them as they rushed through the corridors, Callum still following in the hopes of procuring the herbs and running back to Laena. There could be an entire army waiting outside those gates, and Callum would fight his way through it. There was no *time*.

When they reached the courtyard, the watchman was just opening the gate to admit the newcomer. Not a threat, or so Callum hoped. Thaddeus should really let him come and train the poisonkeepers in proper security protocols.

The man who staggered into the courtyard was tall, with auburn hair and an unruly beard that looked as if it was usually kept neat. He braced himself upon the wall, his chest heaving with the effort of making his way up the hill.

"Regent Riennad," Hawk said, stepping forward to meet him as Thaddeus called for a cup of water. "What happened?"

Regent? No, it wasn't possible. An imposter, at best. Callum eased himself between the king and the newcomer, motioning the guards a step closer. "I left this man an hour's ride behind me," he said. "On the road."

The man was shaking his head, water dripping from his chin as he tried to catch his breath. He did look like Declan Riennad. The man was dirty, disheveled, and exhausted. But it was him.

"What happened?" Callum asked. "Where's Laena?"

"Laena," Declan repeated, shaking his head. "She's why I'm here. I have not seen her since she left Riles."

Callum wanted to lift the man off his feet until his feet dangled in the air. "You were just with the queen. I left her with you."

"No." Declan wiped the water away. He looked as if he was about to collapse. "A shadow only. A heart-tithe. I came here to warn you. The queen intends to kill her sister."

CHAPTER 29

*L*aena had not expected to open her eyes again.

The stars were fading when she did, their light still cool and bright even as dawn washed them from the sky, as if they wished they could use their light to soothe the pain that radiated from her core.

She'd seen Callum's face, the hardness in his eyes. He'd asked if she trusted him. The last thing she remembered was the feeling of his arms around her, the desperation to tell him... something. Where was he now? Her thoughts were slippery, her memory fogged. He would not have left her, surely.

Laena rolled over, retching bile into the grass, the soft blades brushing her cheek.

"That's it, sister. Take it slowly."

She startled as Katrina touched her shoulder with a gentleness that sent a surge of suspicion shuddering through her mind. Katrina was many things, but gentle had never been one of them.

Laena was trembling, her body aching as if one more spasm would heave the pain from her core. It took a monumental effort to slide her elbow under her body and work her muscles just enough to tilt herself at an angle so she could look up.

Katrina should not be here. It made no sense. And yet here she was, golden curls shining in the early-morning sun, a smile crinkling the skin around her mouth. As if Laena were the younger sister, and Katrina the indulgent elder.

Why did she not have an entourage, a guard of soldiers? And where was Declan?

Questions. So many questions, and only one that mattered. Laena coughed, and her throat spasmed in pain. "Where... where is he?"

Katrina sat on the grass in front of her, reaching forward to caress her cheek with the back of her hand. "*He,* dear sister, has abandoned you. Just like everyone else."

"He wouldn't."

Katrina stroked her cheek gently, the back of her nails skimming over Laena's skin. Her hand felt cool, though Laena suspected it was only in contrast to her own fevered heat. "And yet he did." Katrina might have been putting a child down to sleep, for the soothing, sing-song tone in her voice. "He was all too eager to leave you here on the side of the road. All too eager to leave you in my care."

"Because I told him I trusted you."

"What an egregious mistake."

Laena's head was spinning. Her thoughts tumbled around as her fevered mind tried to put the pieces together.

Katrina's nails bit into Laena's skin, sharp and stinging. Before Laena could pull away, Kat dug her fingertips deeper into the flesh of her cheek and dragged them down, drawing rivulets of blood down her face.

Laena scrambled back, pushing herself away from her sister and farther into the road. "What the demons was that?"

"They don't like that term, you know." Katrina was examining the blood on her fingertips. "They find it offensive."

Laena squeezed her eyes shut, raising a hand to her stinging cheek. *Who* found it offensive?

But she knew, didn't she? She already knew.

Katrina stood, brushing invisible dirt from her skirts before waltzing over to where Laena lay. Even the simple act of pushing away from her had cost Laena what little energy she had left; she was panting, every breath like a stab to her chest as the inferno continued to crackle within her core. There was still a spark of cold there, like the last spot of frost before the spring. But it would not last long. She could feel it dying.

She didn't know what would happen when it failed.

Kat reached down and took her wrist, and Laena felt something crack as she squeezed, the bones caving to her unnatural strength.

And through the cloying scent of lilies, Laena caught the rank burn of a heart-tithe.

"It's simple, Laena," Kat said. "The mages will return. When they do, they will allow me to keep my throne."

"How?" Laena choked.

"I kill you, and I kill Hawk. Clearing the way for them." She said it like it was just another item on her to-do list. Visit the seamstress. Select new wallpaper. Meet with the council. Kill Laena and Hawk.

"And what of Silerith?"

It might have been her imagination, but she thought Kat's expression darkened. "Silerith is none of *my* concern. My powers will be unmatched, enough to open the barrier. What do I care about Silerith?"

Clearly, she did care.

But the mages could have asked this of anyone; it needn't have been a queen. And Laena? Laena was nothing. Less than nothing. Why unearth her from her life in the middle of nowhere? Why drag her back when she had already been dealt with?

Callum had been right to ask it. He had been right about everything.

Katrina released her arm, dropping her into the dirt. Pain lanced through her as she caught herself with her injured side, and Katrina smiled, drinking in the power of Laena's pain. More pain meant more power, and Kat clearly intended to draw this out.

But Laena was not without her own power.

Digging deep, she scraped the bottom of her reserves, reaching for that final spark of frost, for the last dregs of her power. Bile rose in her throat, thick and hot, as she threw a blast of cold air in her sister's face.

The world flickered, white-hot pain coiling deeper into her, pushing out through her arms, her legs. She was made of pain; it was all there was.

Katrina raised a hand, catching a snowflake on one fingertip and examining it like it was something to be dissected. Something to be used. "You know, I *had* wondered. They seem singularly concerned with your demise. They had me plant the blight in your garden. I suppose that this"—she gestured to the pitiful flurry of snowflakes—"would explain why. They don't like magic that isn't their own."

Kat had allowed the assassins in; she'd attempted to kill them at sea. Had she been waiting there, watching? Ready to scoop them out of the water so she could be the one to end Laena herself? No doubt this was why she had charged Milla with kidnapping Laena, rather than ending her right there in the woods.

Katrina needed the tithe, the sacrifice to the mages.

Laena reached for her magic again, but this time it slid away from her, as if reluctant to poison her with more heat. She was burning from the inside out, sweat trickling down her back, along her hairline.

Kat knelt before her and produced a dagger from within her

sleeve, sliding the blade out like an extension of herself. "Contrary to what you may believe, I *do* love you. It's just that I love power more."

There wasn't much time. Heartbeats only. But Laena would be damned if she was the reason for the mages' return.

Calling on the last reserves of strength her body could offer, Laena launched herself at Kat, surprising her sister enough to wrest the dagger from Kat's hands.

Instead of slashing at Katrina, Laena turned the blade on herself.

Katrina screamed in rage, leaping toward her. But as the blade bit into Laena's neck, she knew she could be content with the fact that her sister would be too late to claim Laena's death as her own.

A body slammed into her from the side, spilling her into the dirt and knocking the knife out of her hands.

"Not yet, my lady." Callum's voice was soft in her ear, the promise of it making her want to weep with relief. "We still have a world to save."

CHAPTER 30

*C*allum had no wish to leave Laena lying on the ground. She was fighting off unconsciousness, blinking rapidly. Bloody scratches marked her cheek, along with an angry scratch across her neck where she'd nearly just slashed the knife into her own flesh to save them all. She was cradling her left wrist against her other arm. He wanted to hold her forever. Lift her into his arms, soothe her pain, and carry her away to safety.

He pushed to his feet reluctantly. Katrina's surprise at their arrival would only last so long.

As Thaddeus knelt beside Laena, Callum forced himself to turn away, keeping his body angled in front of hers. This fight was not over yet. He had no illusions that he could best a heart-tither by himself. But he would damn well try—at least for long enough to distract her until Hawk revealed himself.

Katrina was standing with her hands balled at her sides, like a child preparing to throw a tantrum. "You think I cannot face you all? Because I can."

Dirt swirled around her, forming into a pair of cyclones. The wind whipped her golden curls around her face, and she tipped her head back, basking in the power that was forged through the pain and sacrifice of those she claimed to love.

"Katrina. You need to stop."

At the sound of Declan's voice, the cyclones stilled. They did not crumble; they merely stopped, hovering above the dirt, the wind calming. Katrina tipped her head back down, eyes widening. "Declan," she breathed. "You're alive."

Callum didn't know what had happened to make her think otherwise. Declan claimed she had imprisoned him. Had she left him for dead? Did she care enough for him that his pain would feed her own power? She cared for something in this world; that was evident enough. He knew enough of heart-tithing to know that a few scratches on her sister's cheek and a broken wrist would not be enough to breed the kind of power she now wielded.

The regent came forward, approaching Katrina with a courage Callum would not have expected of the man. When he held out his hands, she accepted them, and he pulled her toward him until their bodies were flush against one another. He lowered his lips to hers, pulling her into an embrace.

Behind Callum, Laena made a sound of disgust. He could only hope that meant Thaddeus's herbs were helping.

Katrina opened her eyes and drew back, placing her hands on Declan's cheeks. "How did you find me?"

For a moment, Callum thought the regent had brought them here only to betray them. That he would join Katrina with power of his own. That he would tell her their secrets, warn her that Hawk waited out of sight to see if Declan could sway her with words. That it was over.

Declan leaned his forehead against Katrina's and whispered, "You can stop now. You have what you need."

Katrina melted against him, pressing her lips to his once more. "Oh, Declan," she said. "I don't think you've ever been more right."

And then Declan slumped against her, a trickle of blood leaking from his mouth as Katrina eased him to the ground, tears in her eyes. She kept one hand on his chest, right beside the dagger she'd plunged into the regent's heart. She gathered the fading man into her arms with a gentleness that was both surprising and horrifying.

For a moment she knelt there, her head bent over her lover's body, her palm pressed against his chest.

And then the dirt began to stir.

Lightning cracked down from the sky, splitting the nearest tree in half. The trunk ignited with a crackle, the wind picking up until sparks whipped into the grass. A line of fire howled out across the ground behind her, wreathing her silhouette in flame.

"I didn't want to kill him," Katrina said, her voice amplified despite the howling wind. "I wanted to kill Laena. But stepping stones work just as well. I *will* have my throne."

The queen strode forward, the childlike mask vanished behind a wall of pure rage. "Stand up and face me, sister. Show me why the mages fear your magic so very much."

Jealousy, Callum realized. Katrina's voice was thick with it, the derision in her tone failing to conceal how much she wanted to be the one with the power. She wanted to be the one with Vales magic.

Perhaps that was why she wasn't.

Laena began to rise, but Thaddeus placed a hand on her arm. "The herbs can only do so much."

Laena nodded, shaking him off gently. Callum moved to stand beside her, to close the gap that had widened as he'd attempted to follow Katrina's movements. But a crack of lightning split the road before him, knocking him back and leaving him half blind as he fell into the dirt.

He'd so rarely encountered a fight he could not win, or at least attempt. But this fight, this was made of magic. He didn't think there was anything he could do to prevent it from consuming them all.

When he looked up, Laena was on her feet.

He'd seen her take down an army of humans and shadow monsters, not a day ago. He'd seen the power emanating from her as she'd taken control, the fresh air of her magic wielded to protect those she cared about, rather than to destroy them.

Now, tears leaked down her cheeks, the effort a strain. How could the magic she wielded with such ferocity... how could it be hurting her?

Callum looked to Thaddeus. "Help her," he said.

But the poisonkeeper only shook his head. This fight was beyond him.

A blast of cold air stirred his hair as Laena raised her shaking hands, unleashing a column of ice and coiling frost at her sister. But Kat's power met hers in midair, shadows unfurling to meet Laena's magic—near-depleted magic, if her shuddering shoulders and rapidly whitening skin were any indication. Kat bared her teeth, and tendrils of shadow carved into Laena's ice, digging black-veined paths toward her heart, until there was no longer a way to tell where Laena's power ended and Kat's began.

There wasn't a damned thing Callum could do about it.

And then, fire.

A wall of fire joined Laena's ice. It should have been impossible, entirely impossible. But instead of melting it, instead of defeating it, the fire melded with her power until it formed a swirling band of ice and fire.

King Hawk strode out of the smoke like a golden hero, hands cupped together in front of his chest, his eyes flashing as he moved to stand beside Laena. They'd planned for him to reveal himself at the last moment, though Callum felt strongly that the king had taken that definition a step farther than he'd have preferred.

Power emanated from the king, and Laena seemed to feed off it, her power strengthening as Hawk fed it.

Together, they forced Katrina back a step.

Sweat poured from Laena's brow, her face contorted in pain. Hawk might be fresh, but she had fought off an army mere hours ago. She was determined, but she was also pale. So pale—like Hawk's paper-thin complexion at Inasvale—that he feared she would collapse once again.

And that when she did, there would be no saving her.

They needed to end this. Now.

With Katrina distracted by the storm of magic, Callum drew his sword. He plunged forward, pushing against the tide of dirt, the heat of the lightning-induced fire that still burned at Katrina's back.

Katrina saw him coming at the last second, sidestepping just in time to avoid the lethal blow he'd intended.

He plunged his sword into her side.

With one last scream of despair, Katrina whipped the dirt into a cyclone, pulling it around herself like a shield and a cloak.

When the dirt settled, the queen was gone.

CHAPTER 31

*L*aena's throat was sore.

Consciousness came and went, but that one fact stayed with her: her throat was sore. And her cheek, her wrist, and, for some reason, the base of her spine.

None of it compared to the pain below her ribs. Not just pain, not just the emptiness of depleting her reserves, which she'd felt before... but a sense of wrongness. Darkness.

It frightened her.

When she finally managed to open her eyes for more than a few heartbeats, she could see from the view that they had made it to Vunmore after all. She may never have visited the city herself, but she recognized the ancient stone towers that rose up around her window, the cone-like mountain that rose in the background like a permanent reminder that the mages had owned this city once. That they might well own it again.

Callum Farrow was asleep in a chair by her bedside, his cheek propped on his knuckles. Even in his sleep, he looked worried, that little crinkle marring the space between his eyebrows.

And she couldn't help it; she reached forward and brushed

her fingertip against it. As though she could smooth it away with a touch.

He opened his eyes. "You are meant to be resting."

"Indeed, touching your face is a terrible exertion. I do not know how I'll ever manage the strain."

He sat up, and when she dropped her hand, he caught it between his. "Laena," he said. He looked so serious she wondered if he was going to report someone's death. Someone other than Declan, whose dying breaths still rattled in her ears like a curse.

"Hawk," Callum said. "He has magic."

Laena sat back in the bed, releasing his hand. That was it? As if she would not have noticed the king throwing fireballs at her sister. The king's fire had melded with her ice, in fact. She didn't think she would have been able to call forth any ice at all, any magic, had he not joined his power with hers. His reserves had answered hers, balanced it. Responded to her need.

"Yes," she said. "I do recall King Hawk's magic."

He scrubbed his hand over his face, wincing. Mages, but he looked tired. She wondered how much he'd slept reaching the city. "I wasn't sure how much you would remember."

She pursed her lips, attempting to paint her expression with disapproval. It wasn't easy, considering she wanted to beam at him, throw her arms around him. He was alive. She could have wept with joy.

Still, she could at least attempt it. "I remember trying to *tell* you that Hawk had magic. Before the attack on the camp."

She also remembered implying that she suspected him of treachery, when her own sister had been to blame.

"No, no." Callum shook his head. "Your memory is definitely faulty. I don't recall that at all."

The man had the audacity to *smile* at her.

"So," Laena said. "Are we arrested? Hawk and I?"

"No, my lady. You are free to go. If you wish it."

Go. Go where? To save Etra, but how? The idea of Katrina returning there to wreak havoc on the place she claimed to love... What destruction could she bring if she loved it as much as she said she did?

The look in Katrina's eyes as she'd bent down to kill Laena... she didn't think she would ever forget it. How could a heart-tithe work, truly? If you loved someone enough to gain power from their pain, how could you ever want power enough to kill them? It was a dilemma that could not be solved. Maybe that was why it could produce such destructive power.

She'd watched Kat kill Declan with her own hands.

Perhaps Callum was right. Perhaps all magic was evil. At the thought, a new darkness in her core writhed, as if awakening for the first time. Hungry.

He met her eyes more seriously now. "Hawk and Thaddeus have been studying magic. Apparently for just over two years now, ever since Hawk's magic began to show itself. They can help you."

Laena looked at her hands, focusing on the feel of the blankets beneath her fingers. She felt no coolness within her core. Despite Hawk's intervention, she was nothing but hollow. "I'm not sure I still have any magic."

"According to Thad, Vales magic feeds on itself. There's still a price, Laena. It just... comes from you. Instead of from some unwitting victim you supposedly love."

That didn't sound like it was much better.

"Maybe I burned it out of me," Laena said. Maybe that was the reason for the dark feeling, the tingle that prickled her spine. Her body wasn't searing with pain any longer, but her abdomen still felt sore. When she dared to prod at the space beneath her ribcage, where the magic lived, there was no ice. No cold. No power. Only tender pain, and that thrumming sense of darkness.

"Thaddeus doesn't think so."

Thaddeus, it turned out, knew a great deal more than Laena would have guessed. Who would have anticipated that a poison-keeper, a protector of the Vales, would know so much about magic?

Of course, the monks were nothing if not secretive. It was not beyond the realm of imagination that they all knew, that they protected this knowledge along with the barrier. Somehow, though, she suspected that Thaddeus had proceeded beyond the expectations, and perhaps even the wishes, of his master.

"Why us?" Laena asked. "Hawk and me, I mean. Why gift us with magic?"

Callum blew out a breath. "Well, he's got a theory about that, too. He's got a theory about everything. But you're not going to like it."

She waited. He knew he could not keep it from her; he knew she would want to know.

"You'd have to ask him for the specifics," he said, after a moment. "But it amounts to the idea that the magic of the Vales has been dormant since the mages left. And that it's now responding to a coming threat by arming its rightful heirs."

Laena frowned, trying to understand. "But the Vales were united under the mages."

He lifted his shoulder, as if it made little sense to him. "Hawk is heir to the Aglyean throne. You're heir to the Etran. I don't want to make assumptions, but I suppose we can deduce that the Ruthless King also has some magic in his line. Perhaps that's why Silerith is more lenient toward it."

But she wasn't heir to the Etran throne. Not anymore. A wave of nausea washed over her, thick and tinged with guilt. Thaddeus thought the Vales had chosen her, gifted her with power. While Hawk had embraced his, Laena had abandoned her people.

She'd doubted herself for years, worrying that her secret

store of magic was somehow as evil as the heart-tithes that criminals performed in the dark. Criminals and queens, apparently.

Now that she knew for certain that her magic had never been a threat to Etra, or the rest of the Vales, by abdicating her throne, she'd put them all in danger.

She couldn't guess what Katrina would do next. But certainly, she would do everything possible to increase her powers and finish her task: she would return the mages to the Vales and rule alongside them. Assuming they had not poisoned her with treacherous lies.

She sat on the throne because of Laena.

If the Vales had gifted her with magic because it considered her one of its heirs, and if she had answered that call by giving her throne to someone else, then there was one solution she could not ignore. The thought stuck in her throat, and she reached for the cup of water at her bedside, wishing she could wash it away. Wishing she hadn't yet woken. Wishing that the void in her core felt less like a poison—less like a danger that she would need another power to balance. And keep in check.

Her choices had brought her here. And if she wanted to save Etra, she knew what she would need to do. It might have been the magic, but she had the feeling—she knew, without knowing how—that King Hawk very likely knew it, too.

There was a knock at the door, and Thaddeus stuck his head in. "You're awake. Good. The king would like to see you."

CHAPTER 32

*U*nmore was a city of balconies and bridges, of stone carved like lacework. Positioned at the base of a dormant volcano and the meeting point of two rivers—or their fork, depending on which direction you chose to face—it almost felt as if the city had to be this beautiful to compete with its natural surroundings.

It had been the city of the mages long ago, their headquarters. Callum forgot that, sometimes.

Laena walked beside him in silence, her thoughts clearly elsewhere, and annoyance rippled through him. Hawk might have given her another day or two before summoning her like this. She'd nearly died. Even now, Callum could not stop darting glances at her, to make sure she was well.

"I'm fine, Captain," Laena said, offering him the hint of a smile, though she did it without looking his way. She was entirely focused on the corridor ahead of them, and the grotesquely large double doors that awaited them at the end. Hawk might have met them in the library or the study, but he'd insisted on the formality of the throne room.

Laena might be walking and breathing and smiling—sort of—

but she still didn't seem fine. He couldn't quite put a finger on the reason for his unease. She seemed almost careful, as if she wasn't sure whether her legs would support her next step. And no wonder; she must still be feeling weak, after all she had endured.

Their conversation had started out as normal, teasing. Even affectionate. Enough to make him hope for a renewal of what had started between them at the camp.

He was a fool. It had started the moment he laid eyes on her in Riles.

But since leaving the room, she'd been acting as if she knew something he didn't. She was concerned about the state of her magic, whether it had burned out. But he feared there was something more, something she wasn't telling him. Was Thaddeus's cure working? Or was she still in pain?

As they reached the doors, he could take it no longer. He stepped in front of her, taking her hands and drawing her toward a nearby window alcove. Stained glass painted the stone with abstract ripples of red and blue light. The shape of the window appeared elongated as the late afternoon sun passed.

Laena was looking at him with a question in her green eyes, her brow furrowed ever so slightly. Her curls were bound in a plait, though more than a few tendrils refused to be restrained. They floated around her face, brushing at the bandage on her cheek as if to assure themselves that she was safe.

"I must know if you are well," he said.

Laena met his gaze steadily, raising a hand to his cheek. "I'm well." She gave him a pat, gentle. *And sad*, he thought. "Or I will be, if you'll agree to stop fussing."

He bent over her, pressing his lips to hers. "I will not." He dragged his lips along her jaw. She tipped her head back, gasping as he nipped at her ear. He wanted nothing more than to take her back to her room, to delay this meeting another night.

Demons. He'd need more than a night. He needed all of them.

But the king was waiting. And Laena knew it, too. As he stepped back, she made a noble attempt to return his smile.

She drew in a breath, lifted a shaking hand to pat her hair. He wanted to free it from that restrictive plait, feel those silky curly against his hands, his chest.

"Callum," she said. "I think—"

The enormous doors opened, and a pair of guards stepped out of the throne room. "His Majesty is ready for you," the first one said.

If the man noticed Laena's flushed cheeks, or Callum's glare, he didn't let on. These were Hawk's personal guards; they knew how to be discreet.

Though they would very likely report whatever they'd seen to Hawk. It was likely nothing he didn't already know, after their activities at the camp—tent walls were hardly known to be soundproof—though the attack might have pushed the information out of his informants' minds. At least briefly.

What did it matter, if the king knew? If he could, if Laena would allow it, Callum would tell the world.

Callum gestured for her to enter ahead of him. She patted her hair one more time, then tipped her chin in the air and strode into the throne room. He could have cheered at those purposeful strides, the power in every step as she made her way toward the front of the room. Her skirts swished around her ankles, her footsteps sure and strong.

It was a ridiculously long walk. And she didn't look down once.

Hawk wasn't seated on the throne. As was often his custom when he met Callum and Thaddeus here—when he had done, during his father's reign—he'd seated himself on the bottom step of the dais, his hands propped behind him, his legs stretched out. Slanted stripes of sunlight fell across him, illuminating his hair with patches of molten gold.

And Callum suddenly understood his reason for meeting them here in the throne room rather than his library or a parlor or any of the other hundreds of appropriate rooms in this palace. He was making a point of meeting Callum as he once had, ushering his once-disgraced captain back into his trust. He was meeting Laena as an equal.

The thought should have been relieving. Instead, it only added to his sense of unease.

When Laena reached the front of the room, she did not curtsy. She merely faced Hawk, her hands relaxed at her sides, and met his gaze head on.

"I apologize for my sister's actions," she said. "I was unaware of her... loyalties."

Loyalties to the *mages*. Making deals with them, feeding their hunger to return. Answering it with a wretched hunger of her own. Callum wanted to curse their names, but it suddenly felt like he'd only be calling them. Taunting them.

He was going to need to find some new expletives.

Hawk actually laughed. "There is no need to apologize, Princess Laena. I certainly hope I am not to be held accountable for the actions of those who call me family. And I should not hold you accountable for the actions of yours."

Callum didn't know if he was meant to be included among that number. Hawk's gaze didn't flicker toward him. He might have been speaking of Thaddeus, or even Emilia. He and Callum had never been brothers by blood, after all.

And yet, he might have met with Laena alone.

"Nevertheless," Laena said. "I am bound to offer my apologies. And my service."

Aglye would be lucky to have it. Would Silerith join them in unseating Katrina from her stolen throne? Would the Ruthless King emerge from his hermitage to stand against the rise of the mages? Or would the country remain neutral, even rise against them, as the mages staged their return?

Hawk tilted his head, regarding her with open concern. And no small amount of curiosity, Callum thought. As if he planned to catalog every move she made, every response she gave. "I hope you are much recovered from your illness."

If the change in subject surprised her, she gave no indication. "Indeed, Your Majesty."

"I'm given to understand," he said slowly, "that you are willing to overlook certain knowledge you now have about me."

Laena met his gaze, unflinching. "I do not see any reason to overlook it. I suggest we might choose to embrace it."

Callum nodded, as if the statement had been a test. One that Laena had passed.

"A noble suggestion, Princess. I hope it is not too much to hope that our people will also choose to embrace the power."

"If introduced to it carefully, and by stages, I see no reason to think otherwise," she replied.

Callum had the sense, as he had at the magepool, that there was something happening below the surface of the conversation. Some hidden meaning he could not quite grasp. Some part of him screamed that he did not want to, that he should stay in ignorance as long as he could.

That would do nothing to help Laena, or anyone else.

He stepped forward. "We need..." He cleared his throat. "I hope, Your Majesty, that we may find a way to help Etra."

Hawk studied Callum for a long moment. And then he rose, closing the space between them in two long strides to stand before Laena. He offered her his hands.

She accepted them. Callum's gaze fell on their joined hands. A show of friendship. A show of support.

"We do need to help Etra," Hawk agreed, directing his response to Laena even though the statement had been

Callum's. "As we need to help all the Vales. Which is why I would like to ask for your hand in marriage. Officially."

The room tilted. There was no way he could have heard that correctly.

"That's ridiculous." The words left his mouth before he even knew he'd thought them.

When Laena turned to face him, he could see her response in her eyes, and the answer to why she'd been so quiet during the walk over here.

"It's not that ridiculous," she said.

It felt like the floor was dropping out from beneath his feet, like everything he'd hoped for was being ripped away. She didn't want this. She *couldn't*.

"I suppose Katrina wouldn't have had it in mind, not truly," Hawk said. "But I did. I believe she baited me. Perhaps I would have seen it, if I was not so intent on finding a wife before everyone learned of my magic."

Callum shook his head. His thoughts felt thick, his mind foggy as he fought to contemplate what this meant. What this could possibly mean.

"The king with forbidden magic marries the disgraced princess who can't complain," Laena said. "Do I have that right, Your Majesty?"

She was asking Hawk, but she was looking at Callum. He knew what it meant for her to be forced to say it out loud. Someone less bold would have avoided the truth, would have let Hawk tell her a pretty lie without protesting. But not Laena. Never Laena.

Hawk had the grace to look ashamed, his cheeks reddening. "Happily, it turns out we both have magic," he said, neatly side-stepping the admission. "Undeniably complementary magic. Combined, we can face Queen Katrina. We can stop the mages from returning."

Callum couldn't believe what he was hearing. What they

were both saying, as if they were already a united front. Just as they had been during that fight, their magic blending together so effortlessly.

But she couldn't marry Hawk. Not with the memory of her lips against his seared into his mind, the feel of her hips shifting beneath him, her hands on his body. Not when her laugh echoed in his ears, her teasing, her pain. Her power.

And she felt it, too. By the blazing demon mages, he *knew* that she did.

"You can face her without *marrying*," Callum said. Surely they could. It was just magic, just an alliance. It should not necessitate them binding themselves to one another.

Laena pressed her lips together until they went white with the effort. He thought she might be trying not to cry. "But I do not think we can," she whispered. "The Vales chose us to lead."

And she felt an obligation, once more, to a crown she'd set aside. Not for her own sake, but for someone else's.

Callum shook his head. She was not going to do this. She couldn't sacrifice herself this way.

Laena blinked once, as if clearing the tears from her eyes, then turned back to Hawk. "I accept your proposal," she said. "I'll marry you."

CHAPTER 33

*L*aena practically fled into the hall, leaving Hawk behind to make his wedding plans. She didn't know what story he planned to tell his people, how he'd explain away her history with Ben. She didn't even know how the king would have learned of Ben's faithlessness. Katrina, most likely. He did say she'd been baiting him.

It was a good thing, truly. She could leave the details to the king, to his ready smile, his easy charm. He would work out what to tell his people about the foreign queen, and what had become of her famed lover. Perhaps he'd even tell some portion of the truth. A novel thought, indeed.

And with any luck, Hawk would rope Callum into staying behind to listen to him scheme until she'd had a chance to escape.

"Laena."

His voice scraped through the empty corridor, digging a jab into her gut. No, she couldn't expect Callum to allow her to flee in peace. There was nothing in his nature that gave up without a fight.

She would have felt his presence even had he not called out to her, even had she not recognized the firm confidence of his gait. She'd have felt the prickle of his presence. The depth of his dismay.

It wasn't fair—he deserved an explanation—yet she quickened her pace, as if she could hope to escape facing him. Or put it off, at the very least. But he fell easily into step beside her, his pace measured where she was practically running, her skirts twisting a frenzy around her legs.

"What the *hell* was that?" Callum's voice was a rasp, with an unmistakable edge of anger, and it resonated in the empty hall. "You'll marry him? Truly?"

He wanted her to stop walking. She could feel it in the way he lagged behind her by a step, the way he curled his fingers toward his palms as if to stop himself from reaching out to her. He'd saved her, in so many ways. And now she was betraying him.

"I failed Etra." She didn't quite mean to admit it, hadn't intended to say the words out loud. But with Callum, she was finished pretending. She owed him that much, and more. Far more. "I gave up my crown and I left my people. And look at the result."

"Laena."

"And now there's a path." She'd begun speaking, so she might as well barrel on. Might as well spill the whole truth before it poisoned her from within. "There's a path for me to make it right, to fix what I ruined. I have to take it."

She couldn't allow her determination to falter. She wouldn't. She cared for him, truly she did. But abandoned or not, the weight of the crown remained heavy on her brow, on her conscience. There was no room for mistakes when she carried such dire responsibility upon her shoulders. She'd been a fool to ever think otherwise.

Callum did reach for her now, fingers closing around her elbow and forcing her to slow. She might have pulled away—she knew him well enough to know that he would let her go—but she couldn't quite bring herself to sacrifice this last touch, this last moment with him.

The hallway was deserted, with no one to see, though she knew well what hidden eyes a palace could hold. Anyone could be watching, from a shadowed alcove or a lofted perch.

And Callum knew it, too. He guided her toward the nearest door, one of several that dotted the corridor, now that she noticed them. She'd have walked by without seeing it at all, which she supposed was the point of the gray paint.

The door opened into a simple sitting room, with a liquor cabinet pushed against one wall, a cold hearth on the other. The only other furniture in the room was a round table with two wooden chairs, and a scrap of a rug by the entrance. Laena wondered what Hawk could possibly use a room like this for. Refreshments for the nobility who attended long presentations in the throne room? It hardly seemed large enough, or impressive enough.

Callum shut the door behind them. He was still holding her elbow, his fingers a gentle pressure through the fabric of her dress. "It's a guards' room," he said, noting her confusion. "For meals and breaks."

That made sense... mostly. She glanced at the liquor cabinet, a question on her lips, and he grimaced. "I am, occasionally, one of the guards."

Ah. She licked her lips, her chest tight as she forced herself to look up, to meet his gaze. Whatever he wanted to say to her, she would listen. He deserved that much.

"You *shouldn't* have given up your crown," he said quietly. "On that, we can agree."

Of all the charges he might have leveled at her, that wasn't the one she'd imagined. From their very first meeting, he'd shown so little inclination to judge her. Had he always felt this way about her abdication? Or had he realized it during the battle with Katrina, when he'd seen how terrible her power had become? How dearly Laena's abandonment was going to cost her country?

But Callum wasn't finished. He held to her arm like a lifeline. "Marrying Hawk won't make it right. Embracing your power, embracing what it is that *you* want, that's how you'll save your people, Laena. By first saving yourself. And then by taking your *own* damn crown back."

Because he had so much experience in such matters. She hadn't thought him so naive. "A pretty sentiment."

"A true one."

She flung her free hand to the side, as if she might use it to point into the past and force him to see. To understand. "Putting myself first is what led to this disaster to begin with."

He moved closer, releasing her elbow only to let his hand trail up her arm, his stormy eyes trained on her face. "Certainly," he said, his tone bitter. "But only if you buy into the story they tell about you. The story Katrina tells about how you gave up your crown to fuck some stablehand—"

"Fuck you." Anger spiked through the cracks of her resolve, quick and hot, his crassness erasing any hesitation she might have felt in letting it show. She might have slapped him across the face, but it felt like she'd been frozen in place. Like a victim of her own power.

His fingertips reached her collarbone, his touch dragging electric sensation along the swooped collar of her gown and up, up, until he cradled the side of her neck, his thumb tracing light circles on her throat. "You are running away. Again."

Her breaths were coming too fast for rational thought. She couldn't stop herself from leaning into his touch. Every thought, every nerve, was obsessed with the slow circles of his thumb. Of where they might descend next. "I suppose you claim to have no stake in the choice," she breathed.

He dipped his chin toward her. "I claim no such thing." His breath was hot on her lips, voice rough in her ear as he backed her toward the wall. He crushed her against it, a soft rumble in the back of his throat as he pressed his body to hers. "I am in ruins, my lady."

Ruins.

His mouth was on hers before she could gasp, before she could decide whether she had the strength to protest. Even had she wanted to, her body betrayed her, returning his kiss with a vigor that she could not repress. He tasted of whiskey and woodsmoke, enveloping her in the scent of leather, and she could not stop her lips from parting in response to him, allowing him to taste her, her tongue tangling with his as he pushed further into her mouth.

She clutched the back of his neck, sucking his bottom lip into her mouth and reveling in his answering moan.

"You will martyr yourself, and me with you." His voice was husky, edged with need, his lips on her neck, hands in her hair. The dress was still between them, and his jacket, his shirt, his pants. But the way he pressed against her, the intimacy of it as he dragged his body along her every curve, they might as well have been skin to skin. "I don't want to let you do it."

Laena let her head fall back. "It's not up to you," she said.

He stilled, as if her words had broken some spell, his lips still grazing her throat. "You're right. It isn't." His voice was a rumble against her skin, resonating all the way to her bones. "But your power matters. Your *desires* matter. You needn't run from them to save the world."

She wanted him to be right. She wanted this to last forever.

But he wasn't. It *couldn't*.

"To save Etra from Kat?" She had to choke out the words. They sounded too near to a sob. "From the mages? I have no choice."

Not with her power still drained. Not with that strange new darkness coiling in her gut. She owed Callum her life, it was true, but that life belonged to Etra. She'd been a fool to forget that.

There was no other answer she could possibly give, and Callum seemed to know it. Without preamble, he broke their embrace. She wanted to weep with the loss of him.

He backed away from her, still breathing hard, hands raised as if in surrender. "Then I wish you all the best, my lady."

He didn't turn away until he reached the door, where he finally broke their gaze. In a single, easy movement, he swiped a bottle of whiskey from the top of the liquor cabinet and slipped out of the room.

The door shut behind him with a final click, leaving her to the silence.

THE END

—*—

Keep reading with the epic conclusion to Laena and Callum's story: *Winter's Power (Poisoned Kingdoms #2)*.

Available Now!

A queen's forbidden magic. A captain's impossible choice. A realm on the brink of destruction.

Laena's winter magic is killing her from the inside out, but it may be the only thing standing between her people and total annihilation. When her sister's thirst for power unleashes ancient enemies back into the world, Laena must choose between a political marriage that could save her kingdom and the love that could destroy it.

—✳—

Want to read that final scene from Callum's point of view? Sign up for my newsletter to grab it now!

Join now: https://ameliamacleod.com/winters-fate-bonus-scene/

Thank you for reading!

——*——

ABOUT THE AUTHOR

Amelia MacLeod lives in Upstate New York, where she spends a lot of time wandering around in the woods and chatting with the trees. (They rarely chat back.)

She love bonfires and ghost stories and all kinds of wild things -- from the cardinal who taps on her window every morning to the bats who swoop overhead at dusk, snapping up mosquitos for supper.

(She doesn't much care for the mosquitos.)

She also loves stickers. And tiaras. And hot chocolate piled with marshmallows.

Amelia writes stories where love conquers all, where characters unlock their true power by choosing love over whatever has been holding them back -- and where that love is stronger than the lies they've been telling themselves.

WINTER'S FATE

Extras

GLOSSARY - WF

PEOPLE, PLACES, AND THINGS

Aglye (AG-lie): One of two mainland kingdoms; led by King Hawk.

Brin: Laena's shimmerling companion. (See also: *shimmerlings*.)

Callum Farrow: Famed magic hunter from Aglye. Formerly the Captain of the King's Guard.

Declan Riennad: Regent of Etra; assists in running the country until the queen comes of age.

Etra (EH-trah): A small island nation that takes pride in its long line of queens.

Hawk: King of Aglye.

Heart-tithe: A brand of magic requiring the pain of a loved one to access remnants of the mages' power.

Inasvale: A city in Aglye where the poisonkeepers' monastery is located. (See also: *poisonkeepers*)

Katrina Montrose-Aboret: Sister to Laena and heir to the throne of Etra following Laena's abdication.

Laena Felicia Montrose-Aboret: Former heir to the throne, she abdicated five years ago, supposedly because she loved a commoner. In truth, she left out of fear of her forbidden magical abilities.

Landon Moore: Newly promoted to Aglyean general.

Mages: Banished to the Miragelands after years of controlling humans in the Vales.

Magnus: the late King of Aglye; Hawk's father.

Miragelands: The home world of the mages. After ruling over the people of the Vales for hundreds of years, the corrupt mages were banished back to their native world, known as the Miragelands.

Poisonkeepers: An order of monks charged with guarding the passage between the Vales and the Miragelands.

Riles (rih-LESS): The capital city of Etra.

Shimmerlings: Rare, newt-like creatures with magical properties. Legends say their bones were used to were

used to control humans during the time of the mages —
and that they helped liberate the realms.

Silerith (sih-LER-ehth): The secretive country that
shares the mainland with Aglye. Known to be lenient
toward magic users, they are ruled by an elusive king;
most refer to him as the Ruthless King.

Sunflower Cottage: Laena's home after abdicating the
throne.

Thaddeus: King Hawk's younger brother and a prince of
Aglye, he took orders as a poisonkeeper and lives at the
monastery in Inasvale. (See also: poisonkeeper, Inasvale.)

The Vales: Common terminology for the combined
realms of Aglye, Etra, and Silerith.

Vunmore: The capital city of Aglye.

—*—

BOOK CLUB DISCUSSION QUESTIONS

1. Throughout the novel, we see different types of magic: Laena's ice magic, Katrina's heart-tithe, and Hawk's fire magic. How do these different forms of magic reflect the characters wielding them? What might the source and nature of each type of magic say about power and sacrifice?

2. Laena abdicated her throne partly to protect her kingdom from her magic, which she feared. How does her journey from fear to acceptance of her powers parallel her journey as a leader? What role does self-doubt play in both aspects?

3. The story features multiple sibling relationships (Laena and Katrina, Hawk and Thaddeus). How do these relationships differ? What drives the loyalty or betrayal between each pair?

4. Consider the various forms of love presented in the novel: romantic love, familial love, love of country. How do characters navigate conflicts between these different types of love? What sacrifices do they make in service of each?

5. Duty and personal desire come into conflict throughout the story. How do different characters handle this tension? What does the story suggest about the relationship between individual happiness and responsibility to others?

6. The novel explores themes of betrayal through several characters. Compare how Katrina betrays Laena, how Ben abandons her, and how these betrayals shape her ability to trust others. What role does betrayal play in shaping the story's events?

7. How does power - both magical and political - corrupt or reveal characters' true natures? Consider Katrina's path to villainy versus Laena's and Hawk's approaches to their own magical abilities.

8. What role do secrets play in driving the plot? Consider how different characters' hidden truths (about magic, loyalty, feelings) impact their relationships and choices.

If you'd like to invite Amelia to attend a zoom session with your book club, contact:
admin@ameliamacleod.com

THE ICE
Queen
~Cocktail Version~

- 1.5 OZ VANILLA VODKA
- 1 OZ WHITE CRÈME DE CACAO
- 0.5 OZ BLUE CURAÇAO
- 1 OZ HEAVY CREAM

✦

Combine ingredients in a shaker with ice. Shake vigorously and strain into a sugar-rimmed coupe glass. Dust with edible pearl powder.

✦

For a mocktail version, turn the page!

THE ICE
Queen
~*Mocktail Version*~

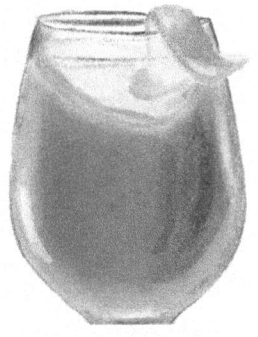

- 1 OZ VANILLA SYRUP
- 1 OZ WHITE CHOCOLATE SYRUP
- 0.5 OZ BLUE BUTTERFLY PEA FLOWER TEA
- 2 OZ COCONUT CREAM
- SODA WATER TO TOP

✦

Combine ingredients in a shaker with ice. Shake vigorously and strain into a sugar-rimmed coupe glass. Dust with edible pearl powder.

The butterfly pea flower tea provides a natural blue color.

www.ingramcontent.com/pod-product-compliance
Lightning Source LLC
Chambersburg PA
CBHW060951030726
47503CB00003B/820